THE ALMOST WIFE

THE ALMOST WIFE

Gail Anderson-Dargatz

HARPER**AVENUE**

Published by Harper Avenue, an imprint of HarperCollins Publishers Ltd

First edition

HarperCollins books may be purchased for educational, business or
sales promotional use through our Special Markets Department.

HarperCollins Publishers Ltd
Bay Adelaide Centre, East Tower
22 Adelaide Street West, 41st Floor
Toronto, Ontario, Canada
M5H 4E3

www.harpercollins.ca

Library and Archives Canada Cataloguing in Publication

Title: The almost wife / Gail Anderson-Dargatz.
Names: Anderson-Dargatz, Gail, 1963- author.
Identifiers: Canadiana (print) 20210166517 | Canadiana (ebook) 20210166525 |
ISBN 9781443458429 (softcover) | ISBN 9781443458436 (ebook)
Classification: LCC PS8551.N3574 A64 2021 | DDC C813/.54—dc23

Printed and bound in the United States of America

LSC/H 9 8 7 6 5 4 3 2 1

For Iris and Jackie

If I gave you my life, you would drop it. Wouldn't you?
—Michael Ondaatje, *The English Patient*

THE ALMOST WIFE

1

I ran to forget. Here, in motion, I was only aware of the early morning light glinting off the water, the beat of my running shoes against asphalt, the rhythm of my breath. There was nothing ahead of me, and the past lagged far behind. I lost all sense of time and, blissfully, of self. There was no *me*. And there was nobody else, either—no Aaron, no Evie, no Nathan and no Madison. But then the buzz of the phone strapped to my arm yanked me out of the flow, and the low sun emerged from the clouds as if rousing from sleep.

I slowed my pace as I removed my phone from the strap, nodding at a woman jogging toward me. A recreational runner, a young mom dressed in blue Lululemon crops and tee, trying to burn off pregnancy fat as she pushed her baby in a Thule jogging stroller. As she passed, her child mewed, and I immediately felt the tingle of letdown. Evie would want to breastfeed as soon as I got home. She was there with Aaron now; they had both been asleep when I left the house in the morning twilight. Evie's eyelids had fluttered when I checked on her before leaving, her tiny hands grasping something in her dream. She had turned her face toward me when I kissed her cheek.

My phone buzzed again, and I unlocked it, thinking Aaron had texted me, wondering where I was. He had, but so had Nathan.

From Aaron: **How long will you be?**

And from Nathan: **Good time to call?**

The serenity I had felt moments ago rapidly disappeared, replaced by a sharp pang of guilt. My fiancé wanted me home. And my old boyfriend wanted to talk.

And then a third message arrived. Madison. Again. She had rarely tried to contact me in the months since I moved in with Aaron, and then it had only been a handful of anxious texts wondering why Olive wasn't replying to her during her weekend visits (**Is Olive okay?**). But since Olive had moved in with us a month ago, Madison's worried messages had become much more frequent. I never answered. Then, in the last week, she had started to send texts not so much about Olive, but for me, wheedling attempts to get us to be friends. **Can we just meet for a coffee?** Or **I think it would be good if we could talk.**

Kira, we really need to talk, she texted now.

No chance. Aaron had warned me what she was like, how persistent she could be. How determined, once she got an idea about something. A real bulldozer of a personality, unlike my own. She probably thought she could convince me to change Aaron's mind and get the custody arrangement reversed. I had no intention of putting myself in the middle of their latest battle.

I looked up at the cars in the nearby parking lot in case Madison meant she wanted to talk to me here, now. Just the week before, on the last day of classes before summer break, she had ambushed Olive as she left the school. I had looked up from my phone to see Madison (dressed in a crisp black blouse, slacks and stiletto heels, always in heels) on the school steps, holding Olive's arm as she

GAIL ANDERSON-DARGATZ

tried to lead the girl to her Volkswagen Beetle, a convertible. Olive, confused, gestured toward my SUV. I left Evie in the car as I ran over to them, crying, "Hey, let go of her!"

When Olive tried to shrug out of Madison's grip, saying, "Ow! You're hurting me!" Madison released her and I quickly wrapped a protective arm around Olive and steered her toward my car, even as she now complained to me: "Jeez, just give me a minute with Maddy, all right?"

"No," I said. "You know your dad doesn't want you talking to her." *Or going anywhere with her*, I thought, as Madison apparently hoped.

"But she's my *mom*," Olive said. "Come on, Kira."

I didn't stop. I knew what was at stake. I hustled Olive to my Mazda, where Evie clapped on seeing her through the window. Madison followed the whole way, saying she just wanted to talk to Olive, she *needed* to talk to Olive. Why were Aaron and I stopping her from seeing her own daughter?

"Stepdaughter," I corrected her. "And you know why."

Once we were inside the car, I locked the door. Madison knocked on my window, yelling repeatedly that she needed to explain some things to Olive, and to me, if I would only listen, that it was important.

But I had heard quite enough of Madison's "explanations," through Aaron. And they were definitely not things Olive needed to hear, not now, not ever. I was determined to protect Olive in the way I wished someone had protected me as a child. Still, I hated conflict and my hands shook as I started the SUV and put it into gear. When I refused to roll down the glass, Madison grew increasingly agitated, banging on my window like a madwoman as I backed up and drove off. In the back seat, Evie fussed and whined.

"Everybody was watching," Olive said, crouching down in her seat.

It was true. As it all came down, I saw students and parents gather in small groups to stare and point and whisper. One boy held up his phone to record Madison's manic outburst beside my car. Weirdly, Madison had been Olive's preschool teacher when she and Aaron first met. It was an occupation that seemed so at odds with her behavior now.

Madison had turned up a second time on the weekend, hovering outside the Starbucks Olive and I frequented as we stood in line, waiting for us to leave so she could snag us. It was sad, really, to see her there. And more than a little frightening. Before Olive had a chance to spot Madison, I'd pulled her from the line, saying it was too long a wait. I handed Evie over to her to distract her, and we slipped out a side entrance into the alleyway. I turned back once to see Madison standing at the end of the alley, framed by dark brick walls on either side, her feet, in heels, planted wide apart like a gunslinger about to draw. The woman freaked me out.

Was Madison here now, lurking along the bike path as I squeezed in my morning run? There were few cars in the nearby parking lot this morning, as it was still early. A figure sat in the driver's seat of an older gray minivan, but the reflecting sunlight obscured my view of them. Madison would never drive anything as prosaic as a minivan anyway, but maybe she had borrowed or rented a vehicle so we wouldn't recognize her when she drove by the house or followed us. I wouldn't put it past her. As I eyed the van, the driver backed out and sped away. The back appeared crammed with gear, like the owner was on a road trip, or homeless; likely homeless, some guy camping out there for the night, spooked by my attention.

My phone buzzed again with another message from Madison. **Please. It's urgent. Pick up!** Then she called. After I declined the call, she rang again. As I again declined, a jogger ran up from behind to bounce in place in front of me. "Mind if I run with you?" he asked. The guy was short, balding, thirty-something, dressed in

GAIL ANDERSON-DARGATZ

navy Adidas sweats and neon-orange runners. He grinned winningly, revealing overly white teeth. It wasn't the first time I'd been hit on by some guy on this path. I turned away from him as I typed on my phone, hoping he'd take the hint and keep going.

Leave me alone, I texted Madison, regretting it as soon as I hit Send. I should have just blocked her.

My phone vibrated again with another text, but from Aaron this time. **Kira, I need you home now.**

Why? What's up? I texted. **Everything all right?**

Aaron took a beat too long to reply. **I'll explain when you get here.**

My heart skipped. **Is Evie okay?**

She's fine. Just hurry.

On my way.

As I turned to head home, I nearly bumped into the jogger, who still waited for me.

"I've seen you at a few races," he said. "You're an elite, right? A pro?"

Sub-elite, and not even that now. I was a long-distance runner, an endurance runner, who had often run near, but not at, the front of the pack. My mother had once dreamed I would go on to make the national team. But the number of long-distance runners who make it to that level is very small, and although I'd had my share of podium finishes in the past, in recent years I'd failed to achieve the times I had been aiming for. As my mother had told me (over and over), I hadn't risen to my potential.

I forced a smile. "I'm just a mom now," I said, hoping that would discourage the guy from talking further.

"You had a baby? But you're looking fit." The jogger's glance lingered over my breasts, which had grown, oranges to grapefruits, from breastfeeding. "Isn't having a baby an advantage for female athletes? Doesn't it change your heart somehow? It gives you an oxygen boost, right?"

Past his shoulder I saw a woman prancing awkwardly across the grass toward me in a pink power suit and stiletto heels that sank into the dirt. *Shit*. Madison.

"Excuse me," I said to the jogger and sprinted off down the pathway in the opposite direction, glancing back once to see Madison throw up her arms in frustration. The jogger followed me, gunning it, an athletic flirtation, but I easily outpaced him, and he gave up. At the light, I crossed the road, taking a shortcut through a park, figuring I would lose Madison there should she try to follow in her car. Aaron, or his lawyer, could deal with her. Whatever she was after, I wanted no part of it. I tried to put her out of my mind.

As I ran the tree-lined residential streets back home, the brief encounter with the jogger on the pathway ate at me instead. *I'm just a mom now*, I'd told the guy. Was that really all I was? A mom? Who *was* I now that I'd given up racing? The jogger had brought up a point Aaron often made when encouraging me to get back into competition, that having a baby might be an advantage for some female athletes. The huge changes a woman's body undergoes to accommodate a pregnancy may increase performance for some time after the baby's birth. The thing is, following my mother's death, I just wanted to leave competition behind.

My mother died suddenly from a brain aneurysm just weeks before Evie was born. I wished, at the time, that I understood the mix of feelings I had after her death. Grief, yes. And something like terror. How would I make it on my own without her? But I also felt . . . relief. After the funeral, I went back to her small house, my pregnant belly snug against the only black dress I owned, and picked up a photo of my mother and me, taken shortly before my parents separated. That image had once been part of a larger photo of my mother, father and me sitting around the firepit behind our summer house on Manitoulin. Following the divorce, my mother had literally cut Dad out of the picture and put this image of just her and me into that small gilded frame. I lay the photo face down on the coffee table and stared at my mother's brag wall, framed photos of us at various long-distance races where I had picked up a medal. In them, cheek pressed to mine, my mother held up the medals as if *she* had placed. I was sweaty in those photos, my hair damp and askew from running, but my mother was always impeccably dressed in white or red jackets with contrasting red or white scarves, broadcasting a national pride that she didn't exhibit at home. *Winning hearts and minds*, she called it. Go, team Mom.

As I looked at those images, the realization slapped me upside the head: I hadn't reached the level of success I had aimed for because I had never raced for myself. I had been drawn into running, biking, swimming, cross-country skiing and kayaking by my father, who loved these outdoor sports as much as he loved hunting and fishing. But while I had inherited his natural athletic ability, I just didn't have the competitive drive necessary to take running to the next level, to become a national or world-class athlete, and it showed. It was my mother who had pushed me to strive, to win, as she had enjoyed the status she gained through my modest success. Now that she was dead, I had no reason to continue. But if I stopped racing competitively, what else would I *do*? Who would I be then? Who was I without her?

I wouldn't, *couldn't*, stop training. I knew that much. It was all I'd done since I was a kid. What else would I do with my days? Now, as I was doing this morning, I ran or cycled my Toronto routes alone or pushed Evie ahead of me in a stroller. When Aaron or Olive was able to take Evie for a few hours, I swam laps at the pool or weight-trained. I *had* to train. I *needed* to train.

Because if I stopped—if I stopped running—the past had a way of hunting me down.

2

A van drove too slowly down the residential street behind me as I jogged the last block before our house, in a way that was always suspect in the rural outskirts of Sudbury, where I had grown up: thieves casing houses, looking for telltale signs that owners weren't home. I faced the vehicle as it approached, thinking it would be Madison. But it was some other woman, driving a gray minivan like the one I'd seen earlier in the parking lot near the bike path, like thousands of others in the city. Through the window, I caught a glimpse of her worn, exhausted face and cloud of frizzy blond hair. She leaned forward, to look at our house number, I imagined, before driving slowly away, presumably checking other numbers along the street.

I often caught people admiring or at least staring up at our house. It was one of those slick, modern homes with two levels of floor-to-ceiling windows hovering over a basement, a shiny box completely at odds with the squat brick bungalows that surrounded it. Living there, I sometimes felt on stage, as if I and my new family were putting on a show for those passing by. Aaron and

Olive didn't seem bothered by it. Olive often lounged in the seating area in front of the huge upstairs window, glued to her phone, as she took in the morning sun. But she wasn't there now. School had just ended for the summer and she was sleeping in.

I unlocked the door, tossed my keys in the marble bowl on the foyer table and kicked off my runners. Then, remembering, I retrieved my shoes and tucked them neatly into the giant closet where Aaron asked that we hide them. The closet had impractical shelves that went higher than any of us could reach, but when the doors were closed, it formed the base of a column that extended to the twelve-foot ceiling, giving the entrance a grand, Greek temple sort of vibe. Everything about the house was sleek, modern and grand. The white marble of the foyer floor was picked up again in the island and countertops of the kitchen, visible from the entrance. Evie and I spent most of our time downstairs at that island, which I covered with placemats for our informal family meals, because, as Aaron reminded me, marble is porous and can stain. Aaron liked evidence of domestic life buttoned away, as he often worked from a home office downstairs and entertained clients at the house on short notice. Even the oven, microwave and espresso machine were built into cupboards, with pocket doors to conceal them.

The living room seating area was framed by an enormous window that faced the street. Light cascaded through it onto an expanse of clean maple floor, making this wide-open space seem even larger.

"I'm home," I called upstairs.

Evie cried out at the sound of my voice, and I again felt my milk let down.

There was a *ping* as something metallic hit the marble tiles on the bathroom floor, likely a cuff link, followed by Evie's gurgles.

"Make me coffee and I'll bring Evie down," Aaron said.

"You got it." I went over to the kitchen to open the cupboard door that hid the large espresso machine, an Italian-made commercial

GAIL ANDERSON-DARGATZ

model. This was the one skill I had outside of athletics, as I had taken on jobs at Starbucks and other coffeehouses to make ends meet. I hadn't gone to university, where I would have gotten more in the way of coaching support, as I didn't have the money. Even elite long-distance runners made little in the way of income from sponsors or racing in this country. Without Aaron's support, I doubt I would have been able to continue competing anyway, Evie or no Evie.

"I thought you said you weren't going for a run this morning," Aaron said from upstairs. Sound bounced around these wide-open spaces like a rubber ball. We regularly carried on conversations between the first and second floor.

"I'm sorry I took off without telling you," I said. "I woke early, couldn't sleep." Thinking about what lay ahead on my trip up to Manitoulin Island later that day, the inevitable painful conversation I would have with Nathan (assuming, of course, I was right about the contents of the mail that awaited me there).

"Evie woke early too, crying for you," Aaron said.

Which meant he had to get up and walk down the hall to pick her up. Evie never slept in the bed with us, as I would have preferred. Aaron didn't like her snacking on me in the night, the milk stains on the Egyptian cotton sheets, the possibility that she might wet the bed. He wanted her to learn to sleep on her own. More importantly, he felt he and I needed a private space where, as he said, we could cultivate our young relationship, focus on just us for a change.

When Aaron had finally left Madison, he and I had moved into this house, an investment property he owned that, at the time, had been up for sale. Aaron had hired a designer to stage the house, and when we took it over, he simply bought the furniture from her. Everything was beige on beige: beige pillows on the beige leather sectional, a beige ottoman, beige leather stools at the kitchen island, beige leather chairs around the maple dining table. Aaron wouldn't let Evie near any of that beige, of course. I lived in fear of her crawling onto the couch, covered in mashed blueberries, when I was distracted.

Aaron appeared at the upstairs landing, wearing a slim-fit Armani suit over a tasteful violet shirt and tie, carrying Evie. He quick-stepped the carpeted stairs. All the way down, Evie reached out her arms to me, mumbling, "Mum-mum-mum." She was wearing one of Olive's old red T-shirts over her ladybug print dress and cardigan set. (It was one of Aaron's many parenting hacks: he threw the T-shirt on her when she ate, as a bib never cut it.) Her hair was so blond it was almost white, as mine had been when I was a girl. She would be flaxen-haired and fair like me, like my father. My grandfather was from Finland, and I could see that ancestry in myself and in Evie, as I had seen it in my father. And my god, Evie's ghostly pale blue eyes. I saw so much of my father in Evie that I often had to look away.

Aaron held Evie at one shoulder so lovingly now, with such experienced ease and tenderness—his long fingers cradling her— that I felt the flutter in my chest I'd felt off and on all week since he'd asked me to marry him. I was engaged to this loving, caring man! The affection and attention he poured on both Olive and Evie was one of the many things I loved about him. He often got down on the floor of Evie's room to play with her and Olive. And he had taught me so much. I'd be the first to admit that Aaron had far more experience as a parent. He'd even had to show me how to put a cloth diaper on Evie (as he had arranged for a diaper service) and how to bathe her, filling the large nursery bathroom sink and cradling her head and upper body with his arm as he gently submerged her in the water.

As Aaron reached the bottom of the stairs, I took Evie from him, handing him his coffee. He had carefully groomed his salt-and-pepper hair, and his expensive suit hung well on him thanks to his slender runner's physique. Our shared passion for long-distance running was one of the many things that had drawn us together. While Aaron wasn't an elite runner or even a sub-elite, he pushed himself in ways most recreational runners didn't. We had met at Ottawa's grueling Winterman marathon, run in the dead of winter.

"You're looking gorgeous," I said, then hesitated before continuing, because I knew what the suit meant. "Are you going somewhere?"

"I've got to catch an early flight to Ottawa this morning to put out a fire. I expect I'll be gone a couple of days."

"On this short notice?"

He took a sip from his espresso. "I just picked up a text from one of my clients when I woke. I may lose the account if I don't get up there."

Aaron was an independent sales rep, selling the products of several manufacturers and wholesalers to retailers throughout the province, so he was always on the road.

"But I'm heading to Manitoulin today," I said.

I had everything arranged. I would fly up to Sudbury that morning, then rent a truck to drive down to the island, to clean out my family cottage. I had booked an appointment with a realtor for later in the week. Then there was the letter from the lab that was undoubtedly at the summer house now, lying on the kitchen table where my next-door neighbor Teresa left my mail after picking it up for me each week. And, of course, once I had opened that, there was Nathan to face. I just wanted to deal with things and get on with my new life.

"Take Olive with you," Aaron said.

Oh god. "She'd be bored up there," I said quickly. "I'll be spending the whole time packing and hauling my mother's crap to the dump. Anyway, you know how Olive is about travel." She was one of those kids who couldn't stand to be confined for any length of time, whether in a plane or a bus. I suspected she was claustrophobic. Aaron resorted to letting her use her phone nonstop when we traveled (a practice that was not allowed at home), as a distraction, a way to cope. Otherwise, she'd freak, crying and begging to be let out.

"You could use the babysitter," Aaron said. "And there's a beach there, right? She'd like that."

"My neighbor will take care of Evie," I said. Teresa, Nathan's mom, thought of herself as Evie's honorary grandma. "Anyway, you know Olive won't want to go." Aaron had planned to take her to the Canada Day fireworks on the waterfront that evening.

"Then Manitoulin will have to wait. Obviously, we can't leave Olive alone in the house, especially now." Now that Madison was determined to get to Olive, and Aaron was determined to stop her.

I nodded, resigned. Aaron was the one paying the bills. I'd fly up to Manitoulin when he returned, as he could keep tabs on Olive when he worked from his home office.

I shifted Evie to my other hip. "Listen, Aaron, I saw Madison this morning, on my run. I mean, she knows my routines. Last week she was at Starbucks, like I told you. This morning she was waiting for me toward the end of my route."

"Seriously?" Aaron pinched the bridge of his nose, as he often did when exasperated, which he usually was when we spoke of Madison. In response, Evie grabbed my nose as if we were all playing "got your nose!"

"She texted first," I said, "and tried phoning. Then she started making her way over to me."

"Please tell me you didn't talk to her."

I *had* answered her text. But he didn't need to know that. "I didn't answer her call," I said.

"That's good. Just ignore her. Keep your distance. I wish to god I had when all this started."

Another wave of guilt welled up as I thought of how I'd talked to Madison at the school the week before, however briefly, when she demanded to know why Aaron and I weren't allowing her to see her daughter. *Stepdaughter*, I'd said. *And you know why.*

"I took off as soon as I saw her," I said.

"I can't believe she's started targeting you now," he said, shaking his head. "I'm so sorry to involve you in this, Kira. I find it all so repugnant, so *embarrassing*."

Madison had been "targeting" Aaron for a few weeks now, ever since Olive moved in with us. She had phoned Aaron's cell phone and our landline repeatedly, demanding to see Olive, and at first Aaron took the bait, answering the phone and yelling at her so his voice boomed around our open-concept house before he hung up on her. I *hated* these brief arguments. I felt as panicked and scared as I had as a kid, trying not to listen when my parents fought. The way he talked about Madison, the way he talked *to* her, with such contempt, and as if she were mad. That was one of the things he called her: *Mad Madison.* But then, wasn't that how people who were going through a bad divorce acted?

After I complained about his fights with Madison, pointing out they must be disturbing for Olive, he promised he would no longer answer her calls. He would engage with her only through his lawyer. He blocked Madison's number and, for a couple of days at least, we had peace in our home. But then Madison turned up at the school, trying to take Olive, and then at Starbucks, and then again on my run. Now that she couldn't get to Aaron, it seemed she was turning to me.

"Is she following me, you think?" I asked Aaron. "Stalking me? How does she know where I regularly go?"

Aaron glanced upstairs, and I knew he was wondering the same thing I was: was Olive still talking to Madison, letting her know where we would be?

"I don't know," he said.

Evie fussed and I bounced her to keep her quiet. "Is Madison likely to do anything stupid while you're away? I mean, should I be afraid of her?" I *was* afraid of her.

He sighed. "I don't know what to tell you," he said. "She phones at all hours. You saw her try to steal Olive away. Now she's stalking you. And of course, she tried to end my relationship with my own daughter. My god, all those terrible lies she tells about me! It seems she's capable of anything."

Strangely, we thought at first that Aaron and Madison would have an amicable divorce. After we first moved into this house in January, Olive continued to live with Madison because she didn't want to leave her friends or start a new school, and Aaron agreed it was too much for her to deal with in the midst of all this change. He also felt we needed a little time to focus on ourselves and our new baby. So he decided that Olive would spend weekdays with Madison and weekends with us, and would move into our house at the end of the school year, when she had become a little more used to me and the new order of things. At least, that was the plan.

But then, shortly after Aaron and I moved into the big house, Olive started giving both Aaron and me the silent treatment. When Aaron picked her up at Madison's for the weekend, she wouldn't even say hello. She just stared out the passenger-side window. Once she arrived at the house, she fled upstairs to her room and would have stayed there if we hadn't tempted her down with pizza and popcorn and movies. Our family dinners with Olive became dull, quiet, tension-filled events where Aaron attempted and failed to start conversations with Olive, and I tried very hard not to make chewing noises. At first I thought she had become jealous of the new baby, and was angry that I had inserted myself into her father's life, breaking her family apart. She had every right to be.

Aaron and I kept trying to pull Olive out of herself, though, and by Sunday afternoon she would start to chat with me, tell me a little about school, her friends. The one thing that was guaranteed to make her smile was holding Evie. I expressed milk so Olive could feed her with bottles. She helped me bathe Evie before bed, the three of us enveloped in the scent of the lavender baby bath soap. During these times, I found myself starting to fall in love with Olive, to think of her as family. I got the feeling she felt the same way.

But on Sunday evening, Aaron drove Olive back to Madison's for the school week, and the next Friday, she was as closed to us as ever. We'd have to start all over again. We began to suspect Madison was attempting to turn Olive against her father, telling lies about him, because she was afraid of losing Olive at the end of the school year. She wouldn't be the first woman to pull that shit. My own mother had.

Then, in the spring, as the end of the school year drew closer, Olive began making excuses, at the last minute, about why she couldn't come for the weekend: upcoming tests, play rehearsals, sleepovers with friends, a date. A *date*? She was only thirteen, or "going on fourteen," as she liked to say. But okay. Then, at the end of May, she stopped replying to Aaron's calls and texts, and when Aaron, panicked, tried phoning Madison to see what the hell was going on, Madison also refused to answer.

Aaron went to Madison's place, his old house, to see if Olive was all right, but Madison wouldn't, at first, let him see his daughter. She told him pointedly that Olive didn't want to spend weekends with him anymore, or to move in with him at the end of the school year, or even to *see* him, because she was afraid of him. Aaron pushed his way in and marched upstairs to find Olive, then told her to pack her things: she was moving in with us full-time starting right then. But Olive told Aaron, almost word for word, the same thing her stepmother just had, as if she'd been coached, and then added, "I don't want to live with you."

Aaron came home, alone, and punched a hole in the foyer wall. Then he sank to his knees and sobbed in my arms.

That was the one and only time I'd ever seen Aaron act out in violence in any way. And yet Madison had led Olive to believe she should fear her father. It was only because she wanted to keep Olive to herself.

"Olive thinks I'm an evil bastard," Aaron said, as I held him. "A *monster*. She's afraid of me. My god, Kira, the way she talks, the way she looks at me now—it's soul-destroying."

Soul-destroying. The words sent a jolt through my body, and all at once I found myself *there* again, looking down at my father's body lying on the frozen ground, his hunter-orange vest and cap, his camouflage pants, the dirty soles of his boots. The pool of blood that oozed onto the snow from the back of his head. A spot of color as brilliant red as a cardinal's plumage in the bleak winter landscape. My dead father turned his head and opened his eyes to look at me.

I had said similar terrible things to my father. I had told him I didn't want to see him anymore. There had been times when my mother stood next to me while I was on the phone with my father and wrote down words I read out loud to him: *I don't love you. I never loved you. Don't phone again.* I had called him an asshole, to his face, mimicking my mother. She called him "the asshole," but never said his name, Krister, and she rarely referred to him as my father. Teresa had once confronted me about it. *I don't ever want to hear you talking like that again*, she had said to me, *especially about your father. Do you hear me?*

I remembered thinking, *You're not my mother.* But I didn't say it. I just stared back at her, with my lips pressed together. Like Olive often did with me now. I'm sure that's what Olive was thinking when she did that. *You're not my mom.*

"It wasn't Olive saying those ugly things to you," I told Aaron. "Those were Madison's words." Just as what I had said to my father had been my mother's words. Madison knew that, as a stepmother, she likely wouldn't gain sole custody of Olive—not unless Aaron was proven abusive—so she had attempted to get emergency custody, unfurling a feeble and desperate list of accusations against him, things that were categorically untrue. When that didn't work, she tried hurling those same accusations at Olive, hoping to convince Olive to choose to live with her, and she had succeeded. "She turned Olive into her own personal weapon to use against you."

Aaron wiped his eyes with the heel of his hand. "Yes, yes, exactly."

"Olive doesn't understand what she's saying. Or the impact it has on you." Any more than I had as a kid. If I *had* understood what I was saying, what I was doing, then . . . then everything would have been my fault. I quickly submerged the thought. "You'll just have to spend time with Olive," I said. "Show her she can trust you. But you'll need to keep her away from Madison for a time—a long time—or that woman will just keep brainwashing her." I had been in my mid-teens before I even began to understand what my mother had done to my father, and even then she continued to exert her influence on me.

Aaron nodded. "You're right, of course. You're absolutely right."

He went back to Madison's house, marched back upstairs to Olive's room and, despite Madison's protests, tried his best to explain the situation. Olive finally agreed to come home with him.

In the few weeks since, we had kept Olive away from Madison while Aaron worked with his lawyer to secure sole custody. Aaron had been trying hard to reestablish Olive's trust and undo the damage Madison had inflicted on their relationship. His efforts seemed to be paying off. Even after just a month of living with us full-time,

Olive talked a lot more and spent much of her day playing with Evie on the floor of the nursery. She seemed more content, but was, at times, still a little wary of us.

So, yes, as Aaron said, Madison was capable of anything, just as my mother was. I *should* be afraid of her.

Aaron placed his espresso cup on the marble counter. "It goes without saying that you'll have to keep a close eye on Olive while I'm away," he said. "If you do go out, make sure Madison isn't following."

I pictured myself eyeing the rearview mirror of my SUV, looking for a tail, like a spy in a thriller.

"She scares me, Aaron," I said. I paused, lowering my gaze to Evie on my hip. "And I don't like being put in this position." Keeping Olive safe from Madison.

"She scares me too," he said. He ran a hand down my arm. "But I've got to work. And we're a family now. We'll just have to find a way to get through this together." He checked the time on his phone again. "I need to grab a bite to eat before I head out. You clear on all this? Are we good?"

"I understand," I said.

I understood I was now Olive's personal bodyguard.

3

As Aaron foraged for breakfast in the kitchen, Evie patted my breast, wanting milk, and I carried her to the couch, holding her warm, sticky little hand so she wouldn't tug up my T-shirt. I put her to breast, and the smell of her scalp—peaches and vanilla and *human*—enveloped me in the memory, as breastfeeding almost always did, of holding her as a newborn that first day in the hospital. Evie, unbelievably tiny, snuggled against my breast, her lips suckling now and again with surprising strength even as she slept. Aaron had left to pick up Olive, and in his absence the flowers he had arranged for were delivered—a bundle of exquisite Cream Yves Piaget roses. They sat on the windowsill, filling the room with their strong, sweet fragrance. I was sure a nurse was about to whisk them from the room, enforcing the no-scent rule. It was snowing outside and the light from the window made the curtains in my hospital room glow. It was just me and Evie in this small, white world. Just us. I hadn't yet bathed Evie, and the birthing scent, mine and hers, still clung to her. I curled over her to smell the top of her tiny head. I couldn't get enough of that primal animal scent.

Bonding, I suppose. My animal brain taking her in, making her my own. I was never more aware of my animal nature than during my pregnancy. The nesting instinct that drove me to compulsively clean house and ready a place for her, and then, during labor, the drive to push that was so strong, so surprisingly separate from my will. Out of my control.

Now, on this couch, just as I had been in that hospital room, I was *compelled* to put my child to breast. The act of breastfeeding filled me with a contentment and peace I had never experienced before. There were times when I wanted only this, to lose myself in this. Before I became pregnant, I had no idea I could love another human this much, that I was *capable* of this kind of love. I would do anything for my child—*anything*. I would build a stable family for her, even if that meant ending Aaron's marriage.

In the early days with Aaron, I never would have considered doing that. I didn't want that for myself. Ours was a casual relationship, and it was enough to fly down to Toronto to meet Aaron at the small furnished apartment he owned that happened to be sitting empty.

But then, just weeks into our affair, I was shocked to find myself pregnant, and everything changed. Suddenly, I wasn't living only for myself anymore. I was a *mom*. I had a child to support and protect, and I had long ago made a vow to myself that I would never let my child grow up in a broken home, as I had. Now I wanted Aaron not just for myself, but for my baby. And so, when I told Aaron about my pregnancy, I also told him something of how my father had died and why it was so important to me that any child of mine—ours—had the chance to know their father, to live with their father, to *love* their father in a way my mother had never allowed. I told him I had lost my father in the worst possible way, that I also felt abandoned by him. I never wanted my child to feel that way.

Aaron took my hand in both of his. "I feel . . ." he started, his eyes watering. Then he shrugged a little at the foolishness of what he was about to say. "I feel I *know* you." He laughed at himself. "I mean, I really know you. I understand now why we felt that instant connection when we first met at the Winterman."

And then he explained. He said he'd made a mistake in marrying Madison so soon after his first wife's death from breast cancer, when he should have allowed both himself and Olive time to heal before entering a new relationship. "It made no sense, I know," he told me. "But when my wife died, I felt angry, betrayed, as if I had been abandoned by her." As he had been abandoned by his mother, he said, who had left him alone with his abusive father when he was a young teen.

We were both orphaned, in our way, forced to live with emotionally stunted parents who weren't capable of real love. I felt, in that moment, that he *did* know me, just as I knew him. We had recognized each other on some subconscious, fundamental level.

The nature of our relationship shifted after that. Aaron unraveled his family life and we moved into the house together in the new year, when Evie was two months old. Olive came to live with us in late May. And just this past week, Aaron had offered me a ring and asked me to marry him! We had to wait until his divorce was finalized, but still. We were a family. I had created a family, for Evie.

Evie was now nearly eight months old, already crawling and pulling herself to standing. Here, breastfeeding in my arms, my baby waved one little hand as if she was a conductor—and, of course, she was. Her conception had orchestrated this seismic shift in all our lives. And now, I knew, it could well send an aftershock, one that had the potential to topple everything. Not long after Evie was born, Nathan had asked for a paternity test, on the chance that Evie was his. I had said no, there was no need, that I knew Evie was Aaron's child. But then I started thinking about the timing of Evie's conception, and the worry ate at me. She *could* have been Nathan's child; we had slept together once when I traveled to Manitoulin around that time. But it was so unlikely. Still, to put my mind at ease, I collected hair from Evie and from Aaron's comb and had a lab run their DNA and mail the results to my summer house on Manitoulin, so there was no chance of Aaron intercepting the letter. Thinking of it now, I felt sick with anxiety and guilt. I shook my head a little to push the thought from my mind. No, I was certain Aaron was Evie's father. He had to be. He, and our life here, was the best thing for Evie.

In the kitchen, Aaron put his cup and plate in the sink, then, wiping his hands on a napkin, he called upstairs. "Olive Oyl, I'm leaving!"

Olive Oyl. Olive wouldn't let me call her that, and she didn't even know what it referred to—Popeye's tall, skinny sweetheart—until I googled it to show her. But she never objected when Aaron said it.

"Olive!" he called again. Then, to me, he said, "She must have gone back to sleep."

"You told her about your trip?" I asked from the couch.

He nodded as he strolled over to me. "She wasn't too happy about the prospect of missing the fireworks. Do take her tonight, okay?"

I might as well, now that I wasn't going to Manitoulin as planned. With the thought, I felt the ache of nostalgia. It would be the first year that I would see the Canada Day fireworks without Nathan. We had gone to the celebrations on Manitoulin together every summer, even the year before, when I was pregnant. I had told Aaron I was visiting my mother.

"Olive!" Aaron called again, louder this time. "I need to go! I've got a flight to catch!"

At his loud voice, Evie unplugged, and I adjusted my bra and T-shirt before standing and putting her over my shoulder to burp her.

"Olive!" Aaron called yet again.

"All right, I'm coming!" Olive thundered down the stairs, wearing the same black yoga pants and pink hoodie she'd worn the day before. Olive was tall, like her father, and appeared more mature than thirteen-going-on-fourteen, especially as she often plastered herself with eighties-glam-inspired eyeliner and blush. But she was a beauty. Her hair was red and curly, a gift from her birth mother, I imagined, as Aaron was dark-haired. But I could see Aaron in her slim build, her long arms and legs, her elegant fingers, her aristocratic features. When she reached us, she planted her lips on Evie's cheek and blew, eliciting a fart sound that never failed to make Evie giggle. A morning ritual.

Aaron gave Olive a goodbye hug. Then he held her shoulders and bent to look her in the eye. "Listen, sweetheart, we've had another incident with Madison."

Olive appeared worried. "What do you mean, an *incident*?"

"She confronted Kira this morning." He glanced at me. *Confronted* was perhaps too strong a word for what had transpired, but I didn't clarify. "You do understand things have changed, right?" he asked Olive. "You need to keep your distance from Madison right now. No phoning, no texts. And we really don't want you passing on any information about our home life to her, like where Kira runs in the morning."

"I don't," she said.

"Have you blocked Madison on your phone like I asked?" Aaron asked her.

Olive nodded, her eyes sliding to either side of Aaron's feet. "Yeah."

"So you're not talking to her. No messaging online either?"

"*No*. But I don't see why I can't—"

When Aaron's face clouded, she fiddled with the zipper on her hoodie. She was a kid with many nervous tics—bouncing knees, a tendency to rashes and hives—and she was forever playing with fidget spinners even though the fad had long passed. Understandable, given how Madison had attempted to alienate her from her father. The last few months must have been so confusing for her. But we simply had to keep her away from her stepmother for the moment.

"I mean it, honey," Aaron said. "I don't want you contacting Madison, not right now."

"We're only trying to keep you safe," I said, doing my bit to support Aaron.

"Maybe you can go back to seeing her again when things have settled." When Madison had settled, he meant. When she got some counseling and wasn't trying to poison Olive's relationship with her father.

"Whatever," Olive said.

He rustled her hair and smiled. "Okay, go back to bed if you want," he said. Then, as she ran up the stairs, he added, "You listen to Kira while I'm gone."

Olive grunted—*Like that's going to happen*—but didn't look back.

Aaron took Evie from me and rubbed noses with her. "I know *you'll* be good for mommy, won't you, sweetheart?" In return, Evie gurgled and patted his face.

After cradling her close to his chest for a last hug, he put Evie on the floor. Then he kissed me, one of his deep, involved, open-mouthed kisses, and for an instant I lost myself. I fell in love with Aaron all over again when he kissed me like that, and I fell again now. He knew it too and used those kisses purposefully, to smooth things over. Jerk. I loved him for it.

But then, too soon, he stepped back and picked up his luggage and, after turning back once to offer me a last smile, he left the house.

I picked Evie up and put her back to breast on the couch, then, after checking that Aaron had driven away in his BMW, pulled out my phone. **Something's come up,** I texted Nathan with one thumb. **Can't make it up today after all.**

I didn't expect an immediate answer, not if Nathan was back at home, as I assumed he would be on this Canada Day holiday. There was no cell service in the beachside village where he lived. Nathan picked up his texts when in town or at job sites within cell tower range. But he surprised me by messaging right back. He must have been waiting for my reply to his earlier text, perhaps at the sweet spot near the crossroads outside the village.

Are you coming later in the week, then? he texted. **I took several days off.**

Doesn't look like it.

Can I call? Nathan texted. **I miss you.**

I hesitated before responding. **I'll phone your landline later.** When I was sure Olive wasn't listening in. **Miss you too.**

I dropped my phone on the couch. Shit. The delay in getting to Manitoulin was killing me. Why had I allowed this situation to drag out? It wasn't fair to Nathan, and if Aaron found out about him, the new life I'd built for Evie and me would implode.

I hadn't sold the family cottage after my mother's death, as I had her house. I told Aaron the cottage would get a higher price if I put it on the market in the summer, when the tourists were there, but in reality I wasn't yet ready to give it up. It had been my second home for most of my life, and Nathan and Teresa were family, there for me in a way my mother never had been. I struggled to let go. While I had tried to end my physical relationship with Nathan several times since I found out I was pregnant with Evie, we continued to fall into old habits during my trips up to Manitoulin, which had become less and less frequent.

But circumstances had changed this past week. Aaron had asked me to marry him, and it was time to finally move on. I had to get up to the island and deal with things there as soon as I could. There were just too many loose ends, ties I needed to cut—with Nathan, Teresa—before everything completely unraveled on me.

4

My phone buzzed as Evie munched a chopped banana from her high-chair tray and I tidied up the kitchen. Aaron, I hoped, texting a last **I love you!** as he often did before he put his phone on airplane mode. But it was Madison again. When I declined the call, she sent four texts, rapid fire:

I saw Aaron leave.

He must be on the plane by now.

So she had waited to contact me again until she knew he couldn't return.

I need to talk to Olive, alone, face to face.

He doesn't have to know.

Of course he had to know. Did she really believe I wouldn't tell him about her texts? I looked out the huge front window from my perch at the kitchen island, all at once feeling exposed. She was watching the house, and from the street she could see all the way into the kitchen. There was no place to hide. And how the hell did she know about Aaron's flight?

I checked to make sure the doors were locked, even though I'd already done that after Aaron left, then scooped up Evie from her high chair. "Want to help Mommy do laundry?" I asked her, trying to keep my tone light, but I thought I could feel Madison's eyes on me as I climbed the stairs.

I stopped to knock on Olive's door. "Olive?" I adjusted Evie on my hip. "Have you been in contact with Madison this morning? Did you let her know about your dad's flight?" But why would she do that, given her father's warnings?

When she didn't answer, I pushed the door open a crack to check on her. She wasn't in her bed, but her bathroom door was closed, and I could hear the shower running. I would have to wait to get answers from her.

But, my god, her room! Clothes and junk-food wrappers were strewn across the floor. I knew Aaron wouldn't get on her case for it, as much as it would bother him, because he now avoided conflict with her at nearly any cost. I put Evie on the floor, grabbed Olive's laundry basket and started collecting her dirty clothes. Evie copied me—monkey see, monkey do—picking up and dropping not only clothes, but a hairbrush, a lipstick and a sanitary napkin still in its pack. I took the pad from her and she merrily carried on, grabbing everything in front of her and dropping it back to the floor.

Then she pulled herself to standing at Olive's bed and I saw her reach for something shiny under Olive's pillow. "No, honey," I said, and she dropped a pair of kitchen scissors to the floor. I picked them up. They were my kitchen scissors. Why had Olive stashed scissors under her pillow? I immediately thought of my own nights spent at my father's hunt camp with a hunting knife hidden under my pillow. *You've got to protect yourself,* my mother had warned me before each visit with my father. *You don't know what he'll do to you. Imagine what he'd do to me if he had the chance.* My mother told me over and over I should fear him, until I came to believe it, until I became afraid of my father, as Olive had. Any moment of anger or bit of discipline that my father directed at me became proof, in my mind, of the danger.

Did Olive keep these scissors under her pillow because of what Madison had told her about Aaron? Was she still afraid of him? I would have to let Aaron know.

Or was I reading my own experience into it? Olive's room was always a mess. She was likely just working on some art project and that's where the scissors landed. I'd found all kinds of things in her bed when I'd changed the sheets. Junk-food wrappers, pop cans, plates, books, the drone controller she thought she'd lost, jammed between the bed and the wall. Her runners were sticking out from between her sheets now, where she'd kicked them off the night before. Olive had not inherited her father's fastidiousness, but she wasn't without her obsessive quirks. All her stuffies were lined up in a neat row far under her bed, against the wall, hidden. I only discovered them when Evie, crawling in Olive's room, spied them and started pulling them out.

I heard a knock on the front door downstairs and placed the scissors on Olive's desk, leaving my hand on them a moment as my heart started pounding in my chest. Madison. I had to get rid of her before Olive got out of the shower.

"Come on, Evie," I said, picking up both her and the laundry basket. "There's someone at the door."

I left the laundry basket in the laundry room (until I moved into this house, it never occurred to me that a laundry room could be on the second floor, or that a teen could have her own bathroom) and carried Evie downstairs. There was another knock on the door, louder this time.

As I reached the bottom of the stairs, Madison peered at me through the window at the side of the door. Her blond hair was carefully arranged in a chignon, and now that I was up close, I saw that her suit was Millennial pink. She'd managed to find stiletto heels in the same tint and carried a matching pink bag. Items bought on Aaron's card before their separation, I imagined. She couldn't afford any of that on a preschool teacher's salary.

"Kira?" she asked, her voice muffled through the glass. "Please let me in."

When I hid behind the door, uncertain what to do, she knocked again.

"Is Olive all right? Is she here? She texted about Aaron's trip and then I didn't hear anything more from her. Aaron didn't take her with him, did he?"

So Olive *was* still in contact with Madison, and lying to Aaron about it. The little shit.

"Olive is okay," I said through the door, hoping that would make her go away. "She's here. She's fine."

"Kira, *please*. I just need a few minutes with her, alone."

To convince Olive that Aaron was dangerous, I was sure, that she should choose to live with Madison instead. That wasn't going to happen.

I checked the door a third time to be certain it was locked.

Madison paused, thinking I was opening it. When I didn't, she shouted at me, "Kira, open this goddamned door!"

"You need to leave," I said. I was trying for a firm tone, but my voice shook. Evie slapped the door with one hand, as if trying to knock.

"Look," Madison said through the glass. "I didn't come until I was sure Aaron was on his flight. He doesn't need to know I was here, or that I talked to Olive. *Please*. I promise I won't tell him."

Say what?

"*I'll* tell him," I said.

"Seriously?" Madison pressed her cheek against the window, trying to get a better look at me. In that moment, she looked like some sort of strange tropical fish. "You really have no idea, do you? I thought you of all people would understand, but then I suppose you're still in the honeymoon stage."

I edged into the corner, out of her line of sight, and held Evie tighter to my chest. "*Please*," I whispered, knowing she couldn't hear. "Please just go away."

There was a long pause during which I thought she might have done just that, walked away. I peeked out the window and then jumped back as her heavily made-up face appeared inches from mine on the other side of the glass. Evie also startled. This close, I could see that the makeup on Madison's face covered the haggard look of someone who was depressed or hadn't slept well in weeks. Her eyes were bloodshot and puffy.

"Kira, let me in. You need to hear what I have to say as much as Olive does, for your own sake, and Evie's too."

Hear what? I wondered. But then I gave my head a shake. I had to stop engaging with this woman. I shouldn't have talked to her in the first place. I should have stayed upstairs, pretended I wasn't home.

Madison waited a moment, hoping, I supposed, that she'd piqued my curiosity, then, getting no response, yelled, "Open the fucking door!" She rapped on the window this time, hard enough that it vibrated, and Evie pointed a finger in her direction, babbling as if trying to tell me something. "You can't keep shutting me out!" Madison cried. Her preschool teacher's voice was high-pitched and singsong even when she was pissed, and she was *pissed*. It somehow made her seem that much more menacing. "You can't stop me from seeing my daughter!"

Evie, unsettled by Madison's banging and yelling, started to cry. I took her into the kitchen and sat her in her high chair, offering her the mushy banana to distract her.

When I swung back to the foyer, Madison was inside, the front door wide open behind her. She trotted, determined, across the expansive floor, her stiletto heels leaving pockmarks in the maple. "Olive!" she called, her voice shrill with desperation. "Olive, come downstairs. Now!"

5

Olive appeared at the top of the stairs, her wet hair snaking around her shoulders. She had changed into a T-shirt, cropped hoodie and joggers. "Maddy?" she said, her face lighting up as she looked down. "What are you doing here?"

"Oh, sweetheart. We have so much to talk about."

"How did you get in?" I demanded. "You copied Olive's key?" And when? She must have done it before Olive moved in with us. The thought chilled me. She might have already been in our house when we were out, rummaging through our things, looking for something she could use against Aaron in court.

Madison waved Olive downstairs. "Quickly," she said. "This is important. You need to come with me, *now*."

"Why?" Olive asked, stepping down.

When I sprinted over to the stairs to block Madison's way, she danced sideways to get around me, but I anticipated her moves, jumping onto the first step to stop her from reaching Olive. From the kitchen, Evie pointed a wet finger in our direction and then clapped, as if we were playing a game. "Mum-mum," she said.

"What's going on?" Olive asked.

"Just—let's go. I'll explain everything once we're out of here."

"What the hell are you trying to pull?" I asked Madison.

She eyed me a moment. "If you want to listen, I'll be happy to tell you once I've spoken privately with Olive. But I know the place you're in, Kira. I've been there. Full denial. Or maybe Aaron just hasn't shown you his true nature yet. Either way, I doubt I can convince you of anything right now." She clapped her hands twice, as she would to gain the attention of her students. "Olive, let's go!"

"Whoa," I said. "She's not going anywhere."

"You have no right to stop me from seeing my daughter."

Stepdaughter. "And yet you feel *you* can stop Aaron from seeing Olive," I said.

"I'm trying to keep my daughter safe. If you cared anything for Olive, you would let us go." She turned to look up at her stepdaughter. "Olive, come down these stairs this instant."

"You really shouldn't be here," Olive said, taking another step down. "When Dad finds out—" Olive looked at me. *And he will find out,* she implied. *Kira will tell him.*

You better believe I will, I thought.

But Madison pushed past me, heading up the stairs, intending, I thought, to force Olive to go with her. I grabbed her arm and pulled her back, and she stumbled on those heels, nearly falling, clutching the railing to right herself.

"Get off me!" she cried. She was petite, nearly a head shorter than me, so much smaller than the image of her I carried in my head. I imagined she wore those ridiculous heels to add some height. In the scuffle, her hair unraveled from the tightly wound bun, and her bloodshot eyes, heavy in eyeliner and mascara, looked wild.

"You need to leave," I said.

"It's okay," Olive said to me, holding out a hand as she stepped cautiously downstairs.

She wasn't really thinking of going with this woman, was she?

"Olive, do you remember what your father told you this morning? You're not allowed to see Madison, not right now."

She looked from me to Madison and back again, feeling torn, I knew. I felt a maternal urge to wrap my arms around Olive and hug her. But I squashed it. The kid wasn't a hugger. At least, not with me. Instead, I held out an arm protectively. "She's not going anywhere with you," I told Madison.

"I said, let's go!" Madison reached past me, took Olive's hand and tried to pull her down the remaining steps, but I pushed her away, hard, and she fell backward to the floor, shrieking in pain as the heels gave out beneath her and she twisted an ankle.

"Maddy!" Olive cried as she rushed to help her.

I stopped her. "Get Evie," I told her. "Take her into the downstairs bathroom and stay there until I tell you to come out. Lock the door." When Olive froze, her eyes on Madison trying, in an ungainly way, to get up from the floor, I said, "Do it! *Now.*"

She jogged over to the island and lifted Evie out of her high chair as Evie snatched a handful of mushy banana for the road.

"Olive," Madison said, tugging her blouse down. "*Please.*" She was almost in tears. "You need to come with me. There are some things—" She glanced at me. "There are things you need to understand."

Olive hesitated, then shook her head. "I'm sorry. I can't." And she hugged Evie, pressing my baby's face to hers, before carrying her to the bathroom.

When Madison took a step in their direction, I grabbed my phone from the kitchen island. "That's it. I'm calling the cops."

It was a bluff. I tapped on Aaron's number instead. The call went to voice mail, as I'd known it would now that he was on the plane. I didn't want the hassle of dealing with the police, explaining this embarrassing situation to them and facing their judgment when they realized I had broken up Madison and Aaron's marriage. More to the point, I was fearful and anxious about dealing with authorities and would do almost anything to avoid talking to lawyers or cops. I had done too much of that as a child, after my father's death.

"Wait," Madison said. She limped to the front door and stood just outside. "Just—wait."

I tapped out of the call and marched to the door, intending to close it on her, but Madison held out both hands to stop me.

"Okay, look, I handled this badly," she said. "I shouldn't have barged in like that. But if you'll just listen—all I want is an hour or two with my daughter. Here, if you want. I was hoping to talk to her privately, but you can listen in. You *should* listen in. You'll understand, then. *Please*." Her eyes had gone watery again.

I pressed the door closed, but she inserted her body into the doorway so I couldn't shut it.

I held up my phone. "I *am* phoning the cops," I said. (Of course I wasn't.)

Madison stepped back and I slammed the door and locked it, though it was a useless exercise now that I knew she had a key. My god, she had broken into my house and tried to take Olive. What the hell was she going to do next?

All at once I ached to hear Aaron's voice. Many nights, when I woke to a panic attack, Aaron talked me down from that bridge railing with his comforting voice. *I'm here*, he said, holding me. *I've got you. I'll take care of you. Just tell me what you need*. He made everything okay. He had to make this okay.

I dialed Aaron's number again and, with the phone still to my ear, squinted through the foyer window to see Madison getting into her VW and beetling away. I didn't expect him to pick up, but he answered so quickly I couldn't help blurting out, "Madison was just here, at the house. I mean, she broke into the house."

"Madison broke in?" he asked.

"You're not in the air?"

"We're still waiting on the tarmac. The flight was delayed. She broke in?"

"She had a key."

"What the hell?"

"She was trying to take Olive out of the house." I focused on my engagement ring as I spoke. My hand shook. "I actually had to fight her off."

"Is Olive okay? Are *you* okay?"

I looked back to the hall, to the bathroom where Olive and Evie were hiding out, and lowered my voice. "Yeah. Olive was scared, though, I think." *I* was scared.

"I'll phone the locksmith, have all the locks changed. But that will likely take a day or two."

"Can you come back home now?"

In the pause behind him, I heard a woman's voice on a PA system. "They won't let me off the plane," he said. "We're about to take off. We're just waiting in queue."

"I don't know how to deal with Madison," I said. "She'll come back. I know she will. What if she breaks in during the night when we're asleep?" I felt the tears well up.

"It's okay," he said. "Everything's going to be fine. Here's what you do." His voice had taken on that confident, take-charge tone I had been waiting for. "Pack a couple of bags and take the girls out of the city—"

"To where?"

"It doesn't matter. Anywhere. You were going to Manitoulin. Take Olive there, like I suggested earlier."

It was still early. We *could* still catch a flight to Sudbury, rent a vehicle and be at my family cottage on Manitoulin Island around suppertime.

"But Olive won't want to go," I said.

"Sell it. Canada Day on the beach."

I heard another muffled announcement over a PA system on his end.

"I've got to go," Aaron said. "The stewardess is eyeing me. We're about to take off. So you'll take the girls to Manitoulin?"

I paused. I didn't want the call to end. "Aaron, are we really getting married?"

"What?" He laughed a little. "Of course we are," he said. "I gave you a ring, didn't I?" Just the week before.

"I know, but . . ."

"But?

"You *are* still married." To this unstable woman who had just broken into my house and scared the shit out of me.

"Kira, you're being a bit . . ." He paused. "Hormonal."

He was right, of course. But still . . .

"When I get back, I'll phone my lawyer and see how we can speed things up. This latest stunt won't help her case. Breaking into the house! We could probably get a restraining order." He sounded almost pleased.

"You know she won't agree to anything less than fifty-fifty custody, and she wants Olive to live with her."

"Well, she won't get it. I'm Olive's father. She's only her stepmother."

"But she'll fight you for it." And the divorce proceedings would drag on.

"Kira, you and I are living together now, with our baby, with Olive. We are a *family*. In every way that matters, you are already my wife."

Almost, I thought, as I twirled the engagement ring around my finger. I was *almost* his wife. After Madison's latest invasion into our lives that morning, I was beginning to wonder if that's all I'd ever be, the almost wife. Was this really what I wanted? Constantly battling for my place in Aaron's life, protecting Evie and Olive from his crazy ex?

After ending the call with Aaron, I pulled up Nathan's landline number, but then, chickening out, I ended the call before it went through. I tapped Message instead. **Coming up after all,** I typed. I hesitated, then added: **I have news.** *News?* I was getting married to another man. I deleted it all. There were some things that couldn't be said in a text or even a phone call. I had to explain myself to Nathan face-to-face.

As I was about to tuck my phone away and call the girls out of hiding, my phone buzzed again, then again and again. Aaron had texted **I LOVE YOU!** a dozen times over. Despite my efforts to stay angry at him, I felt a smile creep onto my face. He always knew exactly what to do, how to fix things.

I texted him back. **I love you too.** But in lowercase, so he'd know I was still pissed.

6

As I drove the last stretch of road before Little Current, I kept an eye on the tenacious grasses and juniper bushes that forced their way up through cracked limestone on either side of the road, watching for deer that might leap in front of the pickup. There were so many deer in the region, and collisions with them were so common, that on this stretch of highway leading to the swing bridge, a row of deer detectors flanked the road. They were strange, futuristic contraptions, a line of black posts each capped with a spacy array. The locals thought they were a joke. Deer wandered across the road when no lights blinked, or the lights flashed when there were no deer in sight. But at least, I supposed, the devices reminded drivers to slow down and watch for danger. Lights flashed now.

In minutes the girls and I would reach the swing bridge that crossed over to Manitoulin, an island filled with lakes that contained islands of their own. I felt a stirring, a little leap of joy inside my belly, as I always did on my return. I was going *home*.

Still, I wasn't looking forward to the tasks ahead. There was that letter from the lab, and then, aside from breaking the news of my engagement to Nathan, I would have to clear out my mother's things from the cottage, selling what I could and taking the rest to the thrift store or garbage dump. I'd rented this pickup with that in mind, and I was more than a little frightened of what I might find as I cleaned the cottage. When I'd readied my mother's house in Sudbury for sale, I had discovered a stack of boxes in her basement, of various sizes, all still wrapped in brown mailing paper, never opened, addressed to me, from my father. After my parents' divorce, and during the infrequent visits my mother allowed (or was forced by court order to allow), my father had sworn he'd sent me letters and small parcels every week. My mother had called him a liar. "He's a cheap bastard," she said. "He's telling you he bought you gifts when he didn't, so he doesn't have to lay out any money on you."

"Maybe they got lost in the mail," I said hopefully, at first. "Maybe they will turn up."

"They won't," she said. "You know what your father is like. Never thinking of anyone but himself. You know that about him, don't you? He doesn't love anyone but himself."

My mother never allowed me to get the mail, either on the island at the rural post office or at our Sudbury house when it arrived at the door. She always insisted on picking it up herself. When I found those parcels, I understood why. She had hidden my father's letters and gifts in the basement, thinking, I imagined, that she would dispose of them at some later date. Or maybe they were strange trophies, evidence of how she had managed to one-up him, take me from him.

In the basement of my mother's house that day, I opened the largest box, wondering what it could be. My father had often bought me sports or hunting gear when my parents were married, so we could do things together. My mother always told me he bought these items because he wanted a boy, not a girl. "But

I wanted you, sweetheart," she said. "I wanted you with all my heart."

Inside the box was a telescope. It would have been a gift for my twelfth birthday, the year of my father's death. I had told him I wanted a telescope, to look up at the Milky Way from the summer house and see a galaxy with my own eyes. Or the moons of Jupiter, the rings of Saturn.

The stars were so much more brilliant on Manitoulin than in Sudbury, as there was little light pollution.

I slipped the paper from the box and a note floated down, in my father's handwriting. *I don't know if this will reach you, Kira. It seems my letters and gifts get waylaid. I hope we have the chance to look at the stars together. I love you so much, and I always will.*

He had loved me. If he had loved me, if my mother had lied about these gifts, then what else had she lied about? Everything, I realized then, in her basement. *Everything.* As a child I had trusted my mother. But as time wore on, I believed in her less and less, especially the things she said about my father. She had done everything she could to destroy my relationship with him.

I wouldn't allow Madison to pull that kind of crap on Olive. I *wouldn't.* I knew what a devoted father Aaron was. I wouldn't let him lose Olive the way my father had lost me.

As we neared the island, the smell of Evie's dirty diaper filled the truck. I would have to change her as soon as we reached the cottage. Beside her, in the back of the crew cab, Olive thumbed her phone with an aggressive obsession, hunched over, peering at the thing at close quarters. She had switched up her favorite hoodie for a brown nylon jacket after she spilled lemonade on the hoodie during our stop in Sudbury. The winged eyeliner she wore made her look so much older.

That morning, when I decided to fly up to Manitoulin to escape Madison, I had counted on the fact that Olive was likely to spend most of our time there on the couch, glued to her laptop. I was thankful, in that moment, for the particular brand of Toronto snobbery that Madison had instilled in the girl, as she was unlikely to talk to any of the locals, to get a sense of who I was when I was here. But now that we had nearly arrived, I worried about how Olive would view me in this context, and what she would pass on to Aaron. I was sure I could leave Evie with her and carve out an hour or two to talk to Nathan, as Olive liked hanging out at the playground with Evie. But we'd have to buy groceries and go out for dinner too, and we'd undoubtedly run into locals I knew, by their faces if not their names.

And what would Olive think of my aging family summer house, the tiny village? There were few amenities there. When I told Olive there was no Starbucks on Manitoulin Island, she had insisted we find one in Sudbury so she could get her Teavana Shaken Peach Citrus White Tea Infusion Lemonade. I rolled my eyes, but it reminded me of Aaron and his little rituals and specific tastes, his Italian coffee always in the same elegant cup with a saucer. If Olive thought of Manitoulin with disdain, Aaron probably would too. What picture would Olive paint of my life here? Worse, what if someone mentioned Nathan?

But I had committed to this trip and here we were.

We reached the lineup of cars waiting to cross the swing bridge over to Manitoulin, and I parked behind the car ahead of me, turning off the ignition. I glanced down at my clothes, brushing them off. I had chosen runners, yoga pants and a matching top for the trip up, for comfort, but the black cotton revealed evidence of a day of travel with a baby: milk stains on my chest, a little spit-up on my shoulder, applesauce on my thigh.

Olive leaned forward to peer out the front window. "Why have we stopped?"

"See for yourself," I said, nodding toward the North Channel.

GAIL ANDERSON-DARGATZ

Up ahead a sign read: *Danger. Keep Clear While Bridge Swinging.* Beyond that, the road had disappeared, leaving a drop into the water, as the elderly swing bridge swiveled away from the road with an arthritic stiffness. It would continue to do so until it was in line with the shore, opening a passage for waiting boaters.

"The bridge usually closes for fifteen minutes at the top of the hour," I told Olive. "It may take a little longer now. Looks like we'll have to wait until all these boats are through." There were more boaters on the water than usual this evening, tourists here for the Canada Day holiday.

My phone rang and I picked it up from the seat to see who it was: Madison. Of course it was Madison. She had called every hour since she broke into the house that morning, trying to wear me down, I imagined. When I didn't answer, she immediately sent two texts. I knew I should just block the woman. I really should. But I felt a sick urge to see what Madison would say or do next. It was the same morbid fascination I might have when encountering a dead body: an instinct to turn away, countered by the compulsion to *look.*

I looked.

Kira, please, for god's sake, answer the fucking phone!

Madison rang again and I dismissed the call. She immediately texted again: **ANSWER THE PHONE!**

I texted, **FUCK YOU!** but deleted the message before sending. I had resisted the urge to reply all the way up. I glanced in the rearview mirror at Olive and tried to keep my voice level. "If Madison texts you, don't respond," I said, as I had several times that day.

"I told you, I'm *not* texting her."

"Who *are* you texting, then?" I smiled in a feeble attempt to tease her, to avoid an argument. "Your boyfriend?"

She lifted one side of her lip in an elegant snarl. "*No.*" She flipped up the hood on her jacket and buried her chin in her chest so her face was hidden as she peered at her phone. She bit a nail. Olive's nails were chewed to the quick. But then, so were mine.

I texted Aaron. **Reached Manitoulin. Having a wonderful time. Olive is such a dear.**

He immediately texted back. **Liar.** Then: **Can I phone? Good time to talk?**

I hadn't really expected him to answer. I'd assumed he would be out to dinner with his client.

We're still in traffic at the bridge, I texted. **Olive will be listening. Understood. Call later?**

The phone rang, and when I refused to pick up Madison's call, it buzzed again and again like an angry hornet caught in an upturned mason jar. I tossed the phone to the seat, then, compulsively, picked it up again to read the latest text. **I know you're at the bridge. I can see you.**

Shit. Madison was *here.* I scanned the lineup of vehicles ahead. Then I hit the steering wheel repeatedly. *Shit, shit, shit, shit, shit.*

I gave the wheel a final slap and caught sight of Olive's worried face, questioning me in the rearview mirror.

She unplugged her earbuds. "What?" she asked. "What happened?"

I stared her down through the mirror. "You told Madison where we were going." I hadn't seen Madison on our flight, but then, I hadn't been looking for her. And she might have taken the one before, or driven up. "Why would you tell her?"

"I just . . ." Olive looked pained, not defiant as usual. "I was just trying to tell her that there was no point coming to the house again because we weren't there. I didn't think she'd *follow* us."

"Olive—"

"I don't want to be in the middle of all this." She sank back into her seat.

Of course, she didn't. No kid would want to spend another weekend caught in a parental battle. I sure as hell hadn't.

I texted Aaron. **Madison's here, on Manitoulin.**

Are you kidding me?

I wish I was. She's here at the bridge now.

My phone rang. Aaron. "I'll meet you there," he said when I answered.

My heart skipped a beat. *No, no, no.* "Is there an Ottawa–Sudbury flight this evening?" I asked.

"I don't know. If not, I'll rent a car and drive there. It will likely be faster in the end."

I glanced back at Olive, who was watching me closely, then lowered my voice, though of course she could still hear everything I said. "Aaron, honestly, there's no need for you to come here. You have things to take care of in Ottawa. I'll make very sure the place is locked up tonight, and we'll head someplace else tomorrow. Maybe Niagara Falls, MarineLand. You could meet us there." We had talked about going there as a family that summer. "In the meantime, I won't let Olive out of my sight."

He paused as if thinking it over. "Are you sure?"

"I'm sure."

He didn't sound sure. "Okay, phone if you run into problems with Madison. Anything at all."

"I will."

We said our goodbyes and I tossed my phone on the seat. Then I searched the cars, trucks and vans lined up ahead of us, looking for any sign of Madison. On the other side of the bridge, the town was busy with tourists, in cars, on foot. Madison could be in any one of those vehicles, watching us now.

7

I gripped the steering wheel as I waited for the swing bridge to close. Behind us, cars lined up one after the other. Tourists and Haweaters—locals born there, named after the hawberries that grew on Manitoulin—heading to the island to hang out in cottages for the holiday. Even when the bridge wasn't swung out of the way for water traffic, there was always a lineup here in the summer, drivers stopped by the lights on either end of the bridge, as the deck was only wide enough for single-lane traffic. Other than the ferry that ran between South Baymouth and Tobermory from May to October, and not at all in the winter, this was the only way on and off the island. There was talk, now, of replacing the century-old bridge with a new structure.

My god, Madison was *here*, in my home territory. I should text Nathan, warn him. I tapped on our conversation. But what would I say? *I'm here, after all. Oh, and by the way, I brought Aaron's daughter, and his crazy ex is here too. A family vacation!* I tossed the phone back to the seat without sending him a message. I would just have to find a way to talk to him alone tonight.

"Have you ever seen a swing bridge in operation before?" I asked Olive, trying to make chitchat, trying to ease my nerves. "I think this one at Little Current is one of the last on the continent, if not *the* last."

I cringed at my chipper, informative voice. I sounded like a teacher, like Madison. No, I sounded like a *mom*. I expected Olive to roll her eyes and snort, but she leaned forward and peered over my shoulder at the bridge. It was surreal, swinging back toward us like a giant art installation.

"How long are we stuck here?" Olive asked.

"We should be on our way shortly," I said. "As soon as the bridge clicks back into place." It was just about there now.

"Evie stinks," she said.

Evie did, indeed, stink. I regretted the brief stop in Sudbury at the Scandinavian bakery, the rice pies and fried jelly pigs—animal-shaped doughnuts filled with jelly—that Olive and I had had as a late lunch. We rarely ate anything like that at home, and the rich food, combined with my nerves and the acrid smell of Evie's dirty diaper, was now making me feel queasy.

I opened the windows, hoping to flush out the smell. But the warm and humid evening air flowed in, making the truck seem even more oppressive.

"I'll change her as soon as we get to the house," I said. Which likely meant taking her out of her outfit. For the trip, I had dressed her in a frilly summer dress and shorts set, something I never would have bought her. The outfit had been a gift from Teresa, and seeing Evie wearing it when we arrived would please her. Anything to soften the blow that the news of my engagement would bring.

I picked up my phone. There were more texts from Madison. But I wouldn't look at them. I *wouldn't*.

I looked.

Stop ignoring me! Madison had texted. **I have to talk to Olive. Please, let's meet somewhere.**

Like *that* was going to happen. I caught Olive staring back at me through the rearview mirror with a haunted expression. My phone buzzed again, and so did Olive's, but neither of us glanced away, an acknowledgment that we were both receiving harassing texts from Madison. Olive seemed to be asking me for something that she couldn't bring herself to say out loud. I should have asked what she wanted from me, what she needed.

She finally looked down to read the texts, and so did I.

Fine then, Madison had texted me. **Ignore me? Face the consequences.**

Olive thumped her head back against the seat. Then she leaned over to kiss Evie, her eyes moist with emotion.

"What's going on?" I asked her.

She grabbed her athletic bag and, after a last look at Evie, flung open the door and jumped out of the pickup. The line of vehicles ahead of us was already starting to roll onto the bridge.

"Goddamn it." I got out of the truck but, hesitant to leave Evie, I yelled out, "Olive, what the hell are you doing? Come back here, right now!"

Olive raised a hand to a car to get it to stop so she could cross the road. Then she jogged at a brisk pace down the shoulder, past the line of waiting cars, heading toward a gray minivan that was parked facing the road back to Espanola and Sudbury. Madison. It must be Madison. I quickly pulled the rental to the side of the road, flicked on the hazard lights and slammed the door shut as the car behind me pulled out into the other lane to pass.

"Mum-mum?" Evie asked through the open truck window, reaching for me, her eyes wide with panic.

"I'll be right back, sweetheart."

I crossed the road in front of a Rio that honked at me, and

sprinted down the shoulder as the cars in line drove slowly by. I was much fitter and faster than Olive, who spent her time in front of one screen or another. But she had a head start, and she jumped into the van before I reached her. The van started moving.

Fuck.

"Hey!" I shouted, waving both hands over my head as I ran after it. "Hey! Stop!"

But the van picked up speed, taking Olive farther and farther away from me.

8

I tapped Olive's number as I ran back to the rental, my mind racing. "Pick up," I said out loud. "Come on, pick up!" But she wasn't answering. I called again and it immediately went to voice mail. I quickly texted, **Stop!** Then, **Is that Madison driving?**

Olive still didn't answer, but of course it was Madison. Who else would it be? My god, what would make Olive get into the van with that woman? What had Madison been telling her, about *me*?

Or was there something else going on here? All through this crisis, I had assumed Olive was as susceptible to Madison's warped suggestions as I had been to my own mother's, and I had felt angry at her for it, but I really didn't know Olive, what made her tick. Now I wondered if she had given up on both her parents. Was she running away? I had certainly thought of doing that many times when my parents argued.

When I reached the rental, Evie gurgled out a laugh on seeing me, a desperate, joyful giggle that made my heart ache. I should never have left her alone, but what else could I have done?

"It's okay, Evie," I said. "Mommy's here."

I jumped into the truck and, after strapping in, tapped Madison's number.

"Come on, come on," I said. But Madison wasn't picking up. Payback, I supposed. Or perhaps she was simply keeping her eyes on the road. Was she even driving that van? If not, where the hell *was* she? And who was Olive with?

I texted, **Do you have Olive?** and stared at the phone, willing her to answer. When she didn't, I tried calling again. The call immediately went to voice mail. Shit. What was I doing, sitting here? It didn't matter who was driving. Olive was in that van. I had to catch up with her. I had to *save* her. I tossed the phone to the seat and, after checking my shoulder again, did a U-turn and peeled down the road after them.

Behind me, Evie mumbled as if asking a question.

"We're going to find Olive," I said. And then, more to myself than Evie, I added, "She's playing hide-and-seek."

I pressed my foot to the gas, speeding along the stretch of road that passed over Goat Island and then Great La Cloche Island. On either side, patches of shallow water alternated with flat, cracked alvar, so I could see a fair distance ahead. The road was busy this holiday weekend, but there were more vehicles heading over to Manitoulin than leaving it. I passed the car ahead of me as I rounded a corner, and then saw it up ahead: the minivan Olive had jumped into. At least, I hoped it was the same van. It was a generic vehicle, silver-gray, one of hundreds exactly like it driving around the region, I was sure. I rode the bumper of the car ahead of me until there was a break in the oncoming traffic, then pressed my foot to the gas pedal to pass two cars, swerving back into my own lane as an oncoming pickup honked. But the minivan also sped up, taking a corner too sharply and drifting into the opposite lane before recovering and shooting off down a straight stretch.

I again pulled out to pass, swinging back into the lane as an oncoming semi shuddered by. The minivan was only one car ahead now. On either side of the road, the deer detectors blinked out a warning, but I saw no deer so I didn't slow. I passed the car ahead and caught up with the van. I honked, then honked again, pulling up within feet of the bumper. When the van only sped up, I pulled out into the oncoming lane, intending to pull up alongside it, but swerved back when a car appeared in front of me. After it passed, I pulled out again and floored it until I had sidled right up to the van. The driver wasn't Madison. It was another woman, with a bush of overprocessed blond hair. Did I have the right van?

I drove ahead a little until I could see into the passenger side, and there was Olive, looking wide-eyed and scared, staring back at me. She bent her head to her phone, and my cell buzzed with a message, likely from her, but I couldn't pick it up. I was barreling down the road in the wrong lane.

I honked and honked again. The woman driving turned to me, her brows furrowed. Her face looked worn and lined, like a smoker's, and she seemed familiar, though I couldn't think from where. I motioned for her to pull over, and when she looked back to the road, I saw her body tense, her eyes widen in shock. In that split second, the deer leapt out of nowhere. It seemed to hang for an instant in the air in front of us, poised like the image on the deer warning signs. The driver of the van and I both swerved to avoid it, and my rental wove back and forth, out of control. In the rearview mirror I saw the minivan bounce into the ditch and roll to a stop on the cracked limestone near the tree line. A long, low, rumbling warning drew my attention back to the road ahead and I saw a semi barreling toward me from the opposite direction. I swung the truck back into my own lane, my heart hammering in my chest. The semi's horn droned a long complaint, changing pitch as it sped by within inches of my rental, rocking the truck.

Fuck.

Shocked by the jarring motion, Evie started crying in the back seat, and I slowed and pulled over to check on her. She was still securely fastened in her car seat, but we had come close, so close, to hitting that deer, and the minivan. "It's okay, sweetie," I said, leaning into the backseat to offer her a soother. "Everything's fine." But I shook with adrenaline and fear.

I checked over my shoulder for cars and did a quick U-turn back to the minivan, parking off the road beside it. As I unbuckled, the woman jumped out of the vehicle, slammed the door behind her and stormed toward me, her hair bouncing. She was too thin, her shoulders bony, as if she had been ill, and her oversized clothes were thrown together as if from a grab bag.

"Are you nuts?" she cried as I got out of the truck. "You almost got us killed! What were you *thinking*?"

It was only then that the full impact of what had just happened hit me in the gut. The truth was, I *hadn't* been thinking. I had acted on instinct. My only thought had been to get to Olive before the minivan disappeared down the road. We *could* have been killed. *Evie* could have been killed. I raked a hand through my hair, loosening it from its ponytail. Jesus, I was losing it. I was still grief-stricken over my mother's death, *hormonal*, as Aaron said, and my mental state seemed to be getting worse the closer I got to Manitoulin Island and the secrets I'd hidden there.

"What were *you* thinking," I spat at the woman, "driving off with my stepdaughter? I should phone the cops."

"You were the one driving recklessly," the woman said.

"No!" Olive cried, getting out of the van. "Don't call the police. This was my fault, not hers."

I squinted at the woman. "Who *are* you?"

She hesitated, uncertain, it appeared, of what I was asking of her. "Sarah," she said, but didn't offer a last name.

"No, I mean, how do you know Olive? Where were you taking her?"

Olive quickly stepped between us, waving both hands. "This was all my idea, okay?"

"Are you all right?" I asked, smoothing a stray ringlet off her face. She pulled her head away. "I'm fine."

"And where's Madison?" I asked, looking over her shoulder to the van. I couldn't see into the back.

Olive shrugged. "I don't know."

I went around to the passenger side and tried the door, but it was locked, so I banged on the van. I was done running from Madison. "Get out of the van, Madison. I know you're in there."

Sarah took a step forward. "Hey, leave my van alone."

"She's in there, though, right?" I asked Olive. "Madison put you up to this? Running off like that?"

"No! God, no." She made a sour face. "I have a brain of my own, you know."

I banged on the van again. "Madison, come out and face me. You wanted to talk, let's talk."

Sarah pushed my shoulder to get me to stop. "I said, leave the van alone!"

I turned to this woman, Sarah. "Are you working with Madison? Did she pay you to pick up Olive?"

Sarah shook her head slightly and looked at Olive, apparently confused.

"Now you're just being paranoid," Olive said.

I cupped my hands to the passenger-side window, trying to see into the back of the van, certain that Madison was in there. But all I could see were piles of household goods—a foam mattress folded in half and stuffed behind the front seats, boxes of pots and pans, books, clothing—as if Sarah was hauling stuff to the thrift store or had just come from there.

"Madison!" I cried, rapping on the window.

"She's not in there," Olive said, crossing her arms. "I told you. This was all my idea."

"But *why*? What's this about?"

Olive exchanged a look with Sarah. "I had plans for this week, all right?" she said. "I was going to catch a bus back to Toronto."

I stepped back and raised a hand, exasperated. "You took off on me so you could meet up with *friends*?"

She shrugged. "You're not really going to call the cops, are you?" she asked.

"I should," I said.

"No, don't do that!" she pleaded, and she started spouting tears. But something was off about them, like she had worked up those tears for her drama class. "Seriously, this was all *my* fault," she said. "I asked her for the ride." She nodded at Sarah. "Please don't phone the cops on her."

Sarah held up both hands. "Look, it's just like the girl said. I was only trying to do the right thing. She said she needed a lift to Espanola, to catch the bus from there. I was worried for her. A girl so young hitchhiking. So I picked her up. Better me than some creep, right?"

"Okay, okay. Both of you just take it easy." I rubbed my temples as my adrenaline-fueled anger abated somewhat. Maybe this woman *was* just a good Samaritan. That would explain why she looked familiar: she was a local heading back home to Espanola after a day at the cottage. God, maybe Olive was right and I was just being paranoid.

"What the hell is wrong with you, then?" I asked Sarah. "You saw me following. You must have heard me honking."

"You were swerving all over the road," she said. "I thought you were some drunk kid in a truck full of Canada Day partiers. I was just trying to stay ahead of you, out of your way. But you're right. I should have pulled over."

"Let's just go," Olive said, stomping to the truck. As she opened the door, she looked back at Sarah. "I'm sorry about this," she said, nodding my way. "You should go." Implying, *Before she does anything stupid.*

"As long as you're all right," Sarah said. "You'll be all right?"

Olive nodded. "I'm okay."

Sarah unlocked the door and got in her van, backed up to maneuver around me and, after holding Olive's gaze, rolled away. Yeah, maybe she was just a good Samaritan, but then maybe not. The timing, with Madison's attempts to take Olive that day, was too coincidental. I pulled out my phone and took a photo of her license plate as she left, in case she tried something. In case Olive ran off again.

I got in the truck with the girls and held the wheel for a moment, feeling jittery. Evie dropped her soother and Olive plugged it back in.

"Don't tell Dad," she begged me. "Please don't tell Dad."

When I didn't answer, she reached into the front seat and grabbed the sleeve of my shirt, knotting up the fabric in her grip. "*Please*, Kira. He'll kill me."

"You should have thought of that before you took off on me."

Of course I was going to tell Aaron that Olive had run off. But I had to gather myself first. I knew he would be pissed, disappointed—not just at Olive, but at me for allowing it to happen. And I couldn't bear his disappointment any more than Olive could.

Olive laid a cheek on the fine hair on Evie's head, her eyes watering. Crying for real this time.

I buckled up and pulled back out onto the road, then looked at Olive through the rearview mirror. "Give me your phone," I said, holding up my right hand.

"No way."

"You are not going to pass on any more information to Madison."

Or, right now, to her father. "I won't give you the opportunity to make travel plans with her, or that woman."

"I told you, she didn't—"

"*Now.*"

"No freaking way."

I ground my teeth. "Give me the fucking phone."

Olive, shocked that I was angry enough to drop the f-bomb in her presence, handed me her phone. I tossed it on the seat next to mine.

"There's no cell service at the cottage anyway," I said.

"Seriously?"

I supposed taking her phone made little difference now. Madison was *here*, in that van or some other vehicle, and was likely following us right now. And it seemed that she might have help.

She was no longer stalking us alone.

9

We drove the few minutes back to Little Current in silence. Evie shifted and whined in discomfort all the way, so after we crossed the swing bridge, I pulled into a gas station.

"I'm changing Evie before we head to the cottage," I told Olive, parking in front of the bathroom.

"Fine."

I unbuckled. "You're coming with me."

"I'm staying in the truck."

"Like hell you are."

I opened the door and lifted Evie from her car seat, slinging the diaper bag over my shoulder. "*Out,*" I said to Olive.

She grudgingly stepped down from the crew cab and slammed the door behind her. I locked up and then, still holding Evie, pushed Olive forward, toward the bathroom. When she jerked away, I grabbed her arm and hauled her to the door, glancing back at the elderly couple watching us from the lineup at the gas pump. The woman leaned into her husband, said something into his ear and scowled at me.

"Get the door, please," I said. Olive opened the bathroom door and went in first. I locked it behind us.

I pulled down the grubby change table and laid Evie on it. "I want to know exactly what is going on."

Olive hugged herself as she looked up at the small, dirty window high above the sink. "So you can tell Dad," she said.

"So I can protect you." I removed Evie's frilly shorts. "Do you know that woman who picked you up? Sarah, was it? She looked familiar."

Olive shook her head, her eyes still on the window. Behind her head, somebody had scrawled *Love stinks*.

I tugged off Evie's disposable diaper and dumped it in the garbage can. "*Is* that woman working with Madison?"

"I said no already."

"Seriously, did she pick you up for Madison? Is she a friend of hers?" Though I couldn't imagine any friend, no matter how close, wanting to help Madison take a kid. "Or is she somebody Madison hired?" Some junkie looking for quick cash. The woman seemed down on her luck, driving that old minivan full of stuff. "Was that woman waiting for you at the bridge? Was she taking you to Madison, or was Madison hiding in that van?"

"*No!* I told you, I just wanted to get back home." Olive breathed out a dramatic sigh as she leaned against the wall. "I was going to see my boyfriend, okay? We planned to meet while Dad was gone, and then you dragged me all the way up here. When we were stuck at the bridge, I saw that van parked on the side of the road, so I jumped out. That lady—Sarah—had just stopped to take a call. I told her I needed a ride to the bus. It was dumb, I know. I didn't think it through. I just wanted to see Tyler. Dad hasn't let me out of the house since school ended."

I eyed her, trying to figure out if she was lying. Then I cleaned

GAIL ANDERSON-DARGATZ

Evie's bum with a disposable wipe. "So you thought, with just me in the house, you could skip out and I wouldn't notice?"

"Before we left, I was going to tell you I was staying over at Camila's place. Camila and I had it all planned."

I let my shoulders fall as I tossed the dirty wipe in the garbage. It *was* the kind of dumb thing a teen would do. I had often camped out with a friend in our backyard so I could slip out of the tent in the night to meet up with Nathan at the beach.

"Don't you understand how dangerous that was, getting a ride from a complete stranger?"

Olive lifted a shoulder, staring not at the mirror behind me, but through it. "She was nice," she said. "I knew she wouldn't hurt me."

I pulled a diaper from the bag. "But what if she was crazy?" I said. She had looked sort of mentally ill, worn to the bone. "Or what if it wasn't that woman who stopped? What if it was like she said, some creep?" God. He could have used Olive and dumped her body. "You could have been *killed*."

Olive snorted. "You're being a drama queen." Something Aaron often accused Olive of.

"Why didn't you answer the phone?"

She gave me a look. *Duh.*

"If Sarah really had nothing to do with it, why didn't *Madison* answer my call?"

"I don't *know*. Maybe she was out of range. Or maybe she just didn't want to talk to you."

I fastened Evie's diaper as I considered that. There *were* big gaps in phone reception in the region. In the small village where my family cottage was situated, I had seen desperate tourists holding their phones to the wind on the beach, hoping to catch a few bars. Occasionally they succeeded in snagging a signal, for fleeting moments. Locals and tourists had to drive into town or stop at the sweet spot at the crossroads to send a text or place a call. I often saw cars parked there, at the crossroads, locals and summer people who knew the drill. If Madison had been in the line ahead of us, she might have had to cross the bridge while I chased after Olive, but then, having seen me take off, she would have waited in Little Current until she could cross back over, and there *was* cell service there. And she had been trying so hard to reach me all day. Why would she suddenly not answer? Unless she had been in the minivan with Olive and Sarah. She must have been.

"Hold Evie for me, will you?" I said.

As I stepped to the sink, Olive took over for me, dressing Evie in her frilly pants.

"So that's your story," I said, washing my hands. "You *weren't* running away from home? You weren't meeting up with Madison?"

"No."

"Huh." I hesitated, turning my back to her as I dried my hands, talking to her through the mirror. "You don't feel you have a reason, do you? To run away?" The scissors under the pillow. "Has Madison been telling you things again, nasty things about your dad? You understand that she lies, right?" As my mother had.

Olive shook her head, but she didn't make eye contact. She tickled Evie's belly, and Evie gurgled as she grabbed her own toes.

"The reason I ask . . ." I chucked the paper towel in the garbage and faced her. "I was cleaning up in your room this morning, picking up laundry. And there were scissors under your pillow."

There was a knock on the bathroom door, and someone tried the knob.

I lowered my voice. "Do you keep the scissors there on purpose?" I smiled, trying to make light of it. "Or are you just a slob?"

As soon as I said it, I wished I could rewind. The comment about being a slob came out meaner than I intended, especially as I had harped on her about her messes many times.

"You snooped around in my room?"

"You haven't answered my question."

As I picked up Evie, Olive stepped back and looked at the door, as if searching for a way to escape.

"Olive," I said, pressing her. "What is Madison telling you? Is she still trying to make you believe your dad is abusive, or talk you into leaving us? Is that what all this is about?"

Olive held my gaze for a long moment. "The scissors must have dropped out of my backpack," she said evenly.

My *kitchen* scissors? It was only then that I became certain Olive had, in fact, put those scissors under her pillow for protection. But protection from what?

There was another knock on the door. "Just a minute!" I said. Then I looked back at Olive. "Listen, when I was a kid, my mother made me afraid of my father. She said he wanted to hurt me. She warned me to be on guard whenever I was alone with him. Even though my father never did anything threatening, I slept with a steak knife under my pillow when I stayed at his house, or one of my hunting knives when I was at the hunt camp. I never trusted him, because she taught me not to."

"I told you, I must have dropped the scissors on my bed," Olive said. "That's all."

But she rubbed her hands on the thighs of her jeans, leaving wet streaks there. She was sweating, nervous. It was a lie. The reason she'd given for running off at the bridge, that was a lie too. I was absolutely sure, in that moment, that Madison had been hiding in that van. But who the hell was that woman, Sarah?

I put the diaper bag over my shoulder as I spoke. "My mother didn't want me to see my dad, or more to the point, she wanted to *hurt* my dad, so she did everything in her power to stop me from spending time with him. I felt I had to go along with what she wanted or I'd lose her. She would even say that: it was either him or her; I couldn't love them both." I paused. "Does Madison make you feel that way, Olive?"

Olive's gaze slid up to the window. "I just want to go *home*," she said, in tears.

I knew it wasn't our big open-concept house she was talking about; it was the home she had shared with Aaron and Madison, the home I'd broken apart. She wanted to go back to the way things were. I knew the feeling. I looked back longingly to even a week ago, before Madison started stalking me, when all I had to worry about was picking up Evie's dropped slimy banana slices and arguing with Olive when she insisted on giving Evie Froot Loops. I wanted to go back *there*. I wanted to go *home*.

GAIL ANDERSON-DARGATZ

10

I became acutely aware of the stink of Evie's discarded diaper in this small gas station bathroom.

"Let's get out of here," I said, carrying Evie out the door.

Olive followed me, holding the door open for the woman waiting outside.

After I buckled Evie into her seat next to Olive, I grabbed both my phone and Olive's from the front seat, pocketing Olive's.

"You're phoning Dad?" Olive asked, her voice rising in alarm. "*Now?*"

"I have some questions," I said. "And he needs to know what just happened."

I closed the passenger door, then stood a few feet away, keeping a close eye on Olive as I called Aaron. He answered right away.

"Is it Madison?" he asked without saying hello. "What has she done now?"

I heard the hum of a vehicle in the space behind him. He was in a taxi, then.

"No . . . yes, likely," I said.

Olive bit her nails as she watched me from the back seat.

"Aaron, Olive jumped out of the truck and ran off on me at the swing bridge. She caught a ride in a minivan—"

His voice rose in alarm. "With Madison?"

"Probably. I chased after it—"

"Olive is *gone*?"

"No, no. She's here, with me." I held out a hand to her as I spoke, as if he could see me. "But there was a deer, and the van she was in swerved off—"

"She was in an accident? My god. Is she okay?"

"She's fine. It wasn't really an accident. The van just drove off the road. But the woman driving the van—"

His voice grew louder. "Why would Olive run off on you like that? Why would she run to Madison?"

"I'm sorry, Aaron. I didn't—"

"Seriously? I can't even trust *you* to keep my daughter safe?"

A semi blew by, shuddering the ground under my feet. "But I brought Olive all the way up here," I said, my voice rising to a childish whine. "I did what you asked. How could I possibly know she'd jump out of the truck?" I repeatedly pressed the toe of my runner against the concrete parking block as I waited for Aaron to respond. In the truck, Olive rocked herself, as she often did when anxious.

Aaron released a long sigh. "Okay, okay, I know," he said finally. "I shouldn't have blasted you like that. I'm just . . ."

"Scared." I nodded as I bit my nail. I would be scared and angry too if something happened to Evie while she was in Aaron's care. I could see her little hands now, clutching a stuffie, waving up and down within the truck.

"But I shouldn't have entrusted you with keeping Olive safe," he said, "not with Madison stalking you like that."

Because I wasn't capable of dealing with it, he was suggesting.

And I wasn't. I had nearly let that strange woman drive away with Olive.

I put my hand under my armpit to stop myself from biting my nails. "What I was trying to ask—at first I was sure it was Madison who had picked her up, but it was this other woman. And I think Madison must have hid in the back of the van when we all stopped. When I tried to open the door to see, it was locked. Could Madison have someone working with her to get to Olive? A friend, maybe?" Although, from the way Sarah presented herself, I doubted it; she didn't look like she belonged in Madison's circle of friends, if Madison even had a circle of friends.

Aaron paused. "Did Olive seem to know this person?"

"I'm not sure. It didn't really seem like it. Olive claimed she was trying to catch a bus back home, to see friends, and the woman said she was only giving her a ride."

"What did she look like?"

"Forty-something, maybe older. Wild hair. She seemed kind of worn-out. Scruffy. The van was older, a minivan, and she was dressed like she shopped at a thrift store or was homeless or something."

I locked gazes with Olive as I realized where I had seen Sarah before. She had driven slowly down the street behind me as I'd run home that morning. Given that Madison had appeared along my running route, it had likely been Sarah's minivan I'd seen parked there as well. She must have given Madison a ride.

"Aaron, I saw her this morning, back in Toronto," I said. "Near our place. I thought she was a homeless person. But she *must* know Madison. Madison must have been in that van with her. Why else would she be up here?" I bit my thumbnail again as I waited for Aaron to respond. When he didn't, I said, "She said her name was Sarah."

"What else did you notice about her?"

"I don't know. She was skinny, bad hair, blond. Dyed." I could see her graying roots. "She looked pretty rough, actually, like a junkie." There was a long pause on Aaron's end. "Are you still there?"

"I'm here." His voice had gone dull. "Did she say anything else to you?"

"No, not really. She was pissed that I had chased after her. And she wanted me to stay away from her van."

"What did she say to *Olive*?"

"I don't know. I'm not sure she had much of a chance to say anything. Olive jumped into the van and then I chased after them. It was only a matter of minutes before we nearly hit that deer."

"Good. Good. That's good."

I locked gazes with Olive. "You know who she is, don't you?" I asked Aaron.

"What's that?"

"That woman, Sarah. You know who she is."

He took a beat too long to respond. "No. No, I don't. I imagine Madison got a friend, or maybe hired someone, to help her. Perhaps she felt having a stranger pick up Olive would make her harder to trace or would deflect the blame away from her."

"So you think Madison was trying to kidnap Olive?"

"I don't know. I just don't know anymore."

"Why were you worried about what this Sarah woman said to Olive?" I hesitated. "*Do* you know her? From where?"

"Oh, for Christ's sake, Kira, don't go hormonal on me." When I stayed silent, reining in the hurt, he softened his voice. "Look, I'm just trying to figure out what the hell is going on."

"Okay," I said, nodding, though of course he couldn't see me. "I get it." He was scared, scared of losing Olive.

"I thought I had worked things out with Olive," he said, "and she runs off like that. I spent all that time with her, getting her to trust me again. This is a nightmare."

"Look, Aaron, I know what Olive is going through. My own mother pulled the same kind of shit on me."

She had taken the gifts my father had offered me during our infrequent visits and thrown them in the garbage. *He's only trying to manipulate you, Kira,* she said. *He's giving you these gifts because he wants something from you. The sick bastard. Has he touched you yet?* He hadn't, but she said he would, he would try to touch me. I wasn't sure what she meant, but I knew it was bad, that he would hurt me in some way. He was an affectionate man, a hugger, and often wrapped an arm around me or hugged me goodbye. After that, I never let him touch me again.

"But we're still in the early days here," I said to Aaron, glancing at Olive. She rocked and rocked, staring straight ahead now. "You're on the right track. We just need to keep Olive away from Madison long enough that she learns to fully trust you and heals up completely. It's only a matter of time."

"I'm heading up there," he said. "I'll rent a car and drive. I should be there in the morning."

"No, Aaron, really, there's no need."

"Don't let Olive out of your sight. Sleep in the same room if you have to. And for god's sake, keep her away from Madison and that other woman."

"I will. I'll keep her safe. I promise. But you don't have to come up here—"

"Phone me if either of those nutjobs turns up again."

"We'll likely be out of cell range soon. I'll have to phone from the landline once we get to the cottage."

"Text me the address now, then."

"But you don't need to—"

"Look, Kira, I'm sorry about losing it earlier. You know I love you."

"I love you too. But—"

He hung up.

"Shit." I banged a hand on the hood of the truck, then turned away from the girls to stare at the bridge over the North Channel, the ribbon of water between us and the way home.

I had managed to keep my old life separate from my new one up to this point. Aaron had never come to Manitoulin with me.

Olive rolled down her window. "What is it? What did he say?"

I hesitated, then plastered on a smile. "Your dad is on his way," I said cheerfully. "He's driving here overnight."

And in the morning, my two worlds would collide.

11

Evie slid into sleep as we drove past the town houses of Little Current, many festooned with Canadian flags. On leaving town, we were surrounded by farmland. There was one deer warning sign after another along this road, featuring the image of a graceful leaping deer and, under it, the warning *Night Danger*. I kept glancing at my side and rearview mirrors, looking for that gray minivan, but the only cars were following at some distance.

In the crew cab behind me, Olive hugged herself.

"Are you ready to tell me who that woman is?" I asked her. "How you know Sarah? Why you ran to her?"

"I told you everything," she said, her voice brittle, on the edge of tears. "I was just looking for a ride."

"I saw her back in Toronto," I said. She'd been casing our house, I realized now. "I assume Madison was with her then too?"

Olive turned away, looking past Evie out the window. "How would I know?" she said.

"Is she a friend of Madison's?"

"No." She paused. "I don't know."

"Madison hired her, then? To pick you up?"

"No! I told you, I don't know who she is."

I hesitated, rubbing the steering wheel with my thumbs, my eyes on the road ahead. "Does your dad know Sarah from somewhere?"

She stopped rocking for a moment. "What? Why would he?"

"Why would you go with her, then?"

"I told you already!" she cried. "Why do you keep asking?"

"I'm just not sure I believe you." I was certain Madison was involved, somehow.

"You never listen to me. Just . . . leave me alone," she said, and her rocking grew more agitated, as it always did right before she freaked out, thrashing and screaming to be let out of the vehicle. That was the last thing I needed right now. I dropped the subject, for the moment.

We glided through a farm landscape pockmarked with aging gray barns, many of which had been toppled by a powerful micro- burst more than a decade before. A few of the old outbuildings that still had roofs sported top hats of darkly glimmering solar panels. Giant white windmills swam lazily in one farmer's field. Every- thing moved more slowly here on the island. No one hurried to get anything done. The locals called it "island time," like it was a whole other time zone. And it was.

As we neared the village, there was a string of cars behind us, heading to the beach, I imagined. Madison and that woman, Sarah, were likely among them, following us in the minivan. I turned off the main road, taking a less-traveled route to the village, and watched through my rearview mirror to see if any of the vehicles followed, but the road seemed empty.

There were even fewer houses out here, and the road was lined with heavy bush. We drove through nothing but trees for a time.

"There's nothing here," Olive said, looking out the window. "*Nothing*," she repeated.

It felt like an insult against this landscape that was so much a part of me. I wanted to push back, set her straight, tell her she knew little about this place or me. I felt jacked up. Pissed. At Madison for following us up, at Aaron for putting me in this position, at Olive for running off, at myself for choosing to bring her up here in the first place.

"Yeah, but it's *my* nothing," I said.

"What?"

"This section of bush we're driving through right now. It's mine."

A hundred acres of it, on one side of the road. It had been my father's hunting property, and I owned it now, though until Olive insinuated it was devoid of interest and worth, I didn't think of it as mine. My father had left the land to me. I could have sold it, as my mother wanted, when I became an adult, but for reasons I couldn't articulate even to myself, I had resisted (not an easy thing to do against my mother). In any case, I didn't want to face my ghosts there, or deal with the contents of that haunted cabin. So the hunt camp had sat empty all these years. Occasionally a hunter approached me for permission to track deer on the land during the November deer hunt. I always said no. I liked the thought that deer and other wildlife had this sanctuary, a place of safety and refuge, even if it wasn't one for me.

"There was a cabin there," I said. "I expect it's still there. And an old barn my father used to hang and butcher the deer—"

"Butcher the deer?" Olive looked horrified.

"Just like a butcher cuts up beef or chicken," I explained. "My father hunted for food more than sport. Anyway, my dad had a nice little camp here: the cabin, the barn, a tree stand, even a sauna."

"A tree stand?"

"Like a tree house. A platform high up in the trees, hidden so deer won't see the hunter." Or smell him as he hunted. As a child, I had played in that tree stand. It was my own personal tree fort. "I imagine it's all still there," I said.

Olive had stopped rocking. "You *imagine*? You don't *know*? If you've got a cabin and sauna here, don't you use it?"

She must have been envisioning the buildings as far swankier than they were. Even years ago, the cabin smelled musty, of mice, and the old barn was sinking into the earth.

"My father took me hunting there." My mother hated that he did that, and argued with him over it, even before they were divorced.

I looked out into the bush, into the past, at my mother zipping up my winter coat just before my father was due to pick me up for that last hunting trip, though I was far too old to need her help. Dad and I would stop at the Scandinavian bakery in Sudbury, as we always did before a hunt. Then we'd drive to Manitoulin, to this hunt camp. *Everything would be so much easier if the asshole wasn't in the picture*, my mother told me as she tugged my toque down into place. *You wouldn't have to go over to his filthy cabin again. He couldn't hurt you. Wouldn't that be wonderful? We'd be free of him.*

"I doubt I'll ever go to that cabin or forest again," I said, more to myself than to Olive. "My father died there, in those woods."

That got Olive's attention. She sat forward in her seat. "He died there?"

I craned my neck to look down the old hunt camp road as we passed it; it was now hopelessly overgrown with grass and young trees. I wasn't sure I could have driven down it, even in this truck. The weathered sign my father had erected was still there, a plywood cutout of a leaping deer, though the paint had long since weathered away. Beyond it, just before the corner that hid the cabin from view, the old barn, miraculously, still stood. It had been there for decades before my father bought the land.

"How did he die?" Olive asked.

"He . . . it was a hunting accident," I said. And in that moment I was a girl again, standing over my father's body. A pool of blood oozed onto the snow from the back of his head. My eyes abruptly clouded with tears, and I shook my head to clear them.

"Look out!" Olive cried.

I jarred to attention and saw the doe first, standing in the middle of the road, then another, smaller deer that turned its eyes on me from the ditch and vanished into the forest. I swerved left to avoid its mother, but the doe leapt right in front of the truck. I had only an instant in which to react, but remembering my father's instruction, I took my foot off the brake and plowed through. If I braked too quickly, I knew the deer would go right through the windshield, injuring or killing us. There was a thud and a grisly splat as blood and tissue hit the glass. I felt the shudder as the truck's wheels rolled over part of the animal's body. *Thud, thud.*

Olive sucked in a gasp of shock. Beside her, Evie startled awake and cried out. I slowed and pulled over, cut the engine, and we sat, stunned, for a moment. My body vibrated. It was a wonder the airbags hadn't deployed. I flicked on the emergency lights and opened the crew cab door to check on Evie, but she seemed unharmed. Scared by the impact, but unharmed. I shushed her, gave her a soother and smoothed her hair, and she settled.

"Are you okay?" I asked Olive. She didn't look okay. She was clinging to the seat in front of her with both hands. Her knuckles were white. "Are you all right?" I asked again.

She turned to me, wide-eyed. "Is it dead?" she asked.

Her voice quivered like it often did when she was about to lose it. *Please don't let her lose it.*

"Stay here with Evie," I said.

I marched back to the deer. Its hind end was smashed. Bone protruded and blood spilled from the wound. The deer was missing part of its front leg, an earlier injury that had healed. Somehow, the handicapped doe had survived the harsh Northern Ontario winter with the injury. It was probably shot by some hungover city boy up here for the November hunt. An experienced hunter would never have let an animal hobble away, bleeding. Nathan kept his beagle in part for that purpose; he'd trained Buddy as a blood-tracking dog, to hunt down wounded deer.

The truck door banged shut and then Olive was there with me, staring down at the deer. "Is it dead?" she asked again.

"Watch yourself." I held out an arm to get her to back up. "It's still alive. It could kick you."

"How?" she said, looking down at the animal's broken body. Then she bent over, bracing her hands against her knees, as if she was about to throw up. "I don't feel so good."

"Are you hurt?" I asked.

She held up a hand as she spit, shook her head. "Seeing that—" She waved at the bloody mess.

The deer roused, lifting its head, struggling feebly to right itself. "I have an emergency kit in the side pocket of my luggage," I said. My father had trained me to take a basic outdoor survival kit wherever I went. "Grab it for me, will you?"

"Why?"

"Just grab it."

The deer settled its head to the ground, its breathing labored. I wanted to smooth a hand over its neck, to comfort it, but of course that would only scare it further. It looked up at me with one frightened eye. And for a terrible moment I was there again, standing over my father's body. The blood that oozed onto the snow from the back of his head.

Olive was suddenly there, pulling me back to the present, offering me the emergency kit, and I took it from her, my heart banging against my chest. In the truck, Evie cried out in the way she often did before falling asleep.

"What will happen to the fawn?" Olive asked. She was in tears now, her lower lip trembling.

"I didn't hit it," I said, opening the kit. "But it was probably still nursing. If it learned to forage on its own, it may survive."

Though it had looked so young—too young to make it on its own. I found the folding survival knife in the kit and flipped it open. Seeing it, Olive jumped back.

"For god's sake, I'm not going to hurt you," I said. Then I softened my voice. "I'm going to put this poor animal out of its misery. Go back to the truck. I don't want you to see this."

I straddled the deer's neck, pulling back its head, then ran the blade of the knife across the underside of its jaw, cutting the jugular in one quick stroke. The knife was sharp, and there was little resistance. Blood pumped from the doe's neck, pooling, oily, across the road. It kicked its front legs again, trying to right its wrecked body, then finally settled, its torso collapsing like a balloon losing air as it passed away. I put a hand over my mouth, the tears stinging. This deer had been alive only moments ago. It had its quiet, secretive forest life ahead of it, and I had taken that away, left its fawn orphaned.

"How can you just *do* that?" Olive cried.

Still holding the knife, I swung around to find Olive standing behind me. She had seen everything. I took a step away from the deer and toward her, one hand out. "It was the kindest thing I could do for the deer. It was in pain. I had to euthanize it." *Euthanize* it? I had *killed* it, slit its throat, in front of a thirteen-year-old city kid who had lost her share of pets but never seen one die. My god, why hadn't I made sure she went back to the truck?

"Get away," she said, backing up. "Get away!"

Then, just like the fawn, she swung around and fled across the ditch, disappearing into the bush.

Exactly like that young deer. Here, and then *gone*.

12

O live!" I called out. "Olive, *please* come back!"
       I went to the truck to make sure Evie was asleep before calling again. "Olive!"

We weren't far from the road to the hunt camp, just a short, brisk walk. Another short hike into the woods and I'd be *there*, in the clearing where my father died. I took a tentative step forward, lost footing and skidded down the slope into the ditch, grabbing a sapling to recover my balance.

"Olive?"

I listened for her, but the buzz of insects and the rustle of leaves as the wind picked up masked her movements. I knew she was close. She couldn't have gone far.

"Olive, come on. You can't wander around in the bush like this. For god's sake. You hear me?" When I still got no reply, I tried another tack: "There are bears here. A young bear was hanging around the campsite just outside the village. It's likely in this patch of bush now." A blackfly bit me and, too late, I smacked it. "The blackflies will get you if a bear doesn't." A mosquito found me, then another, and another, and then a cloud of them swarmed me. *There's going to be a thunderstorm*, I thought as I batted them away and scratched the welts from their bites. Mosquitos and black-flies, drawn out by the moisture in the air, swarmed before a storm. "Olive, honestly, you'll be eaten alive out here."

The wind quickened, passing through the trees, setting every bush in motion. She could run through that bush now and I wouldn't hear her.

I raised my voice, but it was carried away on the wind. "Why are you doing this?" I called out, knowing she likely couldn't hear me now. Olive had seemed terrified of the knife, of *me*. I realized for the second time that evening that I had no idea what was going on in her head.

"Olive, please!" I listened, but heard only the wind blowing through the trees, the groan of branches rubbing against each other. I stepped farther into the bush, ducking beneath a bough. Shapes formed and disappeared again within the shadows. I tried lightening my tone. "If you want to see your boyfriend, we can make that happen." If that was, in fact, what she wanted—if she was telling the truth about that—though I was sure she wasn't. "He can come over to our place for a visit. Do you hear me? Olive?" I wished now that I hadn't taken her phone from her. But then, there was no reception here.

There was a flash of white. "Olive?" But it was only the white undertail of the fawn as it leapt away. It had hidden here, waiting for its mother, who would never come. When I was a child, while hanging out here in the summer with my father, I had heard a fawn mewing for its mother: the unmistakable sorrow of its cry, the grief and fear of any young creature separated from its mother.

"Olive!" I called again. I walked down the tree line, then retraced my steps and checked on Evie before walking along the forest edge in the opposite direction, toward my father's sign, the leaping deer. "Olive!" I cried, over and over. "Olive!"

I found myself standing near the camp road. It was overgrown with small trees that looked like soldiers of an army, ominously waiting for a battle to begin. On either side of the road, forms swam through the bush as the trees shifted in the wind. Farther down, just before the corner, I saw the old barn my father had hung his deer carcasses in. Then movement pulled my attention back to the hunt camp road, the silent sentries standing there. There was something moving ahead, a shape that seemed to churn out of the bush and take form, a shadow running away from me. I squinted in that direction. "Olive?" I called. "Is that you?" It *was* a girl, running. It must be Olive.

The figure sped up, racing down the road, and then leapt into the bush opposite the barn. I sprinted forward, zigzagging between the young trees on the old road, and launched into the bush at the point I had seen the girl disappear. Branches slapped me in the face as I ran. Trees, blown by the wind, shifted back and forth all around me. Clouds overhead deepened the shadows in these woods.

"Olive, stop!" I cried, but my voice was lost to the forest. I ran and ran and then, realizing I wasn't sure where I was anymore, I stopped. I had once known this intricate web of deer paths, as I had hunted them often with my father and explored them alone in summer. But now they were overgrown, and in the wind, everything seemed upside down. I was surrounded by ghostly dancing shapes. "Olive!" I cried out, sobbing a little. "Please!"

Something dashed away in the woods ahead, and I leapt over a log to follow it, watching for windfall and roots that might trip me up. I could see the figure running ahead, though only as movement between trees. Still, it must be Olive.

I ran and ran, dogged by blackflies and mosquitos, until I was deep in the forest, a long way from the rental. In the distance, I heard the sound of a vehicle on the road.

I had left Evie alone in the truck.

I stopped. "Olive, we can't leave Evie. Please come back with me." I listened for a response. "I have to go back!" I cried.

And then I saw the silhouette of a girl double back, heading toward me. I was relieved that Olive had decided to come with me, for Evie, as I'd known she would. But then the figure approached fast, too fast. In the shadows, it seemed to jump locations unnaturally. First there by that tree, then behind another, closer, then just up ahead. A wash of confusion flooded over me, the kind of mental bewilderment that often hit me during panic attacks, leaving me wondering if I was suffering from a stroke, not quite sure where I was or what I had been doing, or even who I was. "Olive?" I called again, straining to see the form in the dense bush. But it wasn't Olive. I knew now it wasn't Olive.

I backed away, and then, as the ghostly shadow jumped again, suddenly appearing within yards of me, I fled. I ran and ran and ran, crying in fear, pushing branches out of my way in panic. I ran through my father's haunted forest until I reached the hunt camp road, and then I ran through the army of small trees all the way back to the main road. I looked back once from the leaping deer sign to see the dark figure standing on the camp road by the barn, but still now, as if it was only a tree, as if I had conjured it out of my own fear. Maybe I had. Maybe what I'd perceived as a girl was only the movement of bush in the wind. Maybe I'd been chasing my own ghosts in those woods. Or maybe I had chased Olive so deep into the forest that she couldn't find her way out, and I, in my panic, had left her there. But there was no way I was going back alone now. I needed help.

I ran to my rental and swung the door open. Evie was still sleeping soundly. I kissed her head and then, closing the door gently so as not to wake her, I tapped Nathan's number. He could bring his beagle, Buddy, out here to track Olive. But there was no cell reception. Of course there wasn't. We were well out of range of the cell tower here. I lifted the phone to the wind but found no bars. I could double back and phone from the sweet spot at the crossroads, but from here it was quicker to drive to the village and track Nathan down there.

"Olive?" I called again, though I was sure that she was deep in the woods now. "I'm going to get help, but I'll be right back. I'm not going to leave you. You hear me?"

There was no response.

I jumped into the truck and sped off. I'd likely find Nathan either at home or already at the beach, where the Canada Day celebrations were held every year. With any luck, we'd be back within minutes and Buddy would sniff out Olive hiding in the bush. That is, if Olive didn't find her way out of the forest and catch a ride first. Luckily, there would be few cars on this back road. Tourists and most locals took the other route, and anyone on the roads that evening would be headed toward the beach for the fireworks, rather than in the other direction, off the island.

Still, I would have to be quick. I was leaving a thirteen-year-old girl alone, terrified, in those haunted woods. And I, more than anyone, knew exactly what that felt like.

13

My mind felt loose as I drove, untethered, unreal, like I was watching myself. The landscape ahead smudged and blurred, and I wiped the tears away with my thumb. This would be over soon, I told myself. Nathan and his beagle would find Olive, and everything would be okay. Maybe I didn't even have to tell Aaron about it. I was sure Olive wouldn't want me to. But then I chided myself for the thought. Of course Aaron needed to know.

I checked in the rearview mirror to see if Evie was still asleep, and then rounded the corner that took us into the village. It was a sleepy little beachside town, quiet even at the height of tourist season. But now it was filled with locals from other parts of the island, summer people and tourists here for the Canada Day outdoor concert and fireworks later in the evening. I passed a stream of foot traffic progressing along the sidewalk. A few of the kids waved Canadian flags like they were on parade. An older couple wore matching red and white top hats emblazoned with the maple leaf. Flags of various sizes flapped in front yards along the road.

I pulled up in front of Nathan's house, a little white bungalow, but he wasn't out on his deck as he often was this time in the evening, nursing a beer with Buddy lying on his bare feet, and the lights were off inside. He'd left the porch light on, which he only did when he was out for the evening. An old baby-blue Ford was parked next to his Dodge Ram. Likely one of the buddies that he worked with in the framing crew. They'd walked to the beach party together. Nathan never missed the Canada Day celebrations, though he and I usually went together. We had since we were teens.

I backed my rental out onto the road and continued down the street, searching the crowd for any sign of him. And then there he was on the sidewalk ahead, walking Buddy on a leash. His ginger hair made him easy to spot. My heart fluttered a little at the sight of him, the feeling in my chest like the kicking of Evie's tiny feet inside my belly during the final months of my pregnancy. As always, whether at work or not, he was dressed in jeans and a T-shirt, forest green this time, and strode with the upright stance of a man used to physical work.

There was a thin, deeply suntanned woman next to him. Were they walking together? There were so many people making their way down the sidewalk to the beach it was hard to tell. But then Nathan reached out and took her hand. *He took her hand.* A sick feeling settled in my stomach. So *she* was the owner of the baby-blue Ford. The woman wore flip-flops, denim shorts and a halter top that showed off tanned, muscular arms. She was a manual laborer of some kind, then, used to working outside, maybe a landscaper. Her hair was tied up in a haphazard bun. She looked familiar, though I couldn't place her.

For a moment, I thought of driving on, as if I hadn't seen them together. But Olive was back in that forest alone, and if she found her way out, she could catch a ride with some stranger or, perhaps worse, with Madison. I had to find her fast. I pulled the truck to the curb just ahead of Nathan and the woman. Buddy lifted his head as if he'd caught a fresh scent.

I got out of the truck and jogged to meet Nathan on the sidewalk. Buddy barked and waved his tail, recognizing me, and, alerted to my presence, Nathan dropped the woman's hand.

"Kira? What the hell are you doing here?" He looked ahead to the truck, as if wondering where Evie was. "You told me you canceled your trip up."

"I need you to come with me right now." I waved at him to follow.

"Why? What's happened?"

I glanced back at the woman, who now skulked nervously behind him. I didn't want to explain anything to her. Nathan, perhaps seeing my look of hurt and confusion, introduced us. "This is Ashley," he said, and then, to her, "This is Kira," his voice level, like he was telling her to watch what she said. I *did* know her. Where did I know her from? Recognition flitted across her face too. And something else. Disdain. It wasn't the first time I'd seen that look from a local.

"I hit a deer," I said, nodding to the truck. I would explain the rest on the way.

Nathan took one look at the front end and said, "Jesus."

From the impact with the deer, a headlight was busted and the front bumper crumpled. Deer hair and bits of flesh were caught in the crushed metal.

"I'll take Buddy," Ashley said, reaching for the dog's leash.

"No!" I said, a little too loud. "Nathan, we need Buddy."

"The deer ran off?" Nathan asked.

"Not exactly."

He tilted his head at me. He knew something else was going on. "Okay. Just give me a minute, all right?"

"Nathan, we really need to *go*."

"I said, *just a minute.*"

I sulked back to the driver's side and got in while he spoke to Ashley on the sidewalk, his back to me. As I watched in the mirror, Ashley raised a hand angrily in my direction. She didn't hug him back when he embraced her, her arms dangling at her sides. I looked away, to the elderly house across the street that listed to the side as its foundation slowly sank into the sand.

Nathan opened the back door to let Buddy in next to Evie, who shifted in her sleep. Then he got into the front. I did a shoulder check and, after waiting for a car to pass, pulled a U-turn. When I looked in the side mirror, I saw Ashley still standing there on the sidewalk, watching us drive away.

"I'm sorry about Ashley," Nathan said quietly. "When you said you weren't coming up . . . I mean, you and I always go to the fireworks together. I guess I was pissed."

I raised a hand. "I don't—I can't talk about this right now," I said. "Nathan, Olive ran off on me."

He shook his head as his mind shifted gears. "Olive? Why did you bring her up here?"

I hesitated. "I'll explain all that later. But right now I need your help. When I stopped to put down the deer, Olive got spooked and ran off into the bush at the hunt camp."

"So she's out there in the woods right now?"

"Yes. Please, Nathan, you've got to find her."

Nathan gestured at his house, just up ahead. "Stop at my place for jackets and flashlights."

"We don't have time." My voice had gone shrill. "We need to get to Olive *now.*"

"Kira, without jackets, we'll be eaten alive by mosquitos and blackflies, and the search may take some time. We could be looking for her in the dark. In that forest, I need to see where I'm going."

"Fine. Fine!" I turned sharply into his driveway, next to Ashley's old blue Ford.

"I'll be right back." He left the truck door open as he jogged into his house.

I drummed the steering wheel as I scanned the passing vehicles, looking for any sign of Madison, or Sarah's van. There were several minivans just like it here already, parked along the side of the road or near the beach, families here for the fireworks. Madison and Sarah could be in any one of them, maybe even watching us now, but in this crowd of people, it would be hard to spot them. It seemed clear now that Madison had driven up from Toronto with Sarah. Tipped off by Olive, they might have reached the island before us and waited at the bridge for us to arrive, knowing we'd have to stop there, that they could get to Olive there. I just hoped they hadn't followed me down the back road and seen Olive take off on me, or they might get to her first.

Nathan jumped into the rental, wearing a rain jacket and carrying a second, along with a couple of flashlights. As he buckled in, I backed up and took off down the road, keeping an eye on the rearview mirror to see if anyone was following. There was a car behind us, but it pulled to the side of the road to park near the dunes.

"Who is she?" I asked.

"Who?" he replied, though I'm sure he knew exactly who I was talking about.

"Ashley."

"I work with her," he said, like I should know. "She's on my crew."

I finally remembered where I'd seen her. In the spring, I had dropped in on one of Nathan's construction jobs, a new beachside cottage, with a surprise lunch, a wicker picnic basket of specialty cheeses and artisan breads that I laid out on a checkered tablecloth, a production that had elicited catcalls from his coworkers on the crew and embarrassed Nathan. Ashley was there that day, working on an outside wall. At the time she wore sunglasses and a red bandana to hold her hair back, a tool belt around her waist. I'd been impressed that she was a carpenter on the crew, but not impressed enough to talk to her. In any case, Nathan hadn't introduced me. He had gulped down my carefully prepared lunch and unceremoniously shooed me away so he could get back to work. I left, hurt, with an empty picnic basket. There was so much about his life I didn't know. So much about this *village* I didn't know. But then, I hadn't taken the time to build a community here, other than with Nathan and Teresa. I had kept my distance.

"No, I mean . . ." I left the rest of my sentence hanging there: *Who is Ashley to you?*

"She's an old friend," he said. "We went to school together."

"A buddy," I said, sarcastically. At the sound of his name, Buddy sat up on the back seat and snuffled, his tongue lolling. "You were holding her hand."

Nathan snorted, shaking his head a little. Here I was, giving *him* shit about seeing a woman on the side? "Seriously?" he said.

"*Are* you seeing her?" I asked.

"I see her every day," he said. "We work together."

"That was noncommittal."

"What do you want me to say?"

As I gripped the steering wheel, I glanced at the engagement ring Aaron had given me. What *did* I want him to say? That he would always be on this island, waiting for me, as he had since we were teens, ready to pick up where we left off in our perennial summer romance, even as I lived with another man?

"How long?" I asked. *How long have you been screwing Ashley, Nathan?*

Nathan hesitated. "A while," he said.

"How long?" I demanded.

GAIL ANDERSON-DARGATZ

"It's been off and on. Since high school."

Since *high school*. "So, all those times we were together, *she* was in the picture?"

He shrugged. "Not always. I dated a few others."

When I gave him a hard look, he said, "You're the one who always wanted to keep things casual. Did you really expect me to wait around while you had someone else's baby?"

My heart skipped a beat as I thought of the letter from the lab that almost certainly waited for me at the summer house.

"In any case, what does it matter?" he said. "You came up here to end things with me once and for all, didn't you?"

I felt a surge of heat in my gut.

"The ring," he said, nodding at my hand. An emerald-cut diamond. *A beauty*, my father would have called it, whistling long and low in that way that made my mother furious at him. *A beauty*.

"I'm so sorry, Nathan. This isn't how I wanted to tell you."

"I would have committed to you if I thought I had a chance," he said, and his voice broke a little. "Do you know how many times I thought of flying down to Toronto and turning up at your house?" From the back of the crew cab, Evie murmured a complaint in her sleep and Buddy whined, both responding to the emotion in his voice. "But I never did. Because even before you got involved with Aaron, I knew the only place you would ever want me is *here*."

"Nathan . . ."

He waited, but I had nothing to offer him. He was part of my life here, but I lived a whole other life when I left the island.

Nathan shook his head angrily. "And the crazy thing is, when you call, I still come running." He held out his hands as if to say, *Look at me now*.

"I'm sorry I have to involve you in this," I said. "It's not fair to you. I just—when Olive ran off, I didn't know who else to turn to."

"Again, why did you bring her up here in the first place?"

"It's complicated. Madison has been hounding us for weeks now, trying to get to Olive."

"But she's the kid's stepmother, right? I mean, she's been Olive's mother for a long time. Why wouldn't you want her to see Olive?"

"Because the woman is absolutely fucking *nuts*. First she wouldn't let Olive come home on weekends. Then, when Aaron brought Olive to live with us, Madison started harassing Aaron, trying to ruin his reputation so she could get Olive back. And now she's stalking me. Nathan, she broke into our house this morning and tried to take Olive."

"She did *what*?"

"Aaron is on the road, so I figured the best thing I could do was get away, bring Olive up here. But then Madison followed us, and Olive took off on me at the bridge."

"At the bridge? She ran off on you *twice*?"

"She jumped into some woman's van."

"Why would she do that?"

"Olive told me the woman in the van was just some stranger, and she ran off because she wanted to go home to see her boyfriend. But I've seen that woman in the van before. She must have come up with Madison."

"And—what? You think Olive is meeting up with Madison and this mysterious other woman at your father's hunt camp, in the bush? Kira, that sounds crazy. More likely she's just throwing a teenage tantrum over being away from her boyfriend, like she said."

I ran a hand over my scalp, feeling a headache coming on. "I don't know. But when I tried to find Olive at the camp, she ran from me." At least, I'd thought it was Olive I was chasing through those woods. Now I wasn't sure of anything. "She may be lost in the bush right now, terrified. If she's not, I worry she might hitch a ride, like she did at the bridge. What if some stranger picks her up, some guy? Nathan, she's only thirteen."

Buddy whined and Nathan reached back to pat his head, to comfort him. But he didn't take my hand to comfort me, as he would have in the past. "We'll find her," he said. "Buddy will find her."

I was counting on it. Buddy was a smart dog with an educated nose. Nathan had trained him as a gun dog, a blood tracker, to find wounded deer during the fall hunt, but Buddy loved tracking so much that Nathan made a game of it at his parties, offering Buddy the scent on clothing belonging to friends who were hidden around his property or in the small patch of bush behind it. Buddy eagerly found Nathan's tipsy, beer-swilling friends as they hid within outbuildings or behind logs or even up in trees.

"Have you got something of Olive's that Buddy can catch her scent from?" he asked.

I nodded. "Her tote bag is in the back."

He reached into the crew cab and unzipped Olive's bag. "Something that hasn't been freshly washed?"

"There's a hoodie in a ziplock." She had put it in there after spilling lemonade on it. It was her favorite pink cropped hoodie that she wore day after day, and often slept in.

Nathan dug out the plastic bag and tossed it to the console. "We'll find her," he said again.

We will find Olive, I reassured myself. But as I drove past a cemetery, I checked the rearview mirror compulsively to see if that minivan was following, and twisted the steering wheel with both hands as if I was wringing it out.

14

I parked the truck near the deer carcass and took a moment to tuck a blanket around Evie. Nathan grabbed Olive's hoodie, still in the plastic bag, and clipped a leash on Buddy.

"I need to stay here, with Evie," I said. I didn't want to go back into that forest or meet the specters that waited for me there.

"We could bring her with us," Nathan said.

A thunderhead boiled ominously overhead, throwing the forest into an early twilight. I shook my head as I stared into the bush, the swirling forms manifesting in the shadows, the memories there. "I would only slow you down."

Nathan reined in Buddy to stop him from taking off, sniffing out the dead deer. "I'm just a stranger to Olive, Kira. If she doesn't want to be found, I may well just push her even further into the forest."

"I can't—" I started. But how to explain? I wasn't brave enough to face my own demons, even to find Olive. I was a coward. "We'll just have to hope she's ready to come out."

"All right," he said doubtfully. He pocketed his flashlight and offered Olive's jacket to Buddy for him to smell. "Find it!" he said. Buddy was engaged by the blood of the deer I'd hit, but Nathan pulled him back to task, offering him another smell of the jacket.

"Olive went into the bush here." I pointed at the newly cut path where she'd leapt the ditch and raced through roadside grass into the woods, the path I'd damped down further when I'd gone in after her.

Nathan nodded once. "Okay. Let's go." As Buddy tongued the trail, Nathan followed along behind him, repeatedly calling Olive's name. The dog bounded all over.

"What's he doing?" I called from the ditch.

"He's distracted," Nathan said, his voice small in the wind. "I can't see Olive—any human—bouncing all over like this."

"There was a fawn with that doe I hit," I said.

"Was it injured?" Nathan asked.

"I don't think so. But it likely walked through its mother's blood trying to get back to her. The road is covered in it."

"Buddy's more interested in that fawn than finding Olive."

Nathan offered the dog Olive's jacket again and called "Find it!" His flashlight swept the trees as Buddy picked up a more direct scent trail, one that swung deeper into the woods along the trajectory Olive must have taken, toward the hunt camp road. And then the light disappeared.

"Nathan?" I yelled after him. "Is Buddy on her scent? Nathan?" I listened and then called again. "Nathan, can you hear me?" But he was too deep in the bush, and the wind drowned my voice.

Shapes took form and dissipated in the forest in front of me. I hugged myself, shivering. After a time, I saw Nathan and Buddy swing up toward the road near the overgrown driveway to my father's cabin. Then Nathan called, "Buddy found something!"

I checked once more on Evie and jogged down the shoulder, catching up with Nathan at the hunt camp road.

He held something out to me. "Is this hers?" he asked.

I took the hair scrunchie from him. It was Olive's favorite, one she carried in her pocket. "That's hers," I said. "Nathan, I saw her—" At least, I thought I'd seen her. "I ran after her, into the forest down there, across from the barn." I found myself tearing up. "I worry I just scared her off, that she got lost in the bush. I got disoriented myself."

"Hey, hey." Nathan put a hand on my arm. "It's okay. We *will* find her. It will just take some time."

"But it was my fault, Nathan. I left her in there. If I had just kept going, maybe I could have led her out."

"She ran off on you. You had Evie to think about. And in this forest, you had little chance of finding Olive, not if she didn't want to be found. Not without Buddy." Hearing his name, the beagle looked up expectantly, tail wagging.

"I should have gone in there after—" I stopped. The figure was there again, on the old camp road by the barn, standing small and dark among the trees. Then it was suddenly closer. Then closer yet. Jumping, somehow, without moving. Beside one tree, then another, hazy, as if rapidly vibrating.

"What?" Nathan said, turning. "What do you see? Is it Olive?"

I shook my head slowly, stepping back. As the figure jumped closer still, my heart raced. *Breathe*, I thought, *just breathe.*

"What's going on?" Nathan asked.

Agitated, I shuffled back and forth in my runners, tears stinging my eyes.

Nathan wrapped his arm around me. "You're shaking," he said. "Oh god, this is your first time back, isn't it? Since your father's death."

I nodded miserably but kept my eyes on the shadowy form, which was now only yards away.

Nathan pulled me close. "I should have remembered," he said, and I hid in his arms.

The hazy figure was almost on us now, right *there*, and then it came into focus. Her delicate features and pale, almost white hair were so at odds with the heavy, oversized camouflage pants and jacket she wore, the hunter-orange vest and cap, the rifle she carried, her heavy boots. A child dressing up as a soldier. The girl walked right by me as if she didn't see me, and made her way up the road to wait for help, as she had countless times in my memory. It was a walk she never completed; she had been stuck in this forest for fifteen years, replaying her father's death over and over. Since the overcast November day when my father died, this part of me had never left.

"Does Aaron know?" Nathan asked. "What happened in this forest? Did you tell him?"

"What?" I asked, wiping my face with my sleeve. It felt like a test. It *was* a test. Who did I trust more? Who was I more intimate with, Nathan or Aaron? I hesitated before answering.

Buddy sat up, eyeing something in the bush that only he could see.

"No one knows the full story," I said.

Even Nathan, my oldest, dearest friend, didn't know the whole truth. I had never dared to tell him, for the same reason I had never told him how serious things were with Aaron—because I didn't want to lose him. For so many years, he and Teresa had been the only real family I had. I craned my neck to kiss him on the cheek, hoping that would make it clear to him: whatever else happened, I didn't want to lose him. Nathan kissed me back, full on the mouth, and there we were again, back in our old love.

"I should get back to Evie," I said, pulling back. "I've left her too long."

"Yeah, okay." He nodded, looking a little hurt. "We'll try picking up Olive's trail again." He offered Olive's jacket to Buddy. "Find it!"

As Buddy sniffed back and forth, unable, it seemed, to pick up a scent, I pushed through the bush to the road and sprinted back to the truck. Evie wasn't crying, thank god, so hopefully she was still asleep. I couldn't bear the thought of her waking in the truck, in the twilight of this lonely rural road, to find I wasn't there. My heart skipped a beat as I thought, again, of how I'd left Olive in the forest alone. My god, if she was still in those woods, she would be out of her mind with panic by now. I felt my own panic start to well up again.

When I opened the back door of the rental, it took me a fraction of a second too long to register what was wrong. Evie's car seat wasn't there. My baby wasn't there.

I felt the adrenaline really kick in then, the thundering rush as it spilled into my bloodstream, the hot prickle of sweat. I gasped.

"Nathan!" I cried. "Nathan!" He didn't hear me, but Buddy did. The dog ran through the bush onto the road to bark in my direction, and Nathan followed to see what he'd spotted. I waved both arms, calling out to Nathan again, and he quickly ran the length of road between us, with Buddy leading the way.

As he reached me, I cried, "Evie's gone!" Sobbing now.

"What? *What?*" He looked into the back of the crew cab as if he didn't believe me. The truck still smelled of Evie, her peachy baby scent. "Who—"

"Madison," I said. "It has to be Madison."

I hoped to god it was Madison, and not some stranger. But then, Madison had broken into our house, tried to steal Olive away, and had followed me all the way up here. Who knew what she was capable of?

Anything, Aaron had said. She was capable of anything.

15

I jumped into the truck. "We've got to get to the sweet spot," I said, starting the engine. My hands shook.

"To phone Madison?" Nathan asked, ushering Buddy into the crew cab.

"If she doesn't have Evie—" My throat caught. Oh god.

"And if she does?"

"Then she wants something. She wants Olive."

"But we haven't found Olive yet." He buckled himself in.

I didn't have even that bargaining chip, not that I would use it. At least, I didn't think I would use it. Then again, in that moment, I would have done anything to get Evie back.

The forest fled by us as I sped down the road, and then the corridor of trees opened and we were once again in farmland, rows of fence line ticking by on either side of us. Something raced across the road. A cat, or a fox.

"You need to slow down," Nathan said. "The deer—"

"You don't need to tell me how to drive," I said, my voice rising. "And you don't need to tell me about the frickin' deer."

I took a turnoff down a gravel sideroad too fast, skidding toward the ditch, nearly losing control.

Nathan grabbed the handle again. "Slow down!" he said.

But I sped on down the dirt road, counting on cutting a few minutes of driving time with this shortcut to the sweet spot. I eased off on the gas only to make the turn back onto the paved road, then floored it again until I reached the crossroads, what had once been a bustling little hub servicing the old-time community. An empty and dilapidated general store slumped sadly to one side.

I parked the truck at the sweet spot, checking to see that I had bars. Then I tapped on Madison's number. In the seat behind us, Buddy whined.

The call went to voice mail. "She's not answering," I said.

"She may still be out of range," Nathan said.

I texted her. **Do you have Evie?**

When she didn't immediately respond, I tried again. **Please, let me know if you have Evie.**

I stared at my message as the seconds ticked by at a painfully slow speed. My question seemed so innocent sitting there, so rational, so ridiculously *polite*. Then time snapped back into place as my phone finally rang. It was Madison.

"Do you have her?" I asked, before she had a chance to say anything.

"So, *now* you want to talk," she said.

"Do you have Evie?" I yelled, punching each word.

Nathan pushed a hand down on air to tell me to cool it.

In the background of Madison's call, I heard the rumble of the vehicle she was in and, behind her, Evie's cries. Was she driving while talking on the phone? No, she would be in Sarah's van; Sarah would be driving.

"Yes, I have her," Madison said.

"Oh, thank god." I tried to keep my voice calm and level, *sane*, though I felt anything but sane. "Evie's crying. Is she okay?"

"Of course she's okay! What? You think I would hurt her? You think I'm some kind of monster?"

I left that one unanswered.

Then she laughed, a little hysterically. "But of course, you *would* think I'm a monster, wouldn't you? You believe all that bullshit Aaron tells you. *Mad Madison*, right? Aaron started calling me that during arguments almost as soon as we were married. Any time I disagreed with him or pointed out just what kind of asshole he was, he accused me of being hormonal and unbalanced and said I needed help."

Hormonal. Aaron had called me that a time or two. But then, I *was* too sensitive and quick to take offense, wasn't I? Pregnancy and then lactation hormones talking.

"For a while there, he convinced me I *was* crazy," Madison went on. "Hear it enough and you come to believe it."

Shut the fuck up, I thought. "I just want my baby back."

On the other end, Evie's cries had become eardrum-shattering howls. Madison had to raise her voice over them. "Believe me, I just want to give her back."

Fuck. "Then why the hell did you take her in the first place?"

Nathan shook his head, warning me, again, to bring it down. I waved a hand in return. *Stop distracting me.*

"I didn't know what else to *do*," Madison said. "You wouldn't let me see my daughter." She whined as if she was about to burst into tears herself. "I had to find a way to get to Olive." Then her tone took on a sharper edge. "In any case, you were the one who left your baby all alone in a parked truck by the side of the road. Anyone could have taken her. It was unbelievably irresponsible."

"I didn't think—" I stopped there. I had done so much that day—in my life, really—without thinking things through, reckless things, dangerous things. But *she* was lecturing *me* about being irresponsible?

"I'll tell the cops that, if you try to call them on me," she said, speaking too fast, like she had been chewing on this worry. "I'll tell them you left your baby in a parked truck and I was only taking her to safety."

"I didn't say anything about involving the police." I closed my eyes and pinched the bridge of my nose, as I had so often seen Aaron do when he talked to this woman on the phone. "Look, Madison, bring Evie back to me right now and I'll forget the whole thing. It never happened."

"What's that?" she said. "You cut out there for a second."

"Just bring Evie to me," I repeated, louder.

"No!" she said shrilly, then she said it again, as if convincing herself. "No, I'll only give Evie back if I get Olive in return."

"Why are you *doing* this to us?"

"What would *you* do if you believed your child was in danger?" Her voice caught. "What would you do to save your child?"

I was there now, and we both already knew what I would say. What would any mother do to save her child? *Anything.*

"What do you want me to do?" I asked.

Madison's voice ratcheted up a notch. "Bring Olive down to the beach in that village of yours," she said. "When we were in town earlier, I saw they were going to have fireworks on the beach. The girls will like that. We can meet there."

"Who's 'we'?" I said quickly. "Is that woman, Sarah, with you? I knew she must have something to do with you!"

"Not now, Kira!" Madison was using her preschool teacher voice on me. "I've been trying to explain everything to you, and to Olive. I'll talk to you both when I see her, and you can take Evie back then."

I glanced up at Nathan, who, sitting this close, was listening in to both sides of the conversation. He shrugged and shook his head.

There was no easy way to tell Madison that I couldn't bring Olive to her.

"You still there, Kira?" Madison asked. Her voice had gone strange, tinny, like a robot, as she started to lose bars. Evie's cries behind her sounded vaguely like an ambulance siren.

"Look, Madison, we have a situation," I said. "I hit a deer and had to stop, and Olive jumped out of the truck. She ran off into the bush. I tried to find her—"

As her phone suddenly regained reception, Madison's voice boomed so loud I held the phone away from my ear. "Olive's *lost*?"

"We were in the process of tracking her down when you took Evie—"

"Tracking her—is that what you were doing? I saw you with a man and a dog. When I didn't find Olive in your truck, I thought—oh god—I thought you had *hidden* her somewhere. But she's out in that forest *alone*? You know how anxious she is. She'll be terrified!"

"I know," I said. "We need to get back to the forest and find her right now. Just meet us—"

"Where did you last see her?"

"Near my father's hunt camp. Where we were stopped, where I hit that deer. There's a leaping deer on the signpost to the camp road."

There was a long pause. "You still there?" I asked.

"Just let me think."

Think? What was there to think about? "Bring Evie to the hunt camp," I said. "We'll find Olive together." There was another long pause, and I thought the call had dropped. "Madison?" I asked.

"No. Olive won't come out of the forest for you, but she will for me."

Sadly, given Olive's actions that day, *my* actions that day, Madison might well be right.

"And I need to talk to Olive alone," she continued. "I need to make her understand, without your interference. It's clear you're still buying into Aaron's bullshit."

"Madison, listen to me—"

"Go back to the village, to the beach—"

"Madison, we don't have time for this. Olive's out there—"

"I'll leave Evie—" The call cut out, and when it picked up again, her voice was tinny. "—maybe at the playground. She can—" And the call dropped.

"Damn it," I said, tossing the phone on the console.

"What's going on?" Nathan asked.

"Madison said something about leaving Evie at the beach." I started the truck.

"Alone? Would she really do that?"

"I don't know."

Nathan shook his head. "This whole situation is so . . ."

I mentally filled in the blank. *Fucked.*

I put the truck in gear and sped toward the village. My baby was only ten minutes down the road, but, my god, a lot could happen in ten minutes.

16

As we reached the outskirts of the village, a gray minivan flew toward us, going as much over the speed limit as I was.

"That van," I said. "It's her van, Sarah's, the woman who picked up Olive at the bridge."

Nathan squinted at it. "Are you sure?" he said. "Those minivans are all over the roads."

But as we met the vehicle, I saw Sarah driving it. Beside her, Madison was leaning forward to stare back at me. She appeared distraught, her mascara tear-smudged, her expression grief-stricken and determined. I imagined I looked much the same. The two of us racing in opposite directions to reach our daughters.

This can't possibly be happening, I thought as I sped past the van, the gas pedal to the floor. Nothing felt real. I had the uncanny sensation that I was awake within a lucid dream. In the field ahead, sandhill cranes high-stepped through the fading twilight, looking for all the world like a herd of feathered dinosaurs.

"Kira, slow down."

"I've got to get to Evie!"

"We can't help her if we hit another deer on the way there."

"She can't get to Olive before we do," I said. "She just can't!" But I eased back on the gas as I picked up my cell, intending to call Madison again as I drove.

Nathan took the phone from my hand.

"What are you doing?" I asked.

"You're distracted enough," he said.

I took a corner too sharply, and we were in town.

"Look out!" Nathan cried.

I braked to avoid hitting a kid wearing a T-shirt with a Canadian flag on it. He scurried across the road to join a few stragglers making their way down to the beach as fireworks exploded in the sky above the bay. It appeared they had started the show a little early, perhaps to get a jump on the storm that loomed overhead, threatening a downpour.

I drove on, but as I reached the parking lot, people walking to the beach crisscrossed the road, blocking traffic. Some ambled down the street right in front of the cars, seemingly unaware of the traffic behind them.

"Come on, come on!" I said and honked to get the vehicles moving. The car ahead of me passed it on, beeping at the group of chubby middle-aged tourists walking in the middle of the road. One of the men lifted a hand and trotted to the sidewalk, grinning. When the line of cars drove straight into the beach parking lot, I followed.

Directly ahead, the playground set was silhouetted against the dark clouds, looking like a miniature castle with turrets. *Please let her be safe*, I prayed. *Please.*

I parked the rental, slung my purse over my shoulder and jogged to the playground with Nathan and Buddy hot on my heels, the sand shifting under my runners. A barrage of red fireworks shot upward, sounding like gunfire, and bloom after bloom of red, blue and green mortars exploded overhead. There were people every-where, seated in camp chairs or on blankets in the sand, leaning against the railings of the boardwalk. Kids wore crowns of eerily colored glow sticks and waved glow-stick swords at one another. Someone must have been selling them or handing them out. A kid spun the sticks, one in each hand, creating a light display. The crowded beach had the atmosphere of a carnival. So many people, and Evie could be anywhere.

"You see her?" Nathan asked, clipping the leash to Buddy's collar.

"No."

Images came in flashes as I scanned the playground and beach for her: a kid climbing up the slide; two teen boys jumping off the top of the bigger playhouse; girls dancing on top of the jungle gym, their arms waving against the stormy sky. Fireworks burst behind, silhouetting them.

"Have you seen a baby crawling around here?" I called to the girls. "She was just here."

The girls shrugged. There were young children everywhere. Evie could have been carried away by any adult, just another sleepy and complaining baby, and no one would have thought twice about it.

I searched the area around the jungle gym as Nathan asked locals he knew if they had seen Evie. The fireworks were so brilliant that, during bursts, the crowded beach was nearly as light as day. But Evie was nowhere in sight.

"Anyone!" I called out. "Have you seen a baby? Evie. Her name is Evie!"

A few people passing close by shook their heads and carried on. Tourists.

"Nathan! Nathan!" A woman's voice rang out across the crowd in between the crackle of fireworks. I swung around to see Nathan jogging toward Ashley, with Buddy running behind him. The dog jumped at her excitedly as Nathan led her back toward me.

"Ashley will help us look," he said.

I nodded. Sure, whatever. I'd take any help I could get.

Ashley looked past me to the playground. "She can't have gone far. You only just got here."

"You don't understand." I spun in a circle, looking for Evie. "Madison said she left her at the playground *alone*." At least, that's what I thought she'd said before the call dropped.

"So, Madison is . . . family?" Ashley asked.

Nathan shook his head to answer her question but also to warn her off.

I realized with a blast of adrenaline that Madison *was* family, through marriage. Or almost family. My future husband's wife, the stepmother of my future stepchild. But I didn't want to explain that to Ashley.

Nathan did it for me, leaning toward Ashley to talk into her ear as fireworks boomed over our heads.

"She was *kidnapped*?" Ashley spoke the word with greedy, breathy horror. A tale to tell a friend over a bottle of Yellow Tail, no doubt.

"We can use Buddy, right?" I asked Nathan. "Can he track Evie in this crowd?"

"We can try," he said. "Have you got something of Evie's?"

I dug into my shoulder bag for Evie's cardigan, which I'd hastily stuck in there. My bag had become a mother's purse, filled with toys and soothers and sippy cups. "Here," I said, handing him the sweater. Nathan, in turn, offered it to Buddy, commanding him with a cheerful "Find it!" Buddy immediately started sniffing the sand, crisscrossing back and forth in front of the play set. The number of human smells must have been overwhelming: dozens and dozens of individual scents flooding the beach. But then Buddy made straight for the swing set and we followed, with Ashley trailing behind. When Buddy got there, he sniffed a circle around the swings and then looked up at Nathan as if to say, *What do you want me to do now?*

"What is it?" I asked. "Why has he stopped?"

"I don't think he's picked up her scent." Nathan offered him Evie's sweater again. "Find it!" he said.

Buddy sniffed the beach, circling the swings, then took off back to the jungle gym. We followed as Buddy wandered from place to place, sniffing everything.

"Either she wasn't here, or there are just too many people," Nathan said.

"But Madison said . . . I thought she said . . ." I blinked back the tears and took in a deep breath to calm myself. The air felt muggy. Lightning flashed over the bay.

Nathan tried offering Evie's scent one more time, pulling Buddy off in another direction. But the dog just zigzagged through the crowd, going nowhere in particular.

"This makes no sense," I said. "She can't have just vanished."

"Someone could have picked her up," Ashley said.

"Or, if she made it to the water . . ." I said.

I turned to the bay. *The water.*

17

I ran toward the water and waded into the lake with my runners on, thrashing around with my hands. It was so cold. My baby in this cold, dark water. "Evie!" I called, then listened.

If Evie had crawled into the lake, she could be dead already. But surely someone would have seen her? There were families everywhere; surely no one would let a baby crawl into the lake alone. She *had* to be along this small section of shore. Didn't she? If she'd made it to the water on her own, she would be right here, in front of the playground. And the waves lapping the shore would keep her body here. *Her body.*

Nathan and Ashley splashed into the water beside me, feeling about in the shallows a few feet away.

"If she *is* here in the water, she doesn't have long," Nathan said. He sloshed back onto shore. "We need more help."

While I flailed around in the water, nearly incoherent, Nathan gathered a few locals to help us search the beachfront. A barrage of fireworks flashed in quick succession, lighting up the bay in staccato bursts.

"Evie!" My voice rang over the water. Something brushed past my leg. I reached down, but whatever it was—likely a fingerling—was gone.

Nathan and the locals he had enlisted waded in with me, the fireworks exploding over our heads, casting shimmering light across the waves. One of the searchers approached a nearby group of teens huddled around a fire they had built with driftwood, even though there were signs everywhere forbidding campfires. The kids shook their heads in response. Beyond them, a row of sandcastles from the Canada Day competition were already crumbling away.

"Anything?" Nathan called out to the searchers in between the bursts of fireworks. And they echoed back:

"Nothing here."

"Nothing here."

"Could she have gone deeper?" I asked Nathan. "Farther into the water?" The bay was shallow. A swimmer could walk far out and still be only waist-deep. "Could she have floated out?" Nathan had lived all his life by this shore. Surely he would know these things. About currents and drownings.

"It's only been a few minutes since Madison left her in the playground, right? It's unlikely. If she's in the water, she would be here."

I splashed and splashed, feeling with my hands in the dark. Someone brought a flashlight and shone it on the waves. That only made it more difficult to see, the light reflecting off the surface.

"Evie!" I cried, and the searchers echoed me down the shoreline. *Evie, Evie, Evie, Evie* . . . Lightning flashed and flashed again over the bay. In the relative quiet between fireworks, I heard the rumble of thunder.

Then there was a holler from just down the shore. "Hey! There's something here!"

Something in the water. Something in that vast expanse of black. Evie. My tiny Evie, lost in all that. I felt like I was trapped in a dream of running but going nowhere, the stretch of dark beach expanding as I struggled to get there. I stumbled once and fell, panting, on all fours.

Ashley helped me up, her thin, cold fingers holding my bare arm. "Are you okay?" she asked.

I shook her off and pushed on without answering, staggering into the group of locals who had gathered on shore to watch a man haul something from the water. Something small and heavy, the size of a child.

18

I pushed through the circle of men on the beach. It took a moment to understand what I was seeing on the sand. Not a child at all. Not Evie. A fawn. Perhaps injured and disoriented, perhaps abandoned, it had fallen into the lake and been washed, wave after wave, to this sandy shore. Now it was little more than a bloated bundle of bones, its legs like twigs, snapped as the carcass was tossed against the rocks at the point.

"I imagine that's a relief," Ashley said.

Relief? "Evie could be anywhere," I said. "She could be anywhere out there! *Dead.*" As dead as this poor young animal.

The men around us shuffled in the sand, embarrassed by my anger. Ashley held both hands beneath her armpits. Her tank top revealed bony shoulders. I had yelled at this woman, just as Aaron had yelled at me when I told him Olive had run off. For no reason. Because she was there. Because I was terrified. Because I blamed myself. Because she also loved Nathan.

Nathan rested one hand on the small of my back. It felt warm and solid there, grounding. "We'll find her," he said. But then, that's what he'd said about Olive.

A barefoot man in a red T-shirt and jeans jogged up to us. He looked familiar, like so many of the locals helping us search for Evie, though I couldn't place him. "Jamie said a couple of women were asking about you, Kira. Where you lived, who your friends were."

Jamie? Who's Jamie? "Just now?" I asked. "I mean, within the last half hour or so?"

"No, earlier in the evening. They were at the ice cream shop."

So they *had* arrived on the island before the girls and me, and had been snooping around in my life, looking for opportunities to get to Olive.

"The questions they were asking Jamie seemed a little strange," the man said. "But he just assumed they were friends of yours, up for a visit and trying to track you down. Jamie pointed them to your place, Kira, and to Teresa's house, as he thought you might be there. Then, just before the fireworks started, he saw the same women, talking to Teresa outside her house. One was holding a baby."

"He's sure it was the same women?"

"He's sure. He said one of them was dressed up, in a pink suit and heels. The other, not so much."

"That's them," I said, jogging toward the boardwalk. As an after-thought, I waved my thanks.

Nathan ran after me, leaving Ashley behind. "Madison wouldn't hurt Mom, would she?" he asked as we climbed the stairs. "I mean, she took Evie, for god's sake."

I didn't answer. She had taken Evie. She had broken into our house. And now, it seemed, she was trying to hurt me through the people I loved.

We jogged down the boardwalk together. I had walked these boards with Nathan many, many times. When we were teens, we had made out on those benches on the beach. I had lost my virginity to him on that dune, under this boardwalk. We had met here at midnight and waded, naked, far out into the shallow bay, the sand deliciously textured under our feet, the dark water around us shining with a thousand reflections of the stars above, the Milky Way cutting a swath through the sky and dipping below the horizon of Lake Huron. But now, under this stormy sky, reddened by flashes of fireworks and crowded with dark figures, the boardwalk felt like the surreal setting of a nightmare.

Teresa's house—and my cottage—was only a short run from the beach, but a small patch of bush, mostly pine and milkweed, covered a sand dune that blocked it from view of the boardwalk. The house was little more than a box with a roof, a two-story structure from the Edwardian era, but without the characteristic Edwardian elements, no veranda or columns.

There were no lights on, but I banged on the door anyway.

Nathan pressed past me and opened the door. "Mom?" he called out. When he got no answer, he said, "She's likely at the beach watching the fireworks."

"We already looked there. I didn't see her."

"But with the crowd—we could have missed her. And we didn't try the ice cream shop."

I raced back to the boardwalk and pushed through the crowd, the smells of beer, sweat and suntan lotion mixing with the scent of the lake that wafted up from those who had spent the day swimming.

The ice cream shop normally closed at nine, but was open late for the fireworks. Families sat at the wooden tables outside, sucking back ice cream cones with their heads tipped upward, their faces rapt, as the dark dome of the sky shattered into a million sparkling pieces, another fireworks barrage exploding overhead. They were bringing out the big guns now as the show came to a close. I waded my way through them to the shop, opened the door and heard a baby's cry.

19

Evie sat on Teresa's lap inside, fussing as she held a mini-cone, her face sticky with ice cream. Her car seat sat at Teresa's feet. "Mum-mum," she said on seeing me. She dropped the cone, holding out her arms as Nathan and I stepped through the door.

"Oh, thank god," I said, rushing toward her.

"There you are!" Teresa said. "We looked all over for you."

I took Evie from Teresa, holding her close and closing my eyes as I breathed in her powder and peach smell. My gut, my breasts filled with the ache of almost losing her, that prickling sensation of letdown. For a moment, the world faded and it was just Evie and me, just us, as it had been in the hospital room the day she was born.

But then Teresa jolted me back to the ice cream shop and the shitty day I was in. "Your friends said you'd only be a few minutes," she said.

"They are *not* my friends," I said.

"Why would they come to you?" Nathan asked his mom. "Why would they leave Evie with you?"

"I assumed you had arranged it," Teresa said to me. "Didn't you?"

"I'll go tell the searchers we found her," Nathan said, and he jogged out the door.

Teresa watched him rush out. "Kira, what's this all about?"

A teen cleaned up the ice cream bar. She didn't appear to be listening, but I knew she likely was. We were the only ones in there. She would be closing soon.

I lowered my voice. "What did they say to you?"

"The women? Not much. They just came by the house and said that Evie and I should wait for you at the fireworks, near the playground."

So perhaps I had misunderstood as Madison's phone cut out. Maybe she had been telling me she was leaving Evie with Teresa.

"She said you'd only be a matter of minutes. But Evie was beside herself, Kira. She wouldn't stop crying. I figured an ice cream would calm her until you found us. I hope you don't mind."

"She's too young for dairy."

"A little ice cream isn't going to hurt her."

"You didn't think to phone?" I didn't try to keep the anger out of my voice. Here she was, feeding my kid ice cream, while I searched the water, thinking Evie could be dead.

A flutter of hurt winged across Teresa's small, heart-shaped face. She had overly large gray eyes, so like Nathan's, and had been pretty in a pixie, elfin sort of way when she was young. I'd seen pictures. Now her face had taken on the soft, peachy texture some older women acquire after menopause.

"You know we don't have reception here," she said. "I didn't see the point."

"You could have tried calling my cell on your landline anyway."

"That woman in pink said you would be here any minute. I was sure you'd find us if we waited. I just assumed you were on your way to see the fireworks with Nathan, as you do every year." *Take it easy,* her tone suggested, *we're on island time.*

I pressed my face to Evie's cheek, the warmth of my daughter in my arms almost too much to bear. She tugged my hair and nuzzled into my neck, humming, "Mum-mum-mum." I sat at the table next to Teresa and put Evie to breast, and all at once the emotion of the day bubbled up in big, shuddering, ugly-face sobs. The girl at the ice cream bar glanced at me and kept wiping the counter.

"Oh, Kira." Teresa handed me a wad of tissue. She never went anywhere without a packet of Kleenex in her pocket, not for her own use, but to hand out to others. Teresa had a way about her that encouraged a quick and easy intimacy and oversharing. She was one of those women who almost always had a smile on her face, even when walking alone, as if she was remembering a private joke. She wore a hippie skirt, a tie-dyed T-shirt, sandals. Happy clothes, she called them, outfits as colorful as the scrubs she wore as a personal support worker. Her wardrobe always made her seem approachable—which was, I supposed, important in her work, where she helped the elderly or people with disabilities in their most vulnerable moments.

"Evie's okay," she assured me. She ran a suntanned hand over Evie's white-blond hair. My baby's eyes were closed. She suckled intermittently, already struggling against sleep. It was late, and the emotional strain of the evening had exhausted her, as it had me. "Now," Teresa said. "Tell me what this is about."

"Madison—"

"Madison?"

"The woman in pink. She's Aaron's wife." I cringed at the gaffe. "His ex." I waved a hand in a circle. "They're going through a divorce."

Teresa lifted her chin in a gesture so like Nathan's. "Ah," she said.

"She took Evie from my truck, then left her here with you."

"Why on earth would she do that?"

The girl at the counter had stopped wiping, her hand still on the cloth, her eyes cast down as she listened in. I lowered my voice further, to a near whisper. "Madison wanted to trade Evie for Olive."

Teresa shook her head. "Who is Olive?"

"Her stepdaughter. Aaron's daughter."

"I don't understand. Why would she want to trade Evie for Olive?"

I wiped my nose with the tissue Teresa had given me. How to explain all this? "Madison came to the house this morning, trying to talk to Olive, trying to *take* Olive while Aaron is away. So I brought Olive up here to get her away from Madison. At least, that was the idea. Madison followed us up. And that other woman you met seems to be working with her somehow. Olive ran off earlier and jumped into her van. I had to chase them down to get Olive. Madison took Evie to get Olive back."

Teresa sat back a moment, working it all out. "So, a nasty divorce, then." She tapped my ring. "You're *engaged* to this man now? But the divorce hasn't gone through yet, right?"

I shifted Evie's weight in my lap, hiding the ring from Teresa's view. "I'm sorry," I said. "I was going to tell you about the engagement after I talked things out with Nathan. Teresa, I'm selling the summer house. I won't be coming up here anymore, not now that Aaron and I are getting married."

"That's it?" she said. "You're just cutting ties with us?"

I looked down to adjust my top to better cover my breast as Evie suckled, but didn't answer, feeling the sting of Teresa's words. She and I were becoming disconnected, and it was my fault. Until that moment I hadn't realized just how much that might matter to me.

Teresa let out a long sigh. "I was never really sure of the nature of things between you and Nathan, if you were just on and off, or if you had one of those open relationships that seem to be all the rage with twenty-somethings and thirty-somethings these days."

An open relationship? Did she really think Aaron was just someone I was seeing on the side? Nathan knew about Aaron. But, of course, he'd neglected to tell me about Ashley, or the other women he'd dated over the years, just as I hadn't told him about my own short-lived affairs. And Aaron would kill me if he knew about Nathan. That would be the end of things.

"But I thought you'd both grow out of it, *grow up*," Teresa said pointedly. "Finally settle down. You and Nathan kept coming back together for so long, I was sure there would be a wedding eventually. Children."

I felt a deep pang of guilt as I thought again of the letter containing the lab results. She wanted grandchildren from me. From Nathan and me. We could have had a family together, a house together, a life together. It was what Nathan wanted. And I loved him. I still loved him. Why had I forced us both to settle for this half-life?

All at once I knew the answer: because if I loved just one of these men, I would have to trust that he and I could make it work. That was one thing I couldn't do—trust anyone that much—not after enduring my parents' relationship, not after living all those years with my mother.

"I never meant to hurt Nathan," I said. "I never meant to hurt either of you."

"Well, right now I'm more concerned about you. You and Evie. What have you gotten yourself into?"

I didn't answer. I wasn't completely sure, and the last thing I needed was for Teresa to involve herself in it.

Nathan appeared at the door to the ice cream shop, with Buddy at his heels. "Everyone is relieved," he said. At the sound of his voice, Evie unplugged from my nipple to look up at him sleepily. When Nathan squatted next to us to kiss her cheek, Evie patted his head with a sticky hand, overjoyed to see him. Buddy licked the ice cream cone she'd dropped on the floor.

"We'll talk about all this later," Teresa said, as I tucked my breast back into place. "I'm just glad everything is all right now."

"It's not all right," I said. "I hit a deer near the hunt camp and Olive took off on me again. She's still out there, in the bush, or at least she was, I think, when Nathan and I left. Madison and that other woman went after her. If they find her, Olive will likely go with them." I turned to Nathan as I laid Evie over my shoulder. "We need to get back to the hunt camp now."

Teresa looked up at the clock on the wall. "You've been here, what? Half an hour? Forty-five minutes? Chances are those women have already found Olive and are gone."

Nathan shook his head. "I'm not so sure. Kira thinks she ran deep into the woods. If she got lost in the dark, she's likely still there."

"That poor girl," Teresa said.

"We've got to find her," I said, standing.

"We should gather a team of searchers," Teresa said.

"I'd like Nathan and Buddy and I to go out first," I said. "A big group of searchers might panic her even more. If we think we need help, we'll get it."

I didn't want any more locals involved in this. They had already let too much slip to Madison. Aaron had repeatedly said that the one thing he couldn't stand was liars. Throughout their marriage, Madison had made a habit of lying to get what she wanted, and she had manipulated Olive into believing her terrible lies. Aaron had made it clear to me that he wouldn't tolerate being lied to ever again. But of course, I had been lying to him all along.

Teresa held out her arms for Evie. "Here, let me take her. I'll get her changed and put her to bed while you take care of this. I assume you still have a supply of diapers in the bathroom." Teresa had a key to the summer house, just as Nathan did. They kept an eye on the place when I was in Toronto.

"Thank you," I said.

Teresa put Evie over her shoulder and hugged me with one arm. The press of her breast against mine was comforting. Like a rare hug from my mother that, when I was a child, had left me far too elated and grateful and desperate. I hung on too long now, as I had then.

I heard flip-flops, and Ashley appeared at the door, bringing with her the overpowering scent of tropical suntan lotion. "I'm so glad you found her!" she said.

I stepped back from Teresa. "Yes," I said, offering Ashley a thin smile. "She was here all along, with Teresa."

Nathan ran a hand down Ashley's bare arm. "We're going back to the hunt camp."

I shook my head, warning him off. I didn't want Ashley to know Olive was out there. She'd tell the locals. But Nathan didn't pick up on it. "Kira's . . . friend, a teen, is lost in the bush."

"What?" Ashley frowned accusingly at me. *You lost two kids in the same evening? What the hell is the matter with you?* "At your dad's place?"

"How do you know about that?" I asked, then I looked at Nathan. He'd told this stranger about my father's hunt camp? *What* had he told her, exactly?

Ashley shrugged. "Everyone knows. A group of us hunt there every November."

"You take hunters onto Dad's property, *my* property?" I asked Nathan. He had taken *Ashley* there?

"It's a waste to let that bush go unused," he said. "All those deer, just waiting to be harvested. It's not only us."

"My dad hunts there," Ashley said. "He has for years."

And yet no one had bothered to ask me, because I was only one of the summer people, an outsider, though I had thought of this village as home. Worse, Nathan had *avoided* telling me. He'd known I wouldn't like it. I didn't want to go near that property. So Nathan took Ashley hunting there instead.

"We didn't think you'd mind," Teresa said soothingly. *We*, she said, speaking for the locals.

I waved both hands beside my ears. This was too much to take in right now. "We've got to go."

"I'll let you know how this plays out," Nathan said to Ashley. "Or if we need help."

"I'll wait at your house," she said, glancing over his shoulder at me.

I didn't like that, how she presumed to wait at Nathan's house, or how he touched her arm, how kindly he spoke to her. Ashley shuffled back and forth in her flip-flops, as if working up the courage to say something else, but then slunk out the door, looking back over her shoulder once at Nathan with sad cocker spaniel eyes.

20

As Nathan and I made our way through the crowd to the truck, the thunderhead hovered over us, black and threatening. I could taste the sour, metallic zing of ozone in the air. Waves stirred up by the wind crashed onto the shore. Lightning flashed immediately overhead, and flashed again, splitting the sky in two. Fat raindrops started to fall, leaving dots the size of quarters on the boardwalk. And then the rain fell in earnest, drenching my hair, pounding against the boardwalk, leaving it slippery. People who were still hanging out on the beach clicked their lawn chairs closed, picked up their blankets and ran for their cars.

We sprinted to my rental. "I'm driving," Nathan said, as if I was a drunk and he was taking away the keys.

"I can drive," I said.

He held out his hand. "Keys."

I was too tired to argue. I tossed Nathan the keys and he opened the back door for Buddy as I took my seat. The dog jumped in, treading wet paw prints across the upholstery. My hair was wet from the downpour. Nathan backed up and drove out of the parking lot, honking to get other vehicles out of the way. The rain pelted down the windshield so quickly that the wipers struggled to keep up. The cars ahead of us were going slowly, too slowly.

Nathan pulled out to pass a string of them, parting a wash of water, and the wheels of the truck caught on the slick, hydroplaning. The anti-lock braking system vibrated as it kicked in, and Nathan regained control.

In the glass of the windshield, I saw my face reflected, lit up from below by the dashboard lights. My blond hair slipping out of my ponytail, my clear, pale skin, which my mother claimed was my best feature. But now I looked ghoulish in the eerie light. My father's ghostly pale blue eyes stared back at me.

As we passed the sweet spot, I quickly checked my messages. Aaron had texted to let me know he was on the road and would arrive in the early morning. I thought of phoning him, but I was with Nathan and there was little time. We'd lose reception again as soon as we sped down the straight stretch. And what was I going to tell him? How was I going to explain any of this? I would have to try later, I knew, but by then I would have Olive back. At least, I hoped so. For now, I tried phoning Madison instead, but she wasn't picking up. She didn't respond to my text either. That could mean anything: that she was out of range or still looking for Olive in the bush, or that she had found her and was driving away with her.

As we neared the hunt camp, I pointed at the gray minivan, its emergency lights flashing. The body of the deer was still lying nearby, its blood washed downhill by the rain.

"That's Sarah's van," I said. "Thank god." Either Madison and Sarah hadn't yet found Olive, or they hadn't brought her back to the van. They might have found a sheltered place, perhaps the cabin, to wait out the storm. But Ashley had said everyone knew about my father's hunt camp, that the locals hunted here. *My god,*

I thought, *anyone could be living in my father's hunting cabin.* I had left it empty since his death. What if Olive had run into a squatter hiding out there? Or, if she had found her way back to the road, anyone could have picked her up. I felt nauseous at the thought. She was just a kid, and an anxious one at that. We had to find her. We simply *had* to find her.

Nathan parked in front of the minivan and flipped up the hood of his coat against the wind and rain as he let Buddy out. I opened the passenger side of the crew cab and rummaged in my bag for a wool sweater to wear under Nathan's spare raincoat. But the rain fell so heavily, I was soaked by the time I got the sweater and coat on. Olive would be drenched too. *Dangerous,* I thought, remembering my wilderness training. It was dangerous to be wet through at night, even in July. Hypothermia could set in so quickly. My father had lectured me on the importance of being dressed properly for the woods—in wool and nylon, not cotton, which stayed wet—and anticipating changes in the weather. He had told me over and over that more people died of hypothermia in the warmer months than at any other time of year. With her slim build, Olive was in even more danger.

I grabbed my bag and locked up. The stream of drivers behind us slowed as they passed, and one driver, a guy in a Canada Day cap, stopped. "Need a hand with that deer, Nathan?" He thought we were there to pick up the carcass.

"No, we're good," Nathan said, raising his voice over the roar of wind and rain. The guy waved and drove on.

Roadkill deer never went to waste on the island. Steady work was hard to come by here, and the meat on a deer would fill a freezer. Once we left, the doe would likely be picked up by a couple of the many unemployed or partly employed men on the island who had a family to feed.

I swung my bag over my shoulder. "Will the rain make it harder for Buddy to catch the scent?" I asked Nathan.

"If we're fast, it will make it easier. Get something wet, and the smell only gets stronger."

I nodded, remembering Buddy's run-in with a skunk. Nathan had bathed him and the stench had eventually disappeared, until Buddy jumped into the lake and came out smelling skunky again, the water refreshing the odor.

"But if the rain continues to be this heavy," Nathan continued, "it could wash the trail away."

"Then we better be quick," I said, pulling the flashlight from my pocket. The rain pelted off the hoods of our jackets, forming rivulets down our backs. The trees around us swayed in the wind, dropping small branches.

Nathan offered Buddy Olive's hoodie again, and we launched into the ditch and then the bush, the beagle leading the way. As Nathan followed Buddy, wading through the wet grass and underbrush ahead, I lagged behind, searching the forest for shapes, the ghost of my young self. Within these woods there was a dark we never experienced in the city, the kind that infiltrates your spine, sends shivers into your scalp.

"You okay?" Nathan called.

I shook my head. "I'm not sure I can do this."

Lightning cracked above our heads, briefly illuminating the old barn ahead, and thunder boomed almost immediately. The storm was on top of us. *We shouldn't be out here*, I thought. *We shouldn't be exposed like this.*

Nathan took my hand and tugged me forward. "We'll do it together," he said.

But then I saw her. Past Nathan, on the hunt camp road, the hazy figure waited for me. "No," I murmured, pulling back.

"Kira," he said firmly. "As you said, we need to find Olive before Madison does. Or we could lose her trail to this rain. Now let's go."

GAIL ANDERSON-DARGATZ

"Okay," I said, breathing deeply. *Okay*, I told myself. *I can do this.* I held Nathan's hand tightly, like a frightened child, and, clutching my bag to my chest, stepped forward, walking the road I had driven with my father when we headed to the cabin on our last hunting trip, keeping my eyes on the figure ahead. She grew clearer and clearer as we came closer. Her hunter-orange cap and vest, the oversized camouflage jacket and pants, the rifle in her hand. When we reached the old barn, its gray boards crumbling at the base as its wood foundation rotted into the ground, the girl, the frightened twelve-year-old girl I had been, nodded once and came to walk beside me, a fetch matching my gait step for step.

I *would* find Olive. I *could* stop Madison from taking her. I could do this.

The long grass parted as we pushed through it, further soaking my yoga pants. My runners were soggy. Rain dribbled down my face and into my cleavage. The drops of water on the young trees reflected the light from our flashlights as we rounded the corner to my father's hunt camp.

The meadow around it was now overgrown with young sugar maple trees. The sauna was still standing. The outhouse was out of view behind the cabin. Beyond that, on the far side of the field, camouflaged and hidden by bush at the forest edge, I knew I'd find the tree stand my father had erected there. I used to love it as a child—I thought of it as *my* treehouse, not a platform for hunting. My father had rarely used it because the deer knew when it was hunting season and disappeared from the main tracks. We no longer saw them along the roads or in the fields. A hunter had to go deep into the forest, where the deer took sanctuary, coming out of hiding only to forage in the dark before the hunters were active at dawn, and again after sundown, when the hunt was over for the day. I marveled, as a child, at the intelligence of these animals, how they learned the rhythms of the hunt, when it began, when it ended. When hunting season was over, the deer returned to their usual foraging patterns, often grazing in farmers' fields or crossing the road in the morning or evening with little fear.

The cabin itself was small, built on a concrete slab that served as its floor. It had cedar siding, and rainwater cascaded from a metal roof that sheltered a small porch in front of the door. Even though it was solidly built, the forest had begun to reclaim it. Rot crept up the siding from the bottom, and a small tree had wedged its way through the floor of the deck on one side.

My fetch looked back in my direction once before climbing the steps. Walking right through the door, she disappeared into the cabin.

"I don't think Buddy's going to pick up Olive's scent now, not in all this rain," Nathan said. "It's too heavy. Or he's picking up too many scents."

Buddy zigzagged through the long grass and young trees around the cabin, excited by several trails, probably not just Olive's, but Madison's and Sarah's as well. Or the many scent trails of the deer that lived in this forest. Oh, to be a dog. To take in the world through smell, to time travel through scent, breathing in events that had happened an hour, a day, a week before. The past lingered like ghosts all around Buddy. But then, this forest had its share of ghosts for me too.

"I'll check the cabin," I said.

"I'll keep working Buddy out here."

I ran up the stairs to the deck and tried the door. It was locked, but the window on it was broken. Recently, by the look of it— either Olive or Madison breaking in. A rock would have done the trick. Rather than retrieve my set of keys from my bag, I reached in and turned the knob from the inside, careful not to cut myself, then took a deep breath and, for the first time since my father's death, walked inside.

21

The cabin was dark, as the power had long ago been shut off, and smelled musty, of mold and mice. There was a layer of dust on the gun cabinet and the phone hanging on the wall, and mouse droppings littered the table. The corners of the ceiling were canopied with spiderwebs. But our mugs were still there on the floor where they had fallen, crusted with the dried remains of coffee. My father sucked his coffee through sugar cubes held between his teeth. I'd learned to do the same, and to drink it at all hours of the day, even in the evening with supper, so that at night I lay wide awake on my cot, vibrating under the influence of caffeine and fear. The bedding on the cots was worn floral sheets cast down from the summer house years before and covered in rough gray camp blankets. A Hudson Bay blanket lay over the back of a chair near the woodstove.

One bed was made up neatly, but the other was rumpled. *Some-body's been sleeping in my bed.* Olive, or Madison or Sarah, trying to warm up, perhaps after being soaked by the rain. I touched a dark spot on a blanket; it was wet. The blankets had been thrown back hurriedly, likely when Olive or one of the women heard us outside, and there were wet shoe prints in the dust leading to the back door. I shone the light on them for a closer look. Runners, I thought. Likely Olive, then, or maybe Sarah. Whoever it was, I must have just spooked her.

"Olive?" I called, though I knew she must be hiding outside in the forest. There was no place to hide in here, and little in the way of furniture. Just the two single beds, a table, two chairs and the small potbellied woodstove that we had used to heat the place. The door on it stood ajar, and wood was arranged inside as if someone had been contemplating making a fire but hadn't gotten around to it. Perhaps Olive hadn't felt confident enough to do so. I doubt she'd ever lit a campfire, much less got a woodstove going.

My father had kept kerosene lanterns on hand for power outages, and I shone the light on two of them on the shelf now, then searched the room with the flashlight until I found a box of Red Bird matches on the windowsill. I lit the lanterns, bringing the inside of the cabin to life—and all at once I was back there on my father's final day.

We had arrived at the camp before lunch, carrying our hunting gear and a bag of rice pies and jelly pigs. The lights were already on inside, and when I opened the cabin door, I found Teresa waiting for us at the small pine table. She'd made a fire and the cabin was warm, a relief from the November cold outside. But even so, Teresa wore a bright-blue puffer jacket.

"What is she doing here?" I asked my father.

"You and I have some things to talk about," he said as he closed the door behind us. "I asked Teresa to help."

"Help? With what?"

It was only much later that I realized Teresa was there as a sort of counselor. Before my parents' separation, my father had had long conversations with Teresa in our summer house kitchen, conversations that came to an end when I entered the room, conversations I now understood were all about me. Teresa was a home care worker, not a social worker, not a counselor, though I thought she viewed herself as one. She was too quick to intervene, to give advice. Even now, I imagined her sitting at the kitchen table with her clients, offering them unaccredited counseling sessions along with a healthy serving of mashed potatoes, applesauce and cabbage rolls. I expect she felt she had missed her calling for lack of an education.

Teresa stood up. "Actually, I asked your father if I could talk with you, with both of you. I've been worried about your dad. He's been very sick for a long time—"

"Sick?" I asked, my heart speeding up.

"Depressed," Teresa said. "Do you understand what that means?"

I gave her *the look*. Of course I knew what it meant. I wasn't a baby. I glanced at my father then. The anguish in his face. I had spent the time since my parents' divorce not really looking at him. He seemed so much older now, and drawn, like he *had* been sick for a long time. He looked smaller, somehow, unkept. *Depressed*, Teresa had said. That meant he was sad, really sad. Sick, but sick in the head.

Teresa smoothed a strand of hair out of my face. "I've also been worried about you, about the things you say about your father, what you call him, things a child shouldn't say or think about a parent. When your dad told me he was worried too, I suggested we all get together and chat about it." She sat back down. "Come sit with me."

My father took a seat on the nearby cot, but I remained standing, wary now. "Look, I'm only here because the judge said I had to visit Dad. That doesn't mean I have to talk to you." I looked pointedly at my father. "Either of you."

My dad reached out to take my hand, but I shook him off. I thought, for a moment, that he might cry, that I might cry, so I turned away, to look out the window. The day was overcast. I could leave, walk back to the summer house, but it was a long walk, and snow had begun to fall. A crow on a nearby branch eyed me through the window, its head tilted. It seemed unnaturally, eerily large.

"What you just said, the way you just acted . . ." My father paused. "That's exactly the kind of thing we'd like to talk to you about. You told the social worker you were afraid of me. Kira, can you remember a time when I hurt you?"

I snorted. "Plenty," I said. It was a response I'd heard so often from my mother.

"Name one."

Had my father ever hurt me? When I wound back through my fragmented childhood memories, nothing of substance surfaced. He got angry at me now and again, mostly over the messes I left on the table and in my room. When my mother yelled at him, he yelled back, and that had scared me. But I couldn't remember a single incident where he had hurt me. I just felt an overwhelming sense of fear in his presence.

"You scare me," I said.

"But why?"

I didn't answer. He leaned forward on the cot and put his head in both hands. We all listened to the crackle of the fire in the pot-bellied stove. The cabin smelled of woodsmoke, creosote.

I finally sat on a chair.

Teresa put a hand on the table between us. "I think your mother led you to believe you should be afraid of your father," she said, "even though there's nothing to be afraid of."

"Why would she do that?" I said. "That's dumb."

"Your mother is very angry at your father," Teresa said.

"Mom has every right to be," I said. "He's is a cheater, an alcoholic. He makes life miserable for her." My mother's words.

"I'm not any of those things," my father said quietly.

I looked to either side of him, but not at his face. I had never seen my father spend time with other women during his marriage to my mother, and he wasn't a heavy drinker, as my mother claimed. But she had never liked how he went off to have a beer with his hunting buddies from the island. They'd always fought about it afterward. So it must have been bad.

"You forced me and Mom to live in poverty after the divorce," I said. Something else my mother claimed.

Dad breathed out heavily. "I pay child support, Kira. But your mother has made her own choices, sometimes foolish choices. She felt she deserved a better lifestyle than she could afford, and overspent. When she ran low, she came running to me. I gave her more money at first, but when it became a habit, I stopped. We are divorced, after all. She has to make her own way."

"You *left* us," I said. "You don't love us anymore."

"Oh, Kira, I may have stopped loving your mother, but I will never stop loving you. It's just . . . your mother doesn't always see things clearly."

My father glanced at Teresa, and she nodded sideways. *Go on, tell her.*

"Your mother is a wounded woman, Kira," he said. "Her father *did* hurt her."

I knew about her father. My mother had told me, too much. Things that made me want to cover my ears. But I listened because I knew Mom wanted me to listen; she needed me to listen.

Teresa took my hand. "Your mother has accused your father of no end of horrible things, to keep you away from him, to keep you to herself. Maybe, in her way, she *is* trying to protect you, but there are no grounds for her accusations."

Dad looked up at me. "Kira, I just couldn't handle the way your mother acted anymore. That's why I left. But I should have taken you with me."

"Your mother has been lying to you," Teresa said. "Your dad isn't scary. And you shouldn't treat him like you do, calling him names and swearing at him. Honey, your dad is afraid he's losing you."

"I'm afraid I *have* lost you," Dad said.

"You have," I said, pulling my hand away from Teresa's. My mother would like that I'd said that. She would think it was funny. I knew even as I said it that I would offer the comment to her as I might a bouquet of wildflowers.

"I don't believe you," Teresa said. "That's your mother talking, isn't it?"

I shook my head as the urge to defend my mother welled up. It had been my job to defend her, against my father and sometimes others, like my teachers, like Teresa. "My mother doesn't tell me what to say. I make up my own mind."

"I believe you still love your father," Teresa said. "But you've pushed your feelings down deep inside, to please your mom."

In that instant, I felt, at first, terrified, because some part of me knew she was right. And then I felt enraged. I *hated* Teresa. This nosy, irritating woman who always spoke her mind and stuck her nose in other people's business. I hated Teresa the way I hated my father. Blindly, for reasons I could never fully define.

"No, I hate him. I hate him!" I shouted, then turned directly to my father. "I *hate* you! I absolutely fucking hate you!"

Teresa, shocked, sucked in air. "Kira!" she said.

I picked up the cast-iron kettle, a clunky black thing still hot from the stove, and wielded it by the handle as if to hit my father with it. But I hesitated and beat the table instead. I hit, hit, hit it, leaving crescent moon–shaped dents in the wood. *Bang, bang, bang.*

Teresa took the kettle from me as if I were a toddler who had gotten hold of her daddy's hammer.

But the storm inside me only grew bigger. I pushed everything off the kitchen table, the mugs filled with coffee, the teaspoons and sugar bowl, the glass salt and pepper shakers. It all clattered to the floor. The shakers spun in the same direction, like ice-skaters.

My father hugged me to stop me from doing any more damage to the cabin or myself, and I struggled in his arms.

"Kira, that's enough," he said slowly, his words thick with fatigue.

"I hate you!" I cried again. "I hate you! I hate you! I hate you!" But I settled into my father's embrace, my head against his shoulder, my arms wrapped around him with such need that I could have been saying *I love you!* My father ran a hand over my hair, shushing me, and kissed my head. The protective numbness inside me started to melt, and something else surfaced through the cracks. I began to shake, overwhelmed by repressed emotion that I fought to dampen. I *couldn't* love him. I *couldn't* love both him and my mother. To do so was a betrayal of my mother. And yet I knew I would feel split in two like this as long as my father was alive. In that moment, I wished he were dead.

It was then, cheek pressed to my father's chest, looking out the window at the crow looking back, that I realized what I must do, here at the hunt camp, before my father took me home. What I must do to prove myself to my mother and protect myself; what I must do to end this torment.

I just wasn't sure yet how I would get away with it.

22

I smoothed a hand over the crescent-shaped marks I'd left in the pine table fifteen years before. Then startled as Nathan appeared at the door.

"Find anything?" he asked. "Was Olive here?"

"I think so. Somebody sure as hell was." I glanced around the room with him at the broken window, the shards of glass on the floorboards, the wet pillow, the opened stove door and the footprints through the dust on the floor. I was still shaking with rage, or grief, or adrenaline—I hardly knew which anymore.

Seeing my face twisted with emotion, Nathan pulled me into a hug. "Hey, hey," he said. "What's going on?"

But I didn't explain. He already knew part of the story, and I had never found a way to tell him, or anyone, the rest.

"My mother always hated this cabin," I said instead, as I pulled away from him to wipe my face. "Even before she and my father were divorced."

"Well, she would, wouldn't she?" he said, looking around. Water dripping from his rain jacket pooled at his feet.

"What do you mean?" I asked.

"This was your dad's getaway. He took you out here to train, or on his hunts, without her. Your mom was jealous of anything that didn't include her, where she wasn't the center of attention. Remember how she bullied her way into managing your training? That was always your dad's thing. After your folks split, she just took right over."

"That's not the way it was." *Not with the training, at least*, I thought. But then here I was, still defending her. "I was living with Mom. It made sense that she would take me to events."

He sunk his hands into his jeans pockets. "And when she did, she pushed me out of the picture."

"You still competed," I said. "We saw each other at races."

"Yeah, but your mom made it clear she didn't want me around."

He's a distraction, my mother had said of Nathan. *You need to focus on your training, on the events.* She said the same of any friend I made, but especially Nathan. She called his mom, Teresa, an interfering bitch, and her dislike of the woman extended to her son. When we stayed at the summer house, I had to sneak out to see Nathan, lie in order to meet up with him. It seemed that habit had extended into my adulthood.

"Did Buddy pick up Olive's scent?" I asked.

Nathan shrugged. "In this heavy rain, he's going in circles."

I headed for the back door. "We need to go farther into the forest, under tree cover. Maybe he can pick up her scent there."

I trained the flashlight outside, across the wall of black. Rain fell in a glossy sheet from the overhang. The storm had only gotten worse. Wind pushed the young trees almost horizontal. Branches fell from the larger trees. Everything was in motion, branches and leaves swirling in the black. And there, standing at the edge of the bush, was a figure in the dark, a girl.

"Olive?" I called. Or was it my doppelgänger?

"You see her?" Nathan asked. "Where?"

"Olive?" I called again. The shadow of a girl ran into the bush, disappearing into the glistening blackness. I launched forward, running through the rain and wind, pushing through the branches as I entered the bush. The dark swallowed me, making it almost impossible to see even a few feet ahead, but there was something moving in front of me, a shadow also pushing through the bush. "Olive," I cried. "Stop!"

Behind me, I heard Buddy barking as he picked up the scent or the chase. As Nathan and his dog ran to catch up with me, I could hear twigs breaking under his feet, the beagle snuffling. The light from Nathan's flashlight bounced off the trees ahead. But I had lost sight of the girl running through the woods. I slowed and shone my light back and forth across the groaning trees. There was a small clearing up ahead, my father's firepit, surrounded by logs, seating where we often had lunch during a hunt. I had waited on one of those logs, rifle in hand, for him to flush out a deer on that last day. As I stepped into the clearing, I saw a figure sitting on that log now. The black outline of a girl. She turned to look at me, and I came face to face with my past.

But then Buddy reached me and barked, and Nathan was there at my shoulder, and my young self faded away.

"Was it Olive?" he asked.

I shook my head fiercely, as if I could shake the ghosts loose. "Nathan, I think I'm losing my mind. I'm seeing ghosts everywhere."

He laughed a little. "I've seen all kinds of things out here in the forest. Heard things. Nutty things. My mind playing tricks on me. Remember what your father always said? *What you think you see in the bush—*"

I finished for him, "*—is rarely what's really there.*"

My father had drummed that saying into me when he took me

hunting. To avoid hunting accidents, he said, wear hunter orange and be aware that what you thought was a deer might very well be another hunter or a hiker. It had been on my mind during that last hunt with my father, after Teresa left, as I waited on the log that was in front of us now, my brown and green pants blending into the leaf mulch dropped by the sugar maple and beech towering above me. But I wore a hunter-orange cap and vest, as my father did. Humans could see it as that brilliant color, while deer experienced it as gray or brown. My father left me there and went to flush out deer, warning me, again, to keep quiet and be ready for the deer when it launched through the bush. It would be my first kill.

As I repositioned the rifle, I purposefully steadied my breath and felt my heart rate settle, the shake in my hands lessen. Slowly I entered that familiar state of grace I so often experienced while running, where I was both hyperaware and oblivious to the passage of time. My sense of self dissipated and then, painfully, snapped back into place as my calf cramped. My right foot had fallen asleep. Had I been sitting here for minutes? Hours? My belly grumbled at the thought of the rice pies and jelly pigs we'd have later.

I scrutinized the bush around me, alert to any movement: the lift of branches shifting in the wind, the flutter of a bird's wings. A chipmunk leapt from one tree to another and ran off, chattering. Somewhere close by, a chickadee sang, *chickadee-dee-dee*.

Then a twig broke in the underbrush ahead and I tensed. My heart raced, thundering in my ears, and my breath grew short. I struggled to calm my nerves as I peered through the rifle scope at the forest beyond. Another twig broke, and I saw my target moving through the bush. The hunter orange. But before the flock of cedar waxwings erupted from the trees into the sky, before the deafening crack of the rifle, even before I squeezed the trigger, the dark shadow of a thought, an *excuse*—a way to get away with it—winged across my mind. An accident, I could say, a hunting accident. A tragic mistake. It happened every year in the province. Most of the time, the victim was a hunter who accidentally hit himself or a buddy. A bullet to the shoulder or foot. But occasionally it was much worse. A hiker had been shot and killed just two years before. She didn't know hunting season had begun, and had gone for a walk with her dog. A hunter had fired at a deer and missed, and the stray bullet had caught the hiker in the chest, killing her. That could happen here, and no one would know otherwise. As my father always said: *What you think you see in the bush is rarely what's really there.*

23

Standing in the dark beside Nathan, in the rain and wind, by the log where I had fired that shot, I started to shake uncontrollably, then, overcome, to cry, and then to wail. I fell to my knees in the muck around the campfire, my hands open on my thighs. Thinking of nothing. Feeling everything. It was like every emotion, the grief, the guilt I'd suppressed as a kid poured out of me. I'd once hiked to a waterfall with my father, one with a gaping cavern behind it that the water seemed to flood out of. Now, with my face tipped up to the rain, my mouth open, I was that cave, and the howl that flooded out was both animal and unearthly. Buddy took up the lament, howling beside me.

"Kira!" Nathan cried, squatting beside me. "For god's sake." He gripped my shoulder so I would look up at him. Rain thundered down from the sky above us. "Kira, what's going on?"

"It was my fault," I said. "I meant to do it!"

He looked with me into the forest, at the path beyond, where my father had walked away from me that day, where the trees had enveloped him. His expression slowly changed as he realized what

I was talking about. What I was telling him, after all this time. Then he pulled me up from the ground and hugged me like he thought I might slip away.

"I'm sorry," he said. "I'm sorry that you never felt safe enough to tell me the truth. I know things with your family were messed up. Whatever happened with your dad, we can talk about it soon. You just let me know when. But it has to wait. Right now, you need to get your shit together. There's a young girl alone and scared in this forest, in this storm, wet through and getting colder by the minute. We need to keep moving."

I nodded. *Breathe*, I thought. *Breathe*.

"I'm right here with you," Nathan said. "You can do this."

I must do this, I thought. For Olive. For myself. As I opened my mouth to tell him we should carry on, I suddenly saw movement in the corner of my eye. Could she be that close?

"Over there!" I pointed.

Nathan pushed into the forest ahead of me, following the trail my father had taken that last day. "Olive!" he called, over and over, and I echoed him. "Olive!"

Buddy took off ahead of us, finding a scent trail now that we were under more cover, and Nathan picked up his pace. When he disappeared into the dark forest ahead of me, I called, "Nathan?"

He pointed his flashlight back in my direction. "I'm right here," he said, his voice warm, reassuring. "I'm right here."

I held a hand up to protect my face from wet branches and followed the orb of Nathan's flashlight, hearing the squish of my own footsteps through mud and wet undergrowth. And then, up ahead, Buddy barked and barked.

"I think he's found her!" Nathan cried from some yards ahead, his voice thin in the wind and rain.

"You see her?" I asked.

"I think Buddy does. Over there!" Nathan shone his flashlight in the direction of Buddy's bark, which was coming from a dense cedar bush. "Kira, you need to come and talk to her. Every time I move forward, she moves back."

Nathan pointed out the section of the woods where he thought she was hiding, and we made our way toward it. Wind swirled the rain, and within it I thought I saw the girl—my younger self. But then the wind retreated, and the fetch dissipated.

"Olive?" I called, then, to Buddy, "Where is she, boy?" He barked and pointed his nose toward the thicket. Branches shook ahead of me.

"Olive, is that you?" I asked. "It's okay. This my friend Nathan and his dog, Buddy. I asked them to help me find you." I heard her move back, farther into the bush. I stopped moving. "It's dangerous to be out here in the rain for long. You must be chilled." I listened. She was close. I could feel her eyes on me. I could feel *someone's* eyes on me, at least. "You must be so scared. Let's get you out of this dark forest, out of this storm."

I trained the light across the patch of bush. There was a flash of white. An arm, and then Olive's young, scared face. A twig snapped as she quickly stepped back, out of the flashlight's glare. I skimmed the light over the undergrowth and found her again, squatting, huddled against a tree trunk, wet through, shivering. She stood and held up a hand to the light, squinting. Buddy's eyes reflected green, like some strange hellhound, as he turned back to us and wagged his tail in triumph. Another successful game of hide-and-seek.

Nathan called the dog to him and made a show of praising Buddy. "Good boy! You're such a good boy! You did so good!" He tossed a treat and Buddy caught it in his mouth. The dog circled Nathan, barking excitedly, wagging his tail.

I held out a hand to Olive. "Let's go inside—" I started.

But then we heard a woman's voice carried on the wind. Madison's voice, calling through the woods in the distance. "Olive! *Olive!*"

"Maddy?" Olive cried. Then, louder, "Maddy?"

"Olive!"

She bolted toward the sound of Madison's voice. I sprinted after her, shining my light forward, pushing branches out of my face. The white of Olive's skin flickered in and out of my beam as she dodged trees, leapt over logs, pushed through bushes. An owl, frightened by our passage, screeched and glided away, a ghost in the rainy night.

I quickly caught up with Olive and took her arm. "Olive, please stop. If you want to see Madison, we can make it happen. We can meet her at the cabin. But for god's sake, stop before you get lost again!"

She yanked her arm out of my grip and stared into the blackness, in the direction of Madison's voice, as if trying to make up her mind.

"That's really why you ran at the bridge, wasn't it? To see Madison?" When she didn't immediately answer, I added, "I know she was in the minivan with you and that woman, Sarah. The van is parked here, at the road. Sarah's here too, somewhere in this forest, looking for you."

Olive's eyes grew large. *Busted*. "I just wanted to see my mom, you know? Dad won't even let me talk to Maddy. But she's my *mom*." She looked up at me. "Will you tell him? I mean, if you let me see Maddy now?"

I looked back at Nathan, and he shook his head. "No," I said. "Aaron doesn't need to know about any of this." About how I had let Olive slip away a second time, about Nathan being here, tracking her down.

Olive eyed Nathan and me, trying to gauge whether she could trust us, I thought. "Okay," she said finally. "Let's go."

I wrapped an arm around her, pushing her wet hair out of her face. "My god, you're freezing. We've got to get you warmed up right away."

She nodded, shivering, and Nathan took off his rain jacket and draped it around her.

"Madison?" I called out into the storm. "Madison, we found Olive. Meet us back at the cabin." I listened a moment. "You hear me?"

There was a pause, as if she didn't quite know how to respond, and then she called back from the black forest. "I heard you."

I squeezed Olive's shoulder. "Come on, let's get out of this rain."

When Nathan snapped Buddy's leash onto his collar for the hike back, Olive bent to scratch Buddy's head. The smell of dog rose up. The beagle, in turn, sniffed her with interest. And for the first time that day—that week, that month—a genuine, spontaneous smile appeared on Olive's face. When we got home, I was going to buy that girl a dog.

24

The rain-peppered cabin windows reflected the flickering amber light of the lanterns within, and I felt a pang of nostalgia, as if I were visiting the past. I half expected to see Dad pass by the window, carrying the kettle from the stove to the small wooden table to make hot chocolate. If I peeked inside, would I see myself, that girl, seated with my father at the table? But, of course, time had moved on, and my father was long dead.

Nathan removed his wet rain jacket from Olive's shoulders and hung it on a hook near the door, next to my father's plaid jacket. I wrapped a gray camp blanket around her and took a good look at her. Her lips had taken on a bluish cast and her makeup was smeared, darkening the area under her eyes. I fished in my purse and handed her a fresh baby wipe. She dabbed her face with it, removing the mascara from beneath her eyes.

"As soon as this storm lets up," I said, "we'll run to the truck and get you back to the house. You can have a hot shower and tuck into bed. I think we're all ready for a good night's sleep."

"I'll get a fire going for now," Nathan said, kneeling near the stove to arrange newspaper and kindling within it. "This place is so small it won't take long to heat up."

It never had taken long, even in November. My father had insulated the walls of the cabin well, and it warmed up within minutes of someone starting a fire.

"When is Maddy going to get here?" Olive asked.

"Soon, I expect," I said.

She sat in a chair at the table to rub Buddy's head. "He's a tracker?" she asked Nathan.

"I trained him myself," Nathan said, grabbing the box of Red Bird matches.

"Buddy's a blood tracker," I explained. "A hunting dog."

"You mean he tracks down wounded deer," she said, wrinkling her nose in disgust as she looked accusingly at me. "So you can *kill* them."

"So they don't endure pain any longer than they have to," I said.

"A good hunter never wants an animal to suffer," Nathan said. He lit a match and held it to the kindling.

"You guys hunt together?" Olive asked, looking first at me and then at Nathan. She was asking how we knew each other.

"We haven't hunted together for a long time," I said. "Not since we were kids." Hunting with my father, though not with rifles. I didn't carry a gun until that final year, after I turned twelve. "Nathan and I grew up together," I said. More or less. I'd spent summers and much of the winter here on Manitoulin when my father was still alive, hunting or cross-country skiing, snowshoeing.

"I've never heard you talk about him," Olive said, pointing a thumb at Nathan.

I exchanged a glance with him. Still kneeling by the fire, he offered her a Snickers from his jacket pocket. "You hungry?" he asked, trying to redirect the conversation. *Awkward.*

Olive didn't bother to answer. Her eyes slid from me to Nathan and back again. The kid was far too attuned to the grown-ups around her, too aware of their associations and concerns, picking up cues other kids would miss. I just hoped she wouldn't mention Nathan to Aaron; if she did, it would become obvious that she'd run away a second time, to get to Madison. We'd have to have a conversation about exactly how much Aaron needed to hear about today's events.

"There," Nathan said, closing the stove door and standing. "That should warm us up in no time." The fire crackled, already throwing some heat.

Olive pulled the blanket snug around her neck and rapped her knuckles against the metal gun cabinet that stood against the wall behind the table. "What *is* this thing?" she asked. "Some kind of safe?"

"That's where my father stored his hunting rifles," I said. One was likely still there, a gun I had never got around to disposing of. I was so foolish, cowardly, not drumming up the courage to venture into my father's hunt camp and deal with this. The low crime rate on Manitoulin was a point of local pride, but anyone could have broken into this cabin over the years and taken the rifle. Kids, even. One hard strike of a rock on the cabinet's lock would have busted it open. I could have been responsible for some dumb kid's death. I rummaged in my bag for my set of keys and flipped through them until I got to the key marked *Guns*. I opened the cabinet to check. My father's Remington Model 700 was still there in the racks, thank god, along with a box of cartridges on the shelf above. The cabinet smelled of mice, and droppings lined its base. I closed the door and put the lock back in place. I would have to come back and clean this cabin out, sell the property finally, rid myself of the memories.

"Your father was seriously into hunting," Olive said. She stood to open the case of hunting knives that hung next to the gun cabinet, dragging the blanket along with her.

"Some of those knives were mine," I said. Gifts from my father. "From when I was about your age, actually."

Her eyes widened. For once I had impressed her. She opened the dusty case, took down a knife and flipped the blade over. "Cool. I mean, it looks like something from one of my games."

"Just what kind of video games does your father let you play?" Nathan asked.

Olive and Aaron played first-person shooter games together, mostly. It only occurred to me then that perhaps this wasn't the most appropriate father-daughter activity, but who was I to judge? My father had taken me out into the forest to kill deer.

"It's not a toy," I said, taking the knife from her. I held it a moment, hearing my mother's voice. *When you're staying with him at the cabin, you'll need to protect yourself,* she'd said. *There are all those knives in the case. He'll never notice if you take one. Keep it under your pillow. When he tries something, you'll be ready.* She'd made a thrusting motion, as if holding on to the hilt of a knife and jabbing. *Always be ready.*

I was always ready. Always watching, wary, on edge. If my father stood too close or stepped toward me too quickly, I would jump away, ready to run.

I put the knife back in the case, turning the latch. Then I steered Olive over to the chair next to the roaring fire and rubbed her arms briskly through the blanket to warm her. "Warming up?" I asked.

"A little."

Buddy barked, alerted by a noise outside, and then there was a knock on the front door and Madison stepped inside. Her hair and pink suit were wet through. She had swapped her heels for a pair of sandals, though they were equally impractical in this forest. Her mascara was completely smudged, giving her racoon eyes, and her lipstick was smeared across her upper lip. She looked deranged.

"Olive," she said, holding out her arms. "Oh, thank god."

Olive ran to her, letting the blanket fall as she wrapped her arms around her stepmother.

"I was so scared," Madison said. "We checked the cabin first—"

"I knew the cabin would be the first place Kira looked," Olive said. "When I heard someone coming, I ran."

Madison smoothed her hair. "We called and called, but with the wind howling—we couldn't find you."

"Then you know how I feel," I said. "You told me to go to the playground. But Evie wasn't there. We searched for her—"

Madison looked perplexed. "But I told you I'd leave Evie with your friend Teresa, and that she would meet you at the playground for the fireworks."

"You took Evie?" Olive asked Madison. As she stepped back, I slipped the blanket around her shoulders.

"But Evie is okay, right?" Madison asked me. She appeared genuinely concerned.

"We found her, but I had no idea where she was at first. We searched the water for her. I was terrified."

"I'm so sorry," she said, with such emotion that I almost believed she meant it. "But you weren't listening to me, and I *had* to find a way to get to Olive. I *had* to."

"Even if that meant taking Evie."

"It did get your attention."

"I could charge you with kidnapping, child endangerment."

"Evie was never in danger, not from me. I found her alone in a parked vehicle on the side of the road. I took her to safety, to your friend's place. *You're* the one who left Evie alone in the truck. *You're* the one who left Olive alone in this forest. *You* should be charged with child endangerment."

"Okay, okay, settle down," Nathan said. "Both of you. The main thing is, Buddy found Olive and everyone's safe now."

Madison glanced from Nathan to his dog.

"Nathan is an old friend," I explained.

"Thank you," Madison said to him, grabbing his hand and shaking it in both of hers. "Thank you for finding my daughter."

Nathan shifted uncomfortably as he withdrew his hand, looking everywhere but at her. She lifted her chin. "I see Kira has told you about me," she said sadly, and then she turned to me. "I imagine you must think I'm crazy."

"The thought has crossed my mind," I said. "You did break into our house, follow us up here and take Evie out of my truck."

"I did, didn't I?" Madison shook her head in wonder and laughed a little, at herself, apparently. "God, I can't *believe* Aaron drove me to do all that."

Wow. Her capacity for self-delusion was astounding. Aaron? *She* was the one who had orchestrated this hell.

"I would have *never* done anything like this before . . ." She looked up at the cobwebs in the corner.

She was passing the blame again, onto me this time. I finished her sentence for her. "Before I arrived on the scene."

Her eyes found my face. "No," she said, like I was being self-indulgent, thinking I was that important. "Before I became a *mother*."

She ran a hand through her hair. Wet and heavy with hairspray, it stayed pushed up on one side of her head, ridiculously so. I hiccupped a giggle: she looked so at odds with the *Real Housewives* image she usually projected. I *giggled*.

"What?" she said, patting her hair.

"You look like shit."

"So do you," she said, and then *she* giggled. That fucking woman and I giggled in my father's haunted cabin. Nerves. The unlikeliness of us finding ourselves here together. And yet here we were. Madison, still smiling, took a compact and tissues from her purse and began wiping away the mascara that was running down her face. I rubbed the nervous laughter from my eyes, no doubt smudging my own mascara further.

"Are you two *okay*?" Olive asked.

Madison waved a hand. "Look, Kira, I just need a little time with Olive, in private. We have some important things to discuss, things she needs to know."

I bet, I thought. More bullshit about Aaron. "And what do you suggest?" I asked. "That Nathan and I wait outside in this storm?" Nathan shuffled backward to the front door as if he wanted to do just that. At his feet, Buddy sniffed the air and scratched the door, asking to be let out.

Madison glanced out the window at the rain hammering down. "Maybe Olive and I could have a little time together at your cottage?"

I shook my head. "Once the storm lets up, Olive is having a hot shower and going straight to bed. And as soon as Aaron gets here in the morning, we're turning around and going right back home."

"Aaron is on his way *here*?" Nathan asked. He looked thunderstruck, but I couldn't talk about that now, not with Madison and Olive in the room with us.

Madison smoothed Olive's wet hair for a moment, then let out a sigh. "Then I guess this is my opportunity."

"There is nothing you have to say that Olive needs to hear," I said. "I won't let you poison her with more lies."

"Lies, huh?"

"You're not going to talk to her."

Madison nodded slowly. "And just how are you going to stop me?"

Nathan and I exchanged a glance as Madison pushed past him to open the front door, revealing a wet figure sheltering on the porch. The smell of rain and wet earth blew in with the wind. "Sarah?" she said gently. "Sarah, it's time."

Nathan pulled the beagle back by the collar as Sarah stepped over the threshold cautiously, like a bristling cat that had just been chased, alert for dangers. Her outfit looked pieced together from a thrift store: gray joggers and an oversized hoodie soaked with rain, men's runners. She pulled back the hood to reveal a wild bush of curly blond hair that she had clearly dyed herself.

"*You,*" I said. "Who the hell *are* you?"

"This is Sarah," Madison said, closing the door behind her. "You met earlier."

At Nathan's feet, Buddy lifted his head, sniffing the air.

"Yes," I said. "But who *are* you? Why were you following me this morning?"

Sarah's eyes grew round and shifted to Olive. Seeing them together like this, I suddenly knew what Madison was about to say, what she had been trying to tell us all along. But how could it be true?

"Olive," Madison said, ignoring me and taking her stepdaughter's hand, "we don't have much time, so I'm just going to say it. I've been trying to arrange for you to meet Sarah for some time now. So here goes. Sarah, this is Olive. And Olive, this is Sarah." She hesitated. "Sweetheart, Sarah is your mom."

25

Olive shook her head and stepped back. Her eyes darted from Madison to Sarah and back again. "No," she said. "Maddy, *you're* my mom."

Madison tucked a loose curl behind Olive's ear. "Of course, I am, sweetheart. That isn't going to change. But Sarah gave birth to you. She lived with you and took care of you until—"

"My mom's name was Victoria."

"Vicki," Sarah said. "I took my middle name, Sarah, when I left your father. Given what happened, I felt I had to start over, leave the person I had been behind."

"But I've seen pictures of my mother," Olive said. "She had red hair, like me. And she didn't look—" She waved a hand, pointing out Sarah's ragged appearance. There were dark circles under the woman's eyes that seemed sunken, as if she hadn't drunk enough water, and her pale, freckled complexion was almost see-through, revealing the blue veins just below the skin. She didn't just look tired, she appeared *consumed*, like the victims of wildfires who had seen not only their homes, but their communities reduced to ashes in the flames.

"I've been ill," Sarah said. She tugged on a curl. "And I dyed my hair. But it was naturally red—auburn, actually—like yours. I couldn't stand to look at it every day in the mirror. It reminded me too much of . . ." Her gaze drifted to Olive's head of red curls.

Olive turned to Madison. "But when you and Sarah picked me up at the bridge—"

"I said she was a friend of mine. I know. This kind of news isn't something I wanted to just blurt out—at least, not under normal circumstances." She glanced at me. "Especially when someone was chasing us down the highway. I was waiting for a moment when we could all sit down together. And apparently this is it." She held out a hand to me. "That's all I was after, Kira. A few minutes to talk to my daughter, to introduce her to Sarah, to explain things to her."

"Why didn't you just tell me that?"

"When did you give me the chance? It's not like I could toss this at you in a text. You wouldn't have believed me, for a start."

Fair enough.

Buddy, excited by our raised voices, started to bark again, and Nathan, holding him back with his leash, petted the dog's head to calm him.

Madison settled into one of the chairs and took a mirror from her handbag to inspect her ruined makeup. "In any case, we didn't want Aaron to know Sarah was back in Olive's life. We're not sure what he'd do—"

"But Dad . . ." Olive said, blinking rapidly. "Dad told me my mother died of—"

"Breast cancer," Madison said. She looked up at me. "When we met, he made himself out to be the grieving widower, to gain my sympathy, and I bought it."

Sarah held her stomach like an insecure teen, the sleeves of her oversized gray hoodie hiding most of her hands. "I did have a breast cancer scare during our marriage," she said. "But I had a biopsy and it turned out I was fine."

"It's what Aaron does," Madison said, looking into the mirror. "He takes bits of truth and twists them into lies."

"No!" Olive said. "He wouldn't do that. He wouldn't lie about my mom."

Madison waved a hand at Sarah. "Honey, he lied to us all. I only found out Sarah was alive when I tried to file for that emergency custody order. Then it took some time to track her down, which wasn't easy—" She looked up at Sarah, unsure, apparently, if she should continue.

"It's okay," Sarah told her. "Olive needs to know why . . . why I haven't been in her life." She turned to the girl, picking nervously at her own sleeve as if there were burrs there. "I've been living out of my van for years," she said. "I didn't have a home or home address. I was embarrassed, scared—"

"You've been living on the *streets*?" Olive said it with something like awe, as if she suddenly had more respect for Sarah.

"I fell apart after . . ." Sarah pushed her sleeve back and forth, looked up as she attempted to rein in her emotions. When she saw me glancing at the track marks that were now exposed on her arm, she pulled her sleeve over them and held her wrist.

Olive's eyes stayed on Sarah's sleeve; she too had seen the injection scars on the woman's arm. "No," she said, shaking her head. "No. Dad wouldn't lie to me about something big like this. You're not my mom. My mom is *dead*."

Sarah made a little chirping chipmunk sound as she gulped in air, and Madison put a hand on her back. "Just give it time," she whispered to Sarah. "It's a shock to her, that's all. We knew it would be."

"This is so hard," Sarah said, tears welling in her eyes. Madison shushed her, rubbed her back.

I glanced at Nathan. He shifted his weight as he eyed the cob-webs on the ceiling, the window to the black storm raging outside, the two empty coffee mugs on the floor, looking anywhere but at the women. I shouldn't have brought him into all this. "Maybe it's best if you wait out on the porch," I said to him quietly.

"Yeah," he said, turning to the door. He sounded both relieved and angry. Buddy followed him onto the front porch. A shard of glass popped out of the frame and fell to the floor as Nathan closed the door a little too hard.

Olive continued to shake her head. "This is some kind of trick." She looked up at Madison. "Dad said you would try to trick me, that you'd lie about stuff. I told him no way, but—"

Madison took her hand. "Olive, honey, Sarah really is your mom. All you have to do is look at her to know it's true. You're the spit-ting image of each other."

They *did* look alike. Similar heart-shaped faces and small indents on their chins. They had the same slight build, though Olive was taller, like her father. I had seen it clearly for myself, a moment before Madison told us who Sarah was.

"I can prove it," Sarah said, wiping her face with her sleeve. She pulled out her phone and scrolled through it. "I have pictures of us when you were little, taken at our old house in Kingston. Here's a photo of all of us together before . . ." She held out her phone to Olive.

I peered over Olive's shoulder to get a look. Aaron and Sarah were cheek to cheek, holding a girl with curly red hair, a toddler, on the deck beside their pool. The girl was unquestionably Olive. Aaron had shown me other pictures of her at about that age. She held one eyebrow up quizzically, as she so often did now, as if to say, *Say what?* Sarah's hair was her natural auburn in the photo, a darker shade of red than Olive's, and her face was much fuller, though she still carried the haunted expression of someone endur-ing grief or mental illness.

"That's me!" Olive said, pointing, and her face lit up in wonder, an expression that was quickly replaced with confusion, then anger.

Shit. Aaron *had* lied to Olive, to me, to all of us, about his first wife. Sarah was very much alive.

Madison squeezed Sarah's shoulder, keeping her hand there as she took over where Sarah had left off. "Olive, honey, Sarah—your mom—her marriage to your dad was very difficult. It made her very unhappy."

"*Depressed*, you mean," Olive said, as if to say, *Don't talk to me like I'm a baby.*

"I was *messed up*," Sarah said. "*Lost*. I thought I was a bad mom. I *knew* I was a bad mom. I thought it was better if I didn't try to be your mom at all. I think maybe that's still the case."

Olive put her hands on her hips in a way Aaron so often did. "So, then what? You just *left* me?"

"No, I—" Sarah was shivering with anxiety. "I thought . . . I honestly thought I was a hazard to you, that I would endanger you."

She looked to Madison for reassurance, and Madison nodded, encouraging her to go on. When she didn't, Madison said, "Sarah had an addiction problem."

"Yeah, I got that."

"But I've been working to get clean," Sarah said, plucking at her sleeve again. "I've been working really hard. But back then . . . I wasn't myself. And one day, there was an accident. I knew it was my fault, and I couldn't live with myself. I didn't think you should live with me either. So I left, and Aaron agreed that he should take care of you. It seemed to be the best thing for everybody. I'm so sorry, Olive."

"But didn't you love me?" Olive asked. Didn't Sarah love her enough to stay?

"Oh, sweetheart, of course I loved you." Sarah reached out and took Olive's hand. "I still love you, so much it hurts."

Olive yanked her hand away. "You didn't bother to phone or message me. You didn't even let me know you were *alive*."

"Your father convinced her that she shouldn't," Madison said.

"I can't blame Aaron for everything," Sarah said. "This is on me. I just . . . at the time I thought leaving was the best thing I could do for you. It was my way of protecting you. And then, later, when I heard Aaron had remarried, I was ashamed. I—oh god—I thought letting you believe I was dead was the best thing for you. Madison was your mother. What would I be to you then?"

"And now?" I asked. "I mean, why are you coming to Olive with all this *now*?" I looked accusingly at Madison.

Sarah held up both hands. "Like I said, I've been working to get clean. And when Madison found me and told me what was going on, I couldn't let the same thing happen to Olive all over again. I couldn't let her lose Maddy too. Now that I understood what her father was doing, I had to help *her* understand it too."

"And what, exactly, is he doing?" I asked, crossing my arms.

Madison held my gaze for a moment, raising her eyebrows as if I should know, but let the question go unanswered. She clasped her hands and leaned on her knees as she looked up at Olive. "Honey, despite what your father may have told you, if you make it clear to the social worker that you want to live with me, that it's safe to live with me, you very likely can."

"You're only Olive's stepmother," I reminded her. "Aaron is Olive's *father*."

Madison breathed out a sigh, pressed her lips together as she stared at me, then articulated her words carefully and slowly, as if I were a child with a processing disorder. "I have been Olive's mother for as long as she can remember," she said. "In every way that counts, I *am* Olive's mother."

Sarah put her head in her hands and started crying in earnest then, and Madison rubbed her back again, whispering, "I'm so sorry, Sarah."

"But what about Dad?" Olive asked. "He wants me to live with him."

"I worry—" Madison glanced at Sarah. "I worry that his home isn't the best place for you." Madison squeezed and let go of Sarah's hand, urging her to take over.

Sarah composed herself and then, with watery eyes and a red nose, looked up at Olive. "Another reason I came back now is that Madison made me realize I still had something to offer you. I know Maddy is your mom, but, Olive, so am I. I won't force anything on you, but sweetheart, if you want to reconnect, I would love that, more than anything."

"It would be good for you," Madison said, standing to put an arm around Olive. "It would be good for you both."

Olive stepped back, appraising Sarah as I was doing, but didn't answer. I imagined she was having as much trouble wrapping her mind around this as I was—perhaps more so. This disheveled woman had been Aaron's *wife*? My god, had Aaron once sent Sarah a dozen *I love you* texts? Or Yves Piaget roses after every argument? Had he sent roses to Sarah's hospital room when Olive was born, as he had for me when I gave birth to Evie? He had. I knew he had. Aaron was a man who kept to his habits and small rituals, the routines that worked for him. When had things changed? And had Aaron really had a hand in what had happened to Sarah, as Madison had implied? Sarah looked *faded*, so much older than she was. Would that be me, I wondered, a decade down the road?

I looked away from her, at a can of Raid that had rolled, long forgotten, under the metal gun cabinet. "But why would Aaron lie about all this?" I asked, dully.

"If Olive knew, if *you* knew Sarah was alive, you'd start asking questions," Madison said. "I sure as hell did. Kira, Aaron wanted

Sarah out of Olive's life, just like he wants me out of her life now. He used Sarah's addictions to gain sole custody and limit her access. And then he used Sarah's guilt to push her away from Olive altogether."

"No, that's not Aaron."

"When Aaron is done with a woman, he's *done*." Madison waved a hand as if batting away a fly. "He just wants us out of the picture and out of Olive's life completely. He keeps us around only so long as we're useful. When he decided he was going to start a new family with you, and wanted Olive living with him, I stopped being useful to him. So now he doesn't want me in the picture. The thing is, Kira, Aaron has been using you too. He convinced you that I was a danger to Olive and used you to keep me away from her."

"Your recent behavior didn't help."

"Fair enough. But you did support Aaron while he cut me out of Olive's life."

Like my mother had cut my father out of mine. All at once, I felt an awful deflating sensation, as if I were a tire with a puncture and was going flat. I sank down to my old cot. *This can't be happening*, I thought, and I felt that old anger welling up, the feeling I had when someone—my father, a teacher, Teresa—criticized my mother and I rushed to defend her. It was my *job* to defend her.

"No," I said, shaking my head. And then, more firmly, pointing a finger at Madison, "No. *You're* the one who tried to turn Olive against her father."

"Kira, I only told her the truth about some of the things he'd done to me. Needless to say, it came as a shock, and she pulled away from him."

"What things?" I asked, looking first at Olive and then back at Madison. "*What things?*"

Madison exchanged a glance with Sarah, then nodded. Sarah answered for her, but spoke directly to Olive. They had clearly planned to have Sarah talk to Olive about this, likely to back up Madison's story. "He started by pushing me," she said, "during an argument, hard enough that I fell."

"It was the same for me," Madison said. "And then a slap. But never a fist," she added. "That would leave a bruise. And never in front of Olive, because she might say something to a friend, or a teacher."

Sarah put a hand to her neck. "Then, when I started talking about leaving him, he squeezed my neck so hard I couldn't breathe."

"He strangled you?" I asked.

"He always claimed to be sorry after," Madison said. "He'd cry and talk about how his old man had hit him, and how he had never wanted that kind of violence in his home. But then, at the same time, he'd blame me for it, say he wouldn't do it at all if I didn't make him angry, if I would just listen to him, do what he wanted."

"So why not phone the cops?" I asked.

"It's hard to explain," Sarah said. "You get to this point where you believe you're not good enough, that no one else would want you, that you can't make it on your own."

I felt a pang in my gut. That had been my mother's tactic with me.

"He tells you that," Madison said. "He convinces you of that."

"And, of course, I had a young child," Sarah continued, "and I had started using. Aaron knew that, threatened me with it. He said he would tell the social workers from Children's Aid if I left. I was afraid I would lose Olive. And then I did."

"I hid the abuse out of embarrassment at first," Madison said. "I was a preschool teacher. I was supposed to have it together. And here my husband was, hitting me, strangling me. I would convince myself that he only lashed out like that when I threatened to leave, which was mostly true. Later I stayed because I knew that if I left, at best I would only have joint custody. Olive would be living with him, alone, most of the time. I wasn't sure what he would do to her. His own father beat him. So I stayed, to protect her. Then you came along and, weirdly, it was a godsend. Aaron seemed content to leave Olive with me while you two had your extended honeymoon in that monstrous house. I figured I could use that time, and the fact that he'd left Olive with me, to fight for full custody. But then I made the mistake of telling Olive about Aaron's abuse, thinking it would help protect her during her weekend visits if she was alert to signs that he might turn violent. She was shocked and pulled away from him, and, well, you know the rest."

"He thought you were alienating Olive. We both thought that."

"Yes. And so he stormed into our house and took Olive and refused to allow me to see her, and then, of course, attempted to turn her against *me*. I had tried for emergency custody, but got nowhere. He hadn't hurt her and had made no threat to take her out of the country or anything like that, so the judge saw no reason to grant the order. But it was in the process of filing for custody that I found out Sarah was still alive and tracked her down. I'm still trying for at least joint custody, but of course Aaron has already painted me as a crazy bitch."

Yeah, about that. I threw up both hands. "How do you expect me to believe any of this after what you just put me through?"

"Look, Kira, I'm sorry about the grief I caused you. But Olive needed to know the truth about Sarah, to meet her and to hear from her what Aaron's capable of. He told Olive her mother was dead, and stuck to that lie for years. At this point, the only way I can get her out of this situation with Aaron is if she wants to move in with me, and away from her father. She's old enough now that a judge will likely allow her to live where she chooses."

"Are you saying she won't even spend weekends with us if she doesn't want to?"

"For her own safety, yes, that's what I'm saying."

I rubbed both eyes with the heels of my hands. *Fuuuck.* Then I shook my head. "She's always been perfectly safe in our house. No, no. If anyone is abusive, it's you. You're the one who broke into my house and took Evie from my truck. You're the one who has been trying to drive a wedge between Olive and her father. *That's* abuse."

Madison hesitated, as if thinking through her response. "Aaron has painted me as a monster. He has lied in an attempt to get both you and Olive onside, to believe I'm unfit as a mother, and he will keep lying until he gains full custody and I lose all access to my daughter. He did the same thing to Sarah. And, Kira, down the road, he'll do the same thing to you."

26

I studied Madison's face. Without her makeup, she didn't look deranged, or like the ridiculously polished woman who had been stalking us. Despite the fact that she had a good decade on me, she was freckled, girlish. I couldn't reconcile the woman in front of me with the one Aaron had made her out to be. But then, she had broken into my house and chased me all the way to Manitoulin. Maybe she *was* a little unbalanced. Then there was Sarah, sitting right there, very much alive. Aaron had lied to me about her, at least. And he knew something of my history with my mother. Had he used that to make me believe Madison was like her so I'd help him take Olive away from her? I glanced at Olive and she quickly looked down at her feet, distraught. My god, if he had, how could I ever forgive him? But if I believed that of him, I stood to lose everything, the life I'd so carefully built. My heart pounded at the thought. I felt jittery, restless.

"I need—I need to talk to Aaron about this," I said, twisting my engagement ring. I wanted him to make it okay. He *had* to make this okay.

"He'll lie, Kira," Madison said. "He'll manipulate you into believing him again, at least for now. Eventually, of course, the veneer wears thin and he can't hide his true self anymore." She glanced at Sarah, who nodded sadly in agreement.

I took out my phone, suddenly feeling pissed, and snapped a photo of Sarah and Olive together, both of them looking a little stunned. "Well, he'll have to explain this," I said, holding up the image.

Madison held out a hand. "Kira, you need to be very careful about how you confront him, what you say. When he feels threatened—"

"You won't know him," Sarah said.

Madison put a hand on Olive's shoulder. "And Olive can't be there when you talk to him. I won't let you put her in danger."

Olive hugged herself as she scanned the dilapidated cabin. "Well, I'm not staying here."

"And you're not taking her anywhere," I told Madison. "Not until I've sorted all this out."

"You should have someone with you, then," Sarah said. "Your friend Nathan, perhaps."

"I don't think that's necessary—"

"Seriously, Kira," Madison said. "Olive isn't safe, *you're* not safe, if you go this alone."

"If someone else is there—" Sarah started.

Madison finished for her. "He'll hide his true nature. But, Kira, as soon as you're alone again—"

Jesus. Just as I had been when I'd hugged my father in this cabin, I was torn by conflicting emotions. I was terrified that Aaron wasn't who I thought he was, but at the same time, I clung desperately to the hope that everything Madison and Sarah had told me about him was a lie. I was both exhausted and overcome with a desire to run, to *move*, to release all the weirdness of the day from my system and lose myself for a while. But I was trapped here, in this cabin, by the storm. I couldn't escape Madison's revelations, the fact that Aaron had lied to me about Sarah. I felt the panic surge again, tightening around my throat, pressing on my chest, making it hard to breathe.

"I need some air," I said, and banged out the door. Once on the porch, I pulled out my phone, tapped on my Favorites album and swiped past photos of Evie until I found one of Aaron and me, one I'd taken of us together at home in Toronto. Aaron took up most of the shot, his handsome face smiling winningly, posed, and I grinned awkwardly, my chin on his shoulder. A silly girl in a ponytail next to a sophisticated older man. The Aaron I knew was an astute businessman, a thoughtful, involved father and an attentive lover. He had it together. It seemed now that I might have been living with someone else entirely.

"I imagine all that was hard to swallow," Nathan said from the bench on the porch.

"You heard?"

"Enough."

Through the broken pane on the door, I could hear Sarah and Madison talking with Olive, though they were speaking quietly enough now that I couldn't make out most of what they were saying. A few words carried to the window. *So sorry . . . custody . . . social worker . . . Home.*

I closed my photos and pocketed my phone as I sat on the bench a foot or so away from Nathan. Buddy, lying over Nathan's feet, thumped his tail but didn't lift his head.

"Madison is right," Nathan said. "It's a good idea to have someone there when you talk to Aaron about all this. I'll stay the night at the summer house—"

"You don't have to do that."

"You heard what they said."

"Women accuse their ex-husbands of abuse all the time, to keep their kids with them. My own mother did that."

"And maybe that experience is blinding you to what's going on here."

"I just need to talk to Aaron and Olive without—" I was going to say *interference*, but Nathan interrupted me.

"And if he does get violent? He's clearly dangerous."

"He's never hurt me."

"Kira, I *will* be there. I'll sleep on the couch, if you want, but I'm not going to let you face that guy alone."

The lantern light filtering through the window above us softened Nathan's features, made him look younger, the boy I had fallen in love with so many years before. Maybe it *was* time to expose the truth, allow my two men to meet each other, even knowing what that would mean.

Strangely, I felt a sense of calm, of *relief*, wash over me at the thought, the prospect that I could end my double life.

Nathan and I sat in silence for a time as the rain intensified again, thundering on the roof, cascading off the eaves. Trees whipped back and forth until I thought they might break.

"Listen, Nathan, about what I said earlier, in the truck—"

He shook his head. "I should have told you about Ashley. I shouldn't have lied about her. I mean, I didn't like it, but at least you were honest with me about Aaron."

Oh god. Honest? I thought again about the lab results that were likely waiting for me at the summer house. I hadn't told Nathan I'd gone ahead with the paternity test. There were so many things I had withheld from him. I smoothed a hand over the bench, the distance between us. I wasn't sure what to say now, how to fix things. "I miss you," I said finally. "I always miss you when I'm gone."

He didn't respond for so long that I thought he wouldn't. Then he said, "I miss you too."

"You asked me if we were over."

He stiffened a little.

"I don't want it to be over," I said.

"I don't think you know what you want."

That stung. "What do you mean?"

He paused. "I think you're scared." He left the rest unsaid: I was scared of being alone, of being a single mom, struggling to make ends meet. He thought I was clinging to him because I feared I was about to lose my life with Aaron. And he was right. I honestly didn't believe I could make it on my own. How the hell had I gotten here?

I was always here, I thought. I had never felt capable enough, good enough, to go it alone. My mother had made sure of that. It was how she kept me close.

I hugged myself and shivered. "God, I'm so cold. I don't remember ever feeling this cold." Even running the Ottawa Winterman. But then I was always properly geared up, and moving.

"Come here," Nathan said. He pulled me to his chest and rested his chin on my head.

"They'll see us," I said, glancing up at the cabin window above us.

"Does it really matter now?"

I supposed it didn't. If Aaron *had* used me to take Olive away from Madison, I wasn't sure how we'd come back from that. But then, hadn't I also wanted Madison out of the picture? I wanted my family to be just that, *mine*, just Aaron and me and the girls.

"Are you ready to talk about it?" Nathan asked quietly.

"What?"

"Your father. What happened out here."

I chewed my thumbnail and shook my head against his chest.

Nathan held me closer and we sat for a time in silence, looking out into the night. The rain lessened somewhat, but the wind shook the wet leaves of a nearby trembling aspen, making it shimmer and rattle like a rain stick. Buddy shifted to lie on both our feet. I felt myself drifting.

"We *could* be together," Nathan said.

"Hmm?"

"I could move to Toronto. I'll sell my bungalow and you'll sell the summer house, and we'll use that as a down payment on a place of our own. We can stay in Mom's guest room when we come for visits."

I looked up at him. "You'd move away, for me?"

"I always would have. You know that."

I ran my fingers across his chest as I considered that one. Had he made this offer to me before, to move? He must have. He had known, then, that I wouldn't settle for living on the island year-round, as much as I loved my time here. But I couldn't imagine Nathan leaving Manitoulin. I had a hard time picturing him off the island. He *was* Manitoulin for me; he was my experience of the place, as much as the beach, the village. What would we be together if we lived elsewhere?

And yet. And *yet*.

"It wouldn't be Toronto," I said. I had landed there only because that was where Aaron lived. "The sale of our two places wouldn't amount to a down payment there in any case."

"Wherever," Nathan said sleepily. "Wherever you want to go."

Where did I want to go? I had no idea. I just felt so very tired, worn to the bone, like I had been running for years. I settled back into Nathan's chest and closed my eyes, the weight of my exhaustion pressing down on me. He was so warm. He was always warm. He smelled of sweat, but pleasantly so. Sandalwood and sawdust. It felt so comfortable, so *ordinary*, to be with him. Nathan had been my first, and though a few others besides Aaron had followed, he was the one I always returned to. I knew every mole on his back, the history behind the white scar on his shin (he'd walked into a log as we helped my father pile firewood at this cabin). I loved his casual physicality, his ease with his own body. I preferred his laid-back shuffle under the covers to Aaron's theatrical and acrobatic lovemaking, which he too often initiated on the cold marble counter in the bathroom or up against the wall of our bedroom. I got the feeling that, even in our most intimate moments, Aaron was putting on a performance—for me, I appreciated, but really, it was a lot of work. Looking back with the new perspective I'd gained tonight, it seemed like Aaron was always playing a part, never himself. Who the hell was he really?

"I'm still not sure what to make of all this," I said. "I mean, did Aaron really fool me all this time?" Or were Madison and Sarah bullshitting me now? "Am I really that blind?"

Nathan sighed a little. "Maybe. Likely. But it wasn't just you, was it? I imagine Aaron has managed to fool a lot of people, including Madison and Sarah at first."

He *had* fooled two women into marrying him, and I was nearly the third. I was almost Aaron's *wife*. I realized in that moment that, as much as I hated them for it, Sarah and Madison might have been doing me a favor, saving me and Evie from a life with that man. I felt the engagement ring tight around my finger and pulled it off to stare down at it.

"I should have seen the signs, read through his lies about Madison," I said. "Especially knowing my mother, how she lied about my father."

"Maybe that's exactly why you *didn't* see what he was doing," Nathan said.

I sat up to look at him. "What do you mean?"

"Have you asked yourself why you inserted yourself into this situation in the first place? I mean, why you *chose* the situation?" I could hear Teresa's words there, her tone. "Doesn't it seem familiar to you?"

"I don't know what you're getting at."

"You're caught between two warring parents, Aaron and Madison, just like you were as a child. It's like some part of you put yourself there, on purpose, to relive it."

No, I thought, looking out into the blackness. Then, *Maybe.* I'd wanted to believe what Aaron told me about Madison for the same reason I had wanted to believe my mother: because to do otherwise was to admit *I* was wrong, *I* was culpable, *I* was responsible. For helping Aaron wrench Olive from Madison. For my father's death.

Oh god, I *was* to blame.

And then I was there again, deep in the forest of my past, sitting on the log at the campfire, searching the bush around me as I waited for my father's return, as he flushed deer in my direction. Branches shifted in the wind. A chipmunk leapt from one tree to another and ran off, chattering. Somewhere close by, a chickadee sang, *chickadee-dee-dee.*

Don't let him see that you're scared, my mother had warned me. *Keep the upper hand. If he sees that you're frightened, then he'll know you're a victim. He'll be more likely to hurt you. And always keep your hunting knife at the ready. Always be ready.*

But ready for what? What would he *do?* I checked the pocket on the leg of my camouflage pants for the hunting knife my father had given me, to slit a deer's throat and put it out of its misery should my shot fail to kill it. But it did little to reassure me, to calm me. Why would my father hurt me? I couldn't reconcile the man my mother talked of with the father I knew. But I knew I should fear him. I knew I shouldn't want to spend time with him. I knew I shouldn't love him. The only person I was allowed to love was my mother. I couldn't love them both. And yet, especially toward the end of our visits, I found myself remembering an old warmth I felt with my father, an ease, a comfort in his presence. Thinking of it, I felt an awful gnawing in my gut, as if a hole were opening up there, and an ache like a hand clenching the side of my head. I yanked off my toque and gripped my forehead as I rocked, cradling the rifle in my arms. This had to stop. I couldn't do this anymore! I hurt like this all the time. I felt torn apart.

A twig broke in the forest, and I tensed. There was a rustle in the underbrush ahead, and another twig broke. My heart raced, thundering in my ears, and my breath grew short. I struggled to calm my nerves as I aimed the gun and peered through the scope at the forest beyond. The hunter orange. I knew, then, that I could get away with it. A hunting accident. They happened every year. Without another thought, I squeezed the trigger and fired. The deafening blast shocked a flock of cedar waxwings into the sky.

27

I woke suddenly, as if shaken awake. I even felt the hand on my shoulder. But it was only a shard of memory slipping to the surface, my father waking me for a November hunt. There in his hunting cabin, he had gotten a fire going in the potbellied stove to make coffee, fry us up a couple of eggs, runny so we could dip our toast in the yolks. He served those eggs with slices of back bacon. A heavy, protein-rich breakfast to keep us warm for the day of hunting ahead.

My stomach rumbled now at the thought of it. There was a time, before my parents' divorce, when I had looked forward to those early mornings in the cabin with my father. I had him to myself; his attention was on me and not my mother. I remembered the fact of that anticipation now, as an adult, but not the emotion, the warmth for my father I must have felt.

Now, in this summer house not far from the beach, the early-morning sun filtered through the warped glass of the elderly windows, casting waves of moving shadows on the bedroom wall. I'd always loved mornings in this house, the birdsong, the light.

In the evening it was the living room at the front of the house that was aflame in lush red light. The builders had understood how to situate a house to make the most of the day's rhythms, the morning sun to wake by, the evening glow to rest by. *I kept this house for the light*, I thought. It certainly wasn't for the family memories.

Olive was asleep in one of the small upstairs bedrooms. She'd gone straight to bed after she'd taken a hot shower to warm up (and after she demanded I give her phone back). I could hear Evie stirring in her crib in the next room; I suspected her cry had been what really woke me. Safe here with Teresa, she was the only one of us who had gotten much sleep the night before. Madison and Nathan had both insisted that Nathan stay the night with Olive and me at the summer house and be there when I talked to Aaron. And so, while Madison and Sarah camped out at the hunt cabin overnight, Nathan and I had driven here with Olive in the early morning, only a few hours before. And then, before she left for the night, Teresa had wanted to hear about Sarah and Madison and what had gone down at the cabin. I finally went to sleep in the bedroom on the first floor that Nathan and I usually shared instead of the master bedroom upstairs. The old house lacked proper insulation, and the summer heat baked the tin roof, trapping the heat in the upstairs rooms, especially the master bedroom, which took in the afternoon and evening sun.

Nathan and I rarely slept at his house anymore, as we once had before my mother's death. Now that I was aware of Ashley, I knew why. Even though she wasn't living with him, his bungalow was *theirs* in the way that, until this trip up, I had come to think of this room as belonging to Nathan and me. It was *ours*, even if this house wasn't exactly ours.

Nathan wasn't sleeping with me this time. He was dozing on the couch, keeping watch over me and the girls, determined to offer protection when Aaron arrived. But this morning, time felt all stretched and weird, like I had come to Manitoulin a year ago, leaving Toronto, and my life with Aaron, far behind.

Evie cried out for me and I flipped the covers back and, still wearing the clean yoga pants and T-shirt I'd slipped on the night before, shuffled across the hall and picked her up. Once I had changed her and washed up, I carried her through the dining room into the kitchen to make coffee. The house had two entrances at the front, one to the kitchen addition and one into the living room, which was the original downstairs of the house. There were also doors on every room. No open concept here. The builders of these old houses understood the need for doors, for privacy, for shutting out other members of the family.

Except for dust and a few cobwebs, the place was as I had left it on my last trip up, before Aaron had offered me a ring. Evie's toys were scattered across the scratched hardwood floor in the dining room, which had become her play area. I kept the Toronto house nearly spotless, spending my days following along behind Evie, picking up the toys, soothers, bottles and bits of half-eaten banana slices she cast in her wake even as she dropped them. Strange, then, that my compulsion to tidy didn't extend to the Manitoulin house. But then, my mother rarely cleaned house here either. She came down to the island to relax and didn't care what the locals thought. They didn't matter. Aside from buying lamps and knickknacks, she had never made improvements to the place. It was almost exactly the same as when she and my father bought it, furnished and decorated, from an elderly couple who had summered there for decades, and they, in turn, had left it pretty much as they found it, even down to the black rotary phone on the gossip table that still functioned as the landline in the kitchen. The place was decorated with antiques that the previous owners and my mother had collected: a dragonfly Tiffany lamp in the living room, a Bakelite radio in the dining room, a Kit-Cat Klock in the kitchen. Old advertising signs were scattered everywhere. There were pressed-glass pieces of all kinds placed near the windows to reflect the light. An impossible setting to bring a young child into, of course. I had to watch Evie constantly.

I put her in the high chair now, with a container of applesauce on her tray, to keep her in one spot. Then I made coffee. While it percolated, I rubbed the sweat from my hands onto my yoga pants and finally picked up the mail Teresa had left on the kitchen table. I couldn't put this off any longer. There was a hydro bill for the house, a tax notice from the municipality, some junk mail and the letter I had been both expecting and dreading. I tossed the other letters to the table and opened the one from the lab, reading it with my heart hammering in my chest as if I was running a race.

Shit.

I picked Evie up, then carried her and the letter to the living room, where Nathan was still asleep on the couch. I stood at the threshold, watching him as he snored lightly. What would I do now? Evie reached out for the dog, and Buddy whined, looking up expectantly at us, his tail thumping, but he stayed on the floor beside the couch. On guard, keeping watch over Nathan.

A vehicle pulled up to the house, and Evie pointed at the window and clapped her hands, babbling.

I quickly pocketed the letter and, still holding Evie, peered through the lace curtain on the living room window to see Aaron stepping out of his rental, a Jeep. Outside, he stopped to inspect the damage to the front end of my own rental. Seeing him there, with the familiar elderly houses of the village around him, I experienced the oddest sensation, like I'd once had when I bumped into another runner I knew, but at a grocery store rather than a race. There was that instant where I recognized her, but wasn't sure from where. It was like that now with Aaron. I knew him, of course. But at the same time, he was a stranger. He didn't belong here, not in this life.

I had hoped for another hour, or at least a cup of coffee to brace myself, before I needed to confront him with Sarah and Madison's allegations. As for the rest, that could wait for another day.

I shook Nathan awake. "He's here," I said.

Nathan rubbed his eyes groggily. "What?" he asked, his tongue thick with sleep.

"Get up," I said. "Aaron's here. Grab yourself a coffee while I let him in."

As I stepped outside, the old screen door's complaints announced my presence and Aaron looked back at me. "I *do* have the right place," he said. "What the hell happened to your rental?"

"I hit a deer," I said.

"Christ."

I forced a smile. "You made good time."

"I only stopped to gas up and grab coffee. I haven't slept."

Aaron was a man who used skin products and expensive moisturizers, who appeared younger than his age. But there were crow's-feet at the corners of his eyes now, and he looked exhausted. It was hard to believe I had seen him just the morning before. His suit was wrinkled and there was a coffee stain on his violet shirt. Such a small thing, but Aaron was so appearance-proud that for a split second it made me ache for him. But then I remembered everything Sarah and Madison had told me.

He held out his hands to take Evie from me. "There's my girl!"

"You really didn't need to come up," I said.

He lifted Evie in the air and spoke with his daddy voice. "I couldn't let that bitch threaten my girls. Could I, munchkin?"

This time, when he called Madison a bitch, I flinched. Evie giggled and he put her to his hip as he gazed toward the bay.

"Wow. It's beautiful here," he said. "I can see why you keep coming back."

The early-morning sun shone through the slats of the boardwalk railing, casting long vertical shadows across the dunes. The few people on the boardwalk this early wore jammies or bathrobes as they walked their dogs or nursed their coffee. The waterfront *was* beautiful, but I was embarrassed by this old house, the flaking white paint, the yellowish lawn that grew on antinfested sand and was dotted with Manitoba maples. Weed trees, my mother had called them, and had them cut down. But they had sprung right back up from the stump, forming wild, bushy mounds. They would keep coming back no matter how many times they were cut at the base. The only way to get rid of them was to dig out the root.

"We've got some things to talk about," I said.

"Oh?" A flicker of worry crossed Aaron's brow, one of those micro-expressions. There and gone. And for the first time in our relationship I felt like I had the upper hand. But then he offered me the smile that always melted me, the one he *knew* always melted me.

I glanced at the vacant faces of the houses across the street. "Let's go inside."

As we passed through the stairwell into the living room, Evie squirmed, and Aaron put her on the floor.

"Aaron—" I started.

But he ran his hands down my arms. "Let's have that kiss first," he said.

I turned my face away.

"What's going on?" he asked.

And then we heard the *tap-tap-tap* of Buddy's nails on the kitchen floor, the beagle's snuffling as he took in the smells of the house. The fridge door opened and closed as Nathan looked for cream for his coffee.

"Kira?" Nathan called from the kitchen. "You okay with coffee whitener?" He spoke louder than he needed to, purposefully letting Aaron know he was there.

"I'll take it black," I said, like there was nothing unusual about Nathan's presence at this hour.

"Who's that?" Aaron asked, looking over my head.

I hesitated as Nathan swaggered into the living room barefoot, carrying two mugs. Buddy trotted out after him, sniffing everything, and Evie squealed on seeing the dog, slapping the floor in her rush to get to him. Nathan handed me my coffee and flopped on the couch, putting his feet on the coffee table like he owned the place. When Buddy jumped up next to him, Evie pulled herself to standing beside him, holding a hand up to Nathan, asking to join them. I quickly swept her up, but Evie's familiarity with Nathan wasn't lost on Aaron.

"Seriously, who are you?" he asked Nathan.

"This is Nathan," I said. When that didn't seem like enough, I added, "He takes care of the house for me." The half-truth felt as tasteless and dry in my mouth as a cotton swab. Nathan's face reddened with anger and his jaw flexed as he looked away. "We've known each other forever," I added.

"Old friends," Aaron said, his voice tense.

"Nathan grew up next door."

Aaron kept his eyes on Nathan. "I thought I'd heard about all of Kira's friends. I don't recall her mentioning you."

Nathan sipped his coffee. "She's certainly mentioned you."

"Nathan helped me find Olive," I said quickly, shifting Evie. "Buddy is a blood dog, a scent dog. Aren't you, boy?" The beagle wagged his tail.

Aaron sniffed the air like he was a scent dog himself. "What do you mean, he helped you *find* Olive?"

Crap. I hadn't told him. In my foggy, sleep-deprived, stressed-out state, the events of the last day were becoming murky. What else had I neglected to tell him? What had I lied about? But then, as Nathan had said, did it even matter now? Did I still want a future with Aaron?

"Olive ran off again last night," I said. "When I hit the deer, she took off into the bush at my father's hunt camp."

"You're telling me she ran away from you a second time?" he asked. "Why? What did you *do*?"

"I didn't—" I took a deep breath to calm myself. "I put down the deer, and it scared her. I didn't think—"

"You killed a deer? In front of her? With what?"

"A knife."

"Jesus, Kira. Where is she?" He looked past me through the dining room to the short hall that led to the downstairs bedrooms. "Is she all right?"

"She's okay. She's upstairs, asleep. We didn't get in until early morning. But, Aaron, she's confused and angry that you—"

He stepped back into the stairwell. "Olive! I'm here!"

Nathan lifted his chin and nodded for me to go on, to tell Aaron. Right. I put Evie on the couch next to Nathan, took out my phone and pulled up the photo of Sarah and Olive I'd taken the night before.

"We met Sarah," I said. "Or Vicki, I should say."

Aaron's head snapped in my direction, and a flicker of fear passed over his face before he reined it in. "Who?" he asked.

I held out my phone to show him the photo.

"You know exactly who," Nathan said, standing.

Aaron waved at him. "Why is he here?" he asked me, but really, he was asking the room, the universe. *Why is this person talking to me?*

I chose my words carefully. "Madison suggested it would be prudent to have someone here while we talked about Sarah—Vicki—your first wife." Among other things. "Nathan volunteered."

"You're shitting me. You're taking advice from Madison now?"

"I'm here to protect Kira," Nathan said flatly. "And the girls." He looked the part too. He stood there by the door with his muscular arms crossed, like a bouncer barring the way to a night-club. Buddy sat beside him, his eyes roaming back and forth between us.

"You presume to protect my own daughters from *me*?" Aaron turned to me, his face twisted in hurt and anger. "What exactly did Vicki tell you?" he asked. "Oh god, what did she tell *Olive*?" He called up the stairs again. "Olive, come downstairs!" When he got no answer, he shouted. "Olive!" There was a rustle of bedsheets from upstairs, an annoyed groan.

"Let's leave Olive out of this," I said.

But Aaron called for her again. "Downstairs, now!"

From above, Olive mumbled, "Okay, okay."

"Why did you lie to Olive about her mother?" I asked him. "Why did you lie to me? Why would you tell us she was *dead*?"

He studied my face a moment, then nodded sideways at Nathan. "I'm not talking about this with him here."

"I'm staying," Nathan said.

"This is a family matter," Aaron said, turning to him.

A private matter, my mother always said of her battles with my father. *A family matter. We don't talk about family matters outside this house.* I didn't want Nathan watching this family drama either. It was embarrassing, and threatened to reveal too much about my life, to both men.

Evie took an interest in the Tiffany lamp, and I scooped her up. "Maybe you should go," I said to Nathan. "We'll be fine, really."

"Seriously?"

I felt Aaron's eyes on me, gauging my interaction with Nathan, and lowered my voice. "Your presence here is only complicating things."

Aaron held out his hand, gesturing for Nathan to leave, but Nathan puffed out his chest and stood his ground. Buddy barked and Nathan did nothing to quiet him. For a tense moment I thought the two men were about to launch into a fist fight. I pictured this for a fraction of a second, with some satisfaction. Burly Nathan whaling on wiry Aaron in his Armani suit. Who would win? Aaron, of course. He would press assault charges and tie Nathan up with legal fees.

I held Evie closer to my chest. "Please," I said to Nathan. "Just *go*."

Nathan shifted his gaze from Aaron to me, his eyes watering. Then the expression on his face changed from anger to resignation, and he pressed his lips together. "All right," he said, nodding slowly. "Sure. Whatever you say." He walked to the stairwell, with Buddy following, then looked back at me and said, "If you need me, I'll be here." He glanced at Aaron briefly before adding, "I'll always be here for you, Kira."

As he slammed the door behind him, I pressed my hand to the pocket in my yoga pants, to the letter hidden there. *Maybe not always*, I thought. Maybe there were some betrayals our old friendship couldn't survive.

28

As soon as Nathan was gone, Aaron turned his anger on me. "How *dare* you bring some stranger into our family business!"

A shower of his spittle sprayed between us, and I stepped back. I tried to sound calm, keeping my eyes on his Adam's apple as I couldn't look him in the eye. He had a nearly day-old beard on him, something I'd rarely seen. He usually shaved even on Sunday mornings. "Nathan is not a stranger," I said. "Not to me." I swallowed.

"I can see that," he said, flipping his suit jacket back to put his hands to his narrow hips. "You want to tell me about him?"

"There's not much to tell," I said, my voice breaking a little. "I've known him and his mom since I was a kid."

"He seems very protective of you. *Possessive* of you, I should say."

"As I said, he's an old friend."

"An old lover, you mean."

Evie began to whine, pulling away from us both, and I lowered my voice as Olive made her way down the stairs. "Is now really the time for this?" I asked.

"He *is* an old lover," Aaron said.

I paused. "From years ago," I said quietly. Not quite lying. "When we were in our teens."

"Are you still lovers?" he asked, hovering over me. "Is that why you keep coming up here?"

Evie whined again, twisting her body away from him. I glanced over his shoulder at Olive, who now watched us from the stairwell, then looked back at Aaron. His neck had started to blotch, like it did when he drank red wine, in big red hives. The blotches moved up his neck and into his cheeks as if some invisible creature with suction cups were climbing up his face.

"Do you still love him?" Aaron asked.

"No," I said. "We're over." I had no idea if I was telling the truth. I'd come here to tell Nathan it was over, but so much had happened since then. I knew which answer Aaron needed to hear, though, if this conversation was going to be about Madison and Sarah, and not about Nathan and me.

"You don't sound very convincing," he said. He lifted his hand and for an instant I thought he might slap me, with my baby still in my arms. But then he caressed my cheek and kissed me, first on the cheek and then, ever so gently, in the way that until this day I adored, full on the mouth. His timing was so off, so strange, that the kiss felt less like a show of affection and more like a territorial display. "We'll talk more about this later," he said, as Olive's footsteps approached. He said it gently, but I knew it was a threat. "Now, where are Madison and Vicki?"

For a fraction of a second, I wondered who he was talking about. Then I remembered: he meant Sarah.

Behind him, Olive shook her head slightly, warning me not to tell him. Wearing no makeup, and with dark shadows under her eyes, she looked exhausted. She had dressed in fresh white joggers and a blue T-shirt, but her hair was a rat's nest from going to bed with it wet after her hot shower.

"I don't know where they are," I told Aaron, lying. They were likely still sleeping in the hunt camp cabin. "I imagine they're back in Toronto by now."

Olive interrupted us, crossing her arms. "Why did you tell me my mother was dead?"

Aaron, standing between us, looked from Olive to me and back again. "Vicki was—is—a very sick woman."

"She's an addict, Dad."

"Yes, exactly. I didn't want you pulled into her ugly world. I knew she would only hurt you."

Olive held her palm out, as if asking for her allowance. "So, *what*? You tell me she's *dead*?"

"She left *us*, Olive." Aaron's voice clotted, thick with emotion. "I didn't want you to think your own mother had deserted you—" He put a hand to his chest. "The way my mother abandoned me. I knew *exactly* what that would do to you."

I shifted from foot to foot to keep Evie quiet. "But telling Olive her mother was *dead*—"

Aaron turned to me. "Look, Vicki chose drugs over me, over her own daughter. She chose to leave us, to live in a stinking van on the streets. She chose *that*, that life, over one with me."

"So you were punishing her," I said.

He eyed me for a long moment, shaking his head slowly. But we both knew it was true.

Olive took her father's arm, turning him in her direction. "You're always telling me how terrible Maddy is, that she lies." She poked a finger into his lapel, the carefully folded silk handkerchief there. "But you're the liar," she said, her voice rising with indignation. "You told me my mom was dead so I wouldn't see her."

"Olive, we've been through this. Madison is the one who has been manipulating you. *She* lies. She lies because she's desperate to keep you in her life. More than that, she wants you to herself. She wants me out of your life." Aaron held out a hand to me. "Kira, help me out here."

Evie, unsettled by the raised voices, leaned away from me and reached for the floor, asking to be let down. I put her down and, as she crawled to the couch, chose my words carefully. "Aaron, I think you were afraid when Olive said she wanted to live with Maddy, afraid of losing her."

"It's *Maddy* now, is it?" he said. "All of a sudden you're friends?"

I chose to ignore that. "I think that because you were afraid, you were willing to say anything, do anything to make sure Olive would stay with us."

"So you think *I* lied." Aaron scrubbed his hands back and forth through his hair in a gesture of frustration, leaving it ruffled. "Christ, I can't *believe* this," he said. "I drove all the way from Ottawa, overnight, to straighten this mess out for you. And here you are, questioning me, doubting my word, defending Madison—"

Olive jabbed a finger at her father. "You lied, Dad. You lied about my mom." She crossed her arms. "You lied about a lot of things."

"What do you mean by that?" When her gaze slid to the floor, he gripped her upper arm. "I said, what do you mean by that? What else did Vicki tell you?"

"Aaron!" I said, pulling him back, but he threw my hands off. He didn't let go of Olive.

"*What did she tell you?*" he roared.

Olive, scared, shook her head rapidly. I knew that look. She was about to lose it. *Aaron* was about to lose it.

"Aaron, stop this, right now."

He turned to me, rage, or fear, darkening his face, but then he let her go. Olive rubbed her arm as she sat on the couch. She put

Evie on her lap, facing out toward the room, and hugged her as if my baby was a teddy bear.

I took Olive's place in front of Aaron, scrutinizing him.

"What?" he asked, smiling a little, as if to say, *What are you looking at?*

"Aaron, did you hurt Madison and Sarah?"

"*What?*"

"Did you hit them, or attempt to strangle them?"

Aaron put his hands on his hips. I could smell his anxiety. He was usually so clean and groomed that I rarely smelled real body odor on him. "Madison has been making up that kind of shit for weeks now, trying to get custody. You know that."

"Yes, but Sarah said you hurt her too."

"*Vicki*, you mean." Aaron threw up both hands. "And of course she did. Madison sought her out, likely paid her off, for exactly that purpose. Please, *please* tell me you don't believe them."

When I didn't immediately answer, he looked to Olive. She hid behind Evie, who clapped, and Aaron's handsome, aristocratic face crumpled into ugly grief as he sank to an armchair and cradled his head in his hands. "You *do* believe them," he said. "God, that woman is bent on *destroying* me. They both are."

"No, Aaron—" I started, but of course, Madison *had* got to me. So had Sarah.

I put my hand on his shoulder as I considered what to say next. From this angle I could see the small circle of shine beneath Aaron's hair where he had started to bald. He had always been so vain about his hair, spending a good half hour on it each morning. But now his hair was mussed, that bald spot making him seem so vulnerable. He started to cry, his shoulders shaking, and the anger and doubt I'd carried with me since the night before began to drain away. Maybe Madison was lying after all. Maybe she *was* using Sarah, and those allegations of abuse, to get full custody of Olive. Maybe she was using *me*. And I was playing right into it.

"Aaron, I'm so sorry—" I started.

But Olive interrupted. "What was the accident that Sarah had? Why did she leave us?"

Evie laughed a little as Olive bounced her on her knee. Or perhaps Olive's knees were bouncing of their own accord, as they often did when she was anxious.

Aaron's face flashed with pain. "She told you about that?"

"She said there was an accident and she had to leave to keep me safe."

Aaron ran a hand across his mouth. "You nearly drowned. You were really little. Vicki got stoned out of her mind with some asshole she was screwing inside *my* house, neglected you and allowed you to wander into our pool. I was away on a business trip. You could have died."

Olive was shocked. "It was me? I had the accident?"

He kept his eyes on his daughter. "Olive, Vicki's addiction, her *illness*, makes her dangerous. She wasn't watching you that day. She was a neglectful parent, and then she simply left us. *That's* why I told you she was dead. I thought it would be easier than knowing she had abandoned you. You don't need a person like that in your life."

"Aaron, I understand your anger, but it's so far in the past now," I said. Evie was reaching for the lamp again. I took her from Olive. "Sarah has been working hard to recover from her addiction. She wants to reconnect with her daughter." I glanced at Olive. "If Olive wants to see her mom, why not just let her?"

"No!" he said. "It's my job to keep Olive safe. I won't allow my daughter to spend any time with that woman."

"You may not have a choice," I said. "Sarah *is* Olive's mother."

"She doesn't have custody," he said. "I made sure of that."

"But she must still have access," I said. "Or be able to get access. And I imagine, now that she's clean, she'll pull it together and try for joint custody."

"She walked out of Olive's life years ago; she doesn't get to share it now. I'll fight her, and I'll win, just like I did before."

"Just like you'll fight Maddy?" Olive asked. She stood. "You're going to take Maddy away from me too, aren't you? Just like you took Sarah."

"Olive, you don't understand—you have Kira now. We're a family."

"For god's sake, Aaron, think about what you're saying here. Olive needs a relationship with Sarah and Maddy as well as with you." I clutched his arm. "Tell me you're not going to force her to make a choice, the way my mother did. Please tell me you're not that kind of person."

Aaron threw me off and I stumbled back, nearly losing my grip on Evie. Shocked, she burst into tears.

Olive, protective of Evie, pushed Aaron in the chest. "You *are* an asshole, just like Maddy and Sarah said!" she cried. "I hate you! I fucking *hate* you!" She pushed him a second time. "I don't want to live with you. I never want to live with you!"

Aaron's eyes narrowed as if he couldn't believe what he'd just heard. "You little bitch," he said, and he slapped his daughter's face, hard. It was a practiced move, no hesitation, no clumsiness, controlled and purposeful. The room shifted as if I were standing on the edge of a sand dune and the waves kicked up by a storm were washing my foothold away. I was certain then that Madison had been telling the truth about Aaron all along.

29

Olive held her face as tears welled up in her eyes. Aaron's slap had left a large red mark on her cheek. "You *hit* me," she said, as if even now she couldn't believe it.

Evie sobbed in my arms, and I held her closer. "Aaron!" I cried.

Aaron, jarred by my voice, looked momentarily confused. He had been lost in his rage, but now his expression shifted as he realized he had given himself away. "I'm sorry," he said to Olive. He closed his eyes a moment, as if trying to regain control of himself. "What you said—it was like Madison was talking. I just—I just *reacted*. You know a little of my history with my father, how he hit me. Sometimes, when I'm tired and stressed, it's like the ghost of my father possesses me, takes over."

"And how many times did you slap Madison like that?" I asked. How many times would he slap me, or Olive, or Evie?

Aaron eyed me, his face red, sweat on his brow, but didn't answer.

"I'm moving back in with Maddy," Olive said.

He shook his head. "Oh, no, you're not."

"The social worker will listen to me, put what I want in her assessment. She gives that to the judge, right? If I want to live with Maddy, I can."

"Who told you that?"

"Maddy."

"Olive, I'm your father and I have custody. Maddy is only a stepmother."

"No, that's not how it works. She's been my mother for years, since I was little. She has rights. She can get custody too."

"You have no idea how family court works."

"When I tell the social worker you hit me, she'll let me live with Maddy for sure."

"What did you say?" he asked, his jaw clenching. But he wasn't asking her to repeat herself. It was a threat, a command to keep her mouth shut.

I shook my head at Olive, warning her off. But she was pissed. "I don't want to live with you ever again," she said. "I'm going to tell the social worker I want to live with Maddy, and that you hurt me and Madison and Sarah. Everybody is going to know."

"You're *threatening* me?" Aaron's face took on the explosive purple hue of fighters or heavy drinkers as he clenched and unclenched his fists. It made him look like another man entirely. I needed to get the girls away from him.

"Aaron, she's not threatening you, she's just upset," I said, trying to placate him, but it looked like he barely heard me. I could tell he was building to another outburst.

"We need to leave," I told Olive quietly. Still carrying Evie, I picked up my bag from the coffee table and slung it over my shoulder. "Let's go."

But Aaron blocked our way to the door and flashed me a charming smile. "Kira, this has nothing to do with you and me. We can talk about this. Alone. Without Olive spying on us for

208   GAIL ANDERSON-DARGATZ

Madison." He held out his hand to Olive. "Give me your phone."

"Why?" Olive asked.

"Just give it to me!" Aaron roared.

"No," Olive said. But Aaron banged a fist against the wall and Olive slid the phone from her pocket and handed it to him.

"No one leaves me," he said. "Do you understand me? No one."

I held out an arm to protect Olive as I backed us away from Aaron. "Go to the kitchen door," I told her. "Now."

As she turned, Aaron shoved me out of the way and grabbed Olive's upper arm so one of her shoulders was lifted at an awkward, uncomfortable angle. "Is there a basement in this place?" Aaron asked me, calmly, sanely, as if he were only asking where the bathroom was.

I shook my head as I thought of the trapdoor on the floor of the laundry room, the stairs below it leading down into a spider-infested dirt-floor cellar where an old cistern still held water. I hadn't been down there in years. It had been the setting of many childhood nightmares.

"There's always a basement in these old houses," Aaron said, hauling Olive along by the arm like a TV cop apprehending a criminal. *You're coming with me.* "Let's go find it."

Olive shrieked, "No, Daddy!"

"Aaron, stop!" I said, pulling on his arm. "Stop this!"

When Olive sank to her knees, he grabbed her by the hair and dragged her across the floor and into the kitchen. Olive shrieked in pain. From my arms, Evie echoed her, crying out in fear.

"What are you *doing*?" I cried. "Aaron, let her go!"

I quickly put Evie in her high chair and tried to yank Aaron's arm, to loosen his hold on Olive. But he easily lifted Olive by the arm and dragged her over to the pantry door under the stairs. He opened it, saw nothing but boxes of cereal, dried beans and pearl barley, and closed it again. He lugged Olive over to the laundry room door and opened it.

"What's this?" he shouted over the girls' screams.

"Just the laundry room," I said. "There's nothing there."

He pulled Olive inside the room and tapped a foot on the trapdoor in the floor. The door to the cellar comprised part of the laundry room floor, but knowing that dark hole lay beneath it, I wouldn't stand on it any more than I would stand on a person's grave. An impressively large spider crawled up from under it.

"What's under this?" Aaron asked.

"Nothing," I said. "The old cistern."

"That'll do."

"No!" Olive screamed, writhing in his grip to escape. "Dad, please, no!"

"Aaron, for god's sake, stop it!" I took his arm again, but he shoved me against the wall, winding me. I sank to the floor as I tried to catch my breath.

Still holding Olive's arm tightly with one hand, Aaron bent down and pulled up the trapdoor to reveal the short flight of stairs. "Go on," he said, pushing Olive toward them.

"Please!" I said, standing. "Aaron, stop it!"

He gave Olive another push and she stumbled toward the stairs, putting a hand on the wall to stop herself from falling.

"Either you walk down," Aaron said, "or I force you down."

"Aaron," I said, raising my voice over Olive's sobs and Evie's screams, "don't do this."

Aaron didn't answer. He all but lifted Olive by the arm and walked her down the steps. When she resisted, crying out, he pushed her down the remaining stairs. She landed in a heap on the cellar floor, her shoulder hitting the packed soil, and grunted in pain.

"Aaron, what are you doing?" I cried.

"You're not thinking straight," Aaron told Olive. "You need a time-out to think about things, about what's best for you. Living with Madison is not what's best for you. When you understand that, and stop all this nonsense, you can come out."

"I understand now," she said, starting to climb the stairs, her voice rising in desperation. "I won't live with Madison. I know she's a crazy bitch."

Crazy bitch. My god. I saw my tween self within Olive, desperate to please my mother, calling my father an asshole and offering her stories of how idiotic he had acted on a visit, to avoid her rage. But it wasn't working for Olive any more than it had for me. Aaron pulled Olive by the arm down the stairs again, then jogged back up.

Olive looked up at me, her face red and tear-streaked, her eyes yellowed and wild in confusion, as if she was snared within a night terror. "Kira, please help—"

But Aaron slammed the door down with a bang, trapping her.

30

A s Olive screamed below us, I tried to pull up the trapdoor, but Aaron pushed me out of the way. The door dropped from my hand, sending up plumes of dust and, wafting from below, the sickly sweet smell of something dead, likely the desiccated body of a mouse that had stumbled on the rodent poison Nathan left out in the cellar.

"Aaron, for god's sake! Let Olive out. She's terrified."

"She threatened to leave me, to live with Madison."

Jesus, he was *pouting*. I studied his face. It was like I was talking to another personality within Aaron, someone I'd never met before, a child. A sulking, dangerous child.

I flung a hand toward the door at our feet. "So you hit her? You drag her across the floor? You throw her in the cellar?"

Olive's whimpers rose from below us.

"She needs to understand," he said. "She can't leave me." He waved a hand before continuing. "Anyway, once you talk to her and to the social workers and help me straighten things out, it'll be fine.

And when custody is all ironed out, we can get married. Then it will just be the four of us. Me and my girls."

He was delusional. How had I never seen it before?

"We're done, Aaron," I said, more to myself than to him. "We are *so* done."

"No," he said. "No. We have our lives ahead of us." He smiled strangely, vacantly, his eyes a little lost, like a person with dementia. "We're going to get married."

I laughed at that, and his smile fell. "You're exactly the man Madison said you were," I said. "I can't *believe* I bought into all your bullshit."

He gripped my arm. "It appears you need a little persuading," he said. He forced me back into the kitchen, but stopped short when he saw Nathan standing there, his hand protectively on Evie's crown.

I felt an overwhelming sense of relief on seeing him. Nathan must have been over at Teresa's, or hiding in between our two houses, listening in, and heard Olive's screams. *If you need me, I'll be here*, he'd said. He never had any intention of leaving me alone with Aaron.

"Let go of her," he said now, gritting his teeth.

"Fuck off." Aaron's hold on me only got stronger. "This is none of your business."

"This is everyone's business," Nathan said. He shoved Aaron's shoulder. "Take your hands off her."

"Get out of this house," Aaron commanded.

Nathan took another swaggering step toward Aaron so they were standing nearly chest to chest. "I said, let go of her!"

When I tried ducking away to get to Evie, Aaron hauled me back and thrust me down into a kitchen chair hard enough that I nearly fell over. From her high chair, Evie cried out.

Nathan didn't hesitate. He took a swing at Aaron, landing a fist to his jaw, and for that instant everything went slow-mo, like those ugly replays of a boxer getting punched. Aaron's face was all bent out of shape, spittle flying, his face turned by the blow. And then time sped up again as Aaron took Nathan by the shoulders and, throwing his body weight against him, bashed the back of Nathan's skull against the wall. Nathan fell on all fours, dazed.

Jesus. "I'm phoning the cops," I said, grabbing my phone from my bag, forgetting for the moment that there was no reception here.

"Oh, no, you're not." Aaron gripped my hand, squeezing until it hurt, and I let the phone drop to the floor. Then he stomped on my cell twice, cracking the casing.

I nursed my bruised hand as I picked up the heavy black receiver of the old rotary phone. Aaron seized the cradle, yanking it until the cord pulled out of the wall, then, seeing Nathan attempting to stand, swung it at him hard. I heard a sickening thud as the phone's base smacked the back of Nathan's head. He collapsed onto the floor, face first.

Aaron slammed the phone back on the gossip table.

When I scrambled to plug the cord back into the wall jack and started dialing, my fingers fumbling in the rotary dial, Aaron picked up Evie from the high chair and carried her over to the old farmhouse sink, turned on the faucet and put in the plug. Water quickly began collecting.

I put the receiver back in its cradle. "Aaron, what are you doing?"

"Persuading you to stay—to cooperate."

"Evie doesn't need a bath," I said, keeping my voice level, trying to inject sanity into the situation. I glanced at Nathan, unconscious but breathing on the floor. A welt had begun to form on the back of his head. "Teresa bathed her last night before bed. Let me have her, please."

When I reached for her, Aaron turned his back on me as he tested the temperature of the water with his wrist, like a good father would. Evie sobbed in his arms.

"For god's sake, Aaron," I said. "Aaron, stop!"

"You're not going to phone the police," he said, like I was being silly. He lay Evie on the kitchen table and smiled as he spoke calmly and assuredly, as if brokering a business deal. "And I know you don't want to leave me."

"You're insane," I said.

"Not insane," he said, pulling off Evie's underpants and diaper. "I'm just a family man who will do whatever it takes to keep his family together." He lifted my baby, naked, to his chest.

I started for the door. "I'm getting my neighbors."

"I wouldn't do that if I were you," he said, carrying Evie to the sink.

"I won't be bullied into staying with you," I said. "Not like Olive." Not like Madison or Sarah.

"Oh, for heaven's sake, Kira, I'm not bullying you," Aaron said. "I'm simply giving my baby a bath, to calm her down."

"Aaron, *please*—" I reached for Evie, but Aaron blocked my way with his body. He sank her lovingly into the water, as he had so many times in the past, careful to support her neck and cooing to her as he did so, only this time he allowed her head to submerge much more fully. The water ringed around her tiny face.

"Now," he said. "You don't really want to leave me, do you?"

Over his shoulder, I watched the water wash over Evie's face, and she looked up at me, wide-eyed, from beneath the surface.

31

As Aaron held Evie under the water, her little arms flailed as she tried to right herself, to find breath. "Aaron!" I cried, clutching his arm, trying desperately to get to my baby, to stop him. "You'll drown her."

Olive, hearing us from below, screamed out. "Daddy, don't hurt Evie!"

"*Please*," I said. "Please don't kill her."

"Only if you promise to stay," he said. "If you leave, there's nothing for me. I won't lose my family again. I *can't* lose my family. Not a fourth time."

A fourth time? He was thinking not just of Sarah, Madison and me, but of the mother who had left him.

"I'll stay!" I cried. "I'll stay with you. Olive and I will both stay with you. Just *stop!*"

"You'll help me convince Olive? You'll support me in court?"

"Yes, yes, of course. Always."

"Because if you don't—"

"Daddy!" Olive cried out again from below, and Aaron lifted Evie's head gently from the water as if the whole thing had been an accident. She sputtered and coughed.

I uttered a sob of relief, my heart slamming against my rib cage.

"She's fine," Aaron said. He smiled down at Evie. "You were born for water, weren't you, sweetpea?"

Evie, catching her breath now, slapped the water as she did when we dunked under at our mom and baby swim sessions at the pool.

"That's my Evie," he said. "She'll be a swimmer, a triathlete. I bet she does the Ironman. Get her a towel, will you?"

I stood there staring at Evie in the sink, shaking, not quite taking everything in.

"A *towel*," Aaron said sharply, and I ran to the bathroom.

When I returned, I held the towel open for Evie. "Please let me take her," I begged.

"Of course," he said.

I wrapped the towel around her and held her close. And then I burst into tears.

When Aaron put a hand on my shoulder, I startled.

"It's okay," he said soothingly. "I'm not going to hurt you, or Evie. I just need you to understand. Come sit." He took my hand and led me back to the kitchen table. I sat with Evie wrapped in my arms. From the cellar below, as if she too were submerged underwater, I heard Olive's muted sobs and pleas to be let out.

"I regret our argument," Aaron said, as if we had only had a lover's spat. "Let's put this to bed, all right? No more tears."

I glanced at Nathan, still unconscious on the floor. Aaron, following my gaze, dismissed Nathan's prone body with a wave of his hand. "I'll say he broke in, accosted me in a jealous rage, and I had to defend myself, and you. You'll confirm my story, of course." When I didn't immediately respond, his voice grew sharp. "You *will* confirm my story."

I held Evie closer and nodded. "Yes," I whispered.

"What was that?"

"Yes," I said.

He reached over and tickled Evie until he got a smile out of her. "I can make you happy, Kira," he said. "I *have* made you happy."

Yes. Yes, he had. Even as he had lied to me and to his daughter about Madison and Sarah, as he had hidden his violent nature from us. He had made me happy even as some part of me must have known there was something deeply wrong with him. What was wrong with *me*?

"Let's make this work," he said. He held out a hand. Was I supposed to shake it, sealing a deal? For Evie, I would. To save Evie, I would. I took his hand and he squeezed it, then swung it as if we were skipping along a beach. "Good." He stood and held out his arms. "Put Evie down," he said.

I shook my head a little, staring at his feet. I wouldn't let her go.

"I said, put Evie down!" he shouted.

I winced and put her on the floor. She left the towel behind and squealed in delight at going unclothed, slapping manically as she crawled across the kitchen floor. She stopped to pat Nathan's head, as if to wake him, then, getting no response, pulled herself to standing at the gossip table and stuck her fingers in the dial of the phone.

Aaron yanked me up and to his chest, so close that I struggled to breathe. I squirmed, but he only held me tighter. He whispered in my ear. "We'll all be happy together, Kira, if you stay." He kissed the top of my head. "But if you don't, we won't be happy."

As he held me, I stared past his shoulder, first at Nathan unconscious on the floor, then at Evie playing with the old rotary phone. When I was a child, I had imagined I could have conversations on it with people from the past, the dead.

Aaron kissed me again, on the lips this time, and I responded like I wanted it, putting on a good show. *Fucking psycho*, I thought.

I kissed him long and lovingly while thinking, *Fucking asshole*. My passion for Aaron had once washed over me, a tsunami, when he arrived home from one of his trips and kissed me like that. Now his kiss made me feel sick with rage. When he stepped back, I wiped my mouth.

"That's worth sticking around for, isn't it?" he asked. He *begged*.

I nodded. But of course, I wasn't planning on sticking around for his kisses. I was just keeping him onside long enough to figure out how we could escape safely, all of us. Evie was so little and trusting, and Olive was the opposite, so sure now of everything she knew and unwilling to play along. How could I get us all out of this house to safety without Aaron hurting anyone again?

Aaron stepped back, releasing me, and smiled that lovely, disarming smile, and there he was again, *my* Aaron, the one I thought I'd known. One of his nostrils was bigger than the other, and his long nose was just slightly bent to one side. Little imperfections that had made him easier to love somehow. I remembered thinking I would do anything—*anything*—to keep him smiling at me like that, to keep his attention focused on me. But now, in this moment, my only thought was how nicely my hands would fit around his slender neck.

32

There was a loud knock on the kitchen door, and then Teresa's worried voice. "Kira?"

In the cellar below us, Olive's pleas for help rose in volume when she heard Teresa.

"Kira, are you all right? Is Nathan still there?"

"Who's that?" Aaron asked.

"Teresa, my neighbor."

"Ah, the babysitter."

"Kira?" Teresa called again, knocking harder this time. "Nathan and I heard screams and yelling. He was coming over to check on you. Is everything okay?"

"Get rid of her," Aaron hissed. When I hesitated, he picked up Evie, wrapped the towel around her and carried her back over to the kitchen sink. "I said, get rid of her!"

I held out both hands. "Okay, okay." Then, wiping the tears from my face as I turned to the door, I called, "Coming!" I opened the door, but just a crack, so that Teresa couldn't see her son lying behind me.

Teresa was wearing a blue bathrobe and slippers, a set I recognized as a Mother's Day gift from Nathan, her face puffy and creased from her pillow.

"Teresa," I said wearily, "this isn't a good time."

She took in my tear-stained face. "I can see that." Then she peered past me at Aaron. "What's going on? Where's Nathan? Do you need help?" From the concerned, determined expression on her face, I knew she meant, *Should I phone the police?*

"Everything's fine," I said quickly. "Nathan came by to check on us, but I convinced him to go home."

"But he didn't come back to my place for Buddy."

"I imagine he forgot," I said.

"He would never forget Buddy."

I knew that. Nathan and that dog were inseparable. He even took Buddy to the construction sites he worked on.

I shrugged. "He said something about going home to see Ashley. Maybe he planned to come right back."

She pursed her lips as we both listened to Olive's cries for help beneath us. I could tell her to phone for help right now, but then what would Aaron do to Evie before the cops arrived? He was standing right there with her, beside the kitchen sink full of water. I thought of bears in that moment: on finding a female with a cub that wasn't his, a male bear would kill the cub.

"The kids are overtired and wound up from last night," I said. "As you can see, Aaron just gave Evie a bath to calm her down."

"Did he now?" Teresa gripped her bathrobe at the neck to close it. "And the girl? Kira, I can hear her screaming for help."

Aaron cleared his throat, reminding me to be careful about what I said next.

"Olive is having something of a temper tantrum," I told Teresa. "Aaron is just giving her a time-out until she cools down."

"A tantrum? At her age? She's, what, thirteen?"

"Can we talk later?" I asked. "We're in the middle of things here. As you can imagine, we have a few matters to discuss."

"Yes, well, I'm sure you do." She glanced at Aaron. "Tell Sarah and Madison that they are welcome to come to my place for coffee and breakfast if they'd like. I'm sure you're not going to want to feed them here, not with all this going on."

I felt a hot jolt of adrenaline rush from my stomach to my skull. I'd told Aaron that Sarah and Madison had headed back to Toronto. Now he knew they were still here. I felt his anger swell behind me. As Teresa padded away in her slippers, I closed the door quietly behind her, pressing my forehead against the frame as I glanced sideways at Nathan lying on the floor. *Shit.*

"Where *are* they?" Aaron roared. I felt his eyes on me, and the hairs on the back of my neck rose. "Where are you hiding them?"

"I'm not hiding them," I said, turning to him.

"But Vicki and Madison *are* still here, on the island."

Below us, Olive was quiet for a moment as she listened in, and then her cries started up again. Evie started to whimper again too, and I reached for her, but Aaron refused to let me hold her.

"Where *are* they?"

"I don't know," I cried over Evie's howls.

Aaron grabbed my neck with one hand and squeezed. "Tell me where they are!"

I grappled with his arm, trying to get him to let go. So this is what it had felt like for Sarah, and for Madison. Now it was my turn. My throat, gripped in his fist, felt as if it were full of sand. I shook my head a little as I struggled for breath, and he loosened his grasp just enough to let me speak.

"I don't know," I said again, my voice hoarse. "I don't know!"

He kept his long, elegant fingers around my neck, scrutinizing my face to gauge whether I was lying. To avoid his gaze, I looked past his shoulder at the view out the window over the sink, the milky early-morning light. Spiderwebs, covered in dew and catching the low sun, were suddenly visible in the long, uncut grass of the yard, hundreds of them, thousands of them. They shimmered, vibrating in the morning breeze. Until now, I'd had no idea they were there—these traps, all these fucking traps.

33

Aaron abruptly let go of my neck and turned sharply, carrying Evie back to the laundry room. With my baby in his arms, he squatted down and opened the trapdoor.

"Aaron—Aaron, what are you doing?" I said, following.

"Get up here!" he shouted at Olive, and she stumbled up the steps, keeping her eyes on Evie as my baby, wearing only a towel, hung from Aaron's arm over that hole. I stepped back as he pushed Olive into the kitchen.

"What did you do to Nathan?" she cried.

But Aaron ignored her question. "Where are Madison and Vicki?" he asked her.

"I don't know." Olive glanced at me. "Is Nathan going to be okay?"

"Where *are* they?" Aaron boomed.

"She doesn't know," I said. "Aaron, for god's sake, leave her alone!"

But he kept his eyes on her. "I know they're still on the island. Tell me where Madison and Vicki are, *now*." He held Evie over the kitchen sink, and her towel dipped into the water. "Or do I need to give Evie another bath?"

"No!" Olive cried, holding out both hands.

"Aaron, *please!*" I said.

"Then tell me where they are!"

Olive froze. Above her, on the kitchen wall, the eyes of the Kit-Cat Klock slid back and forth. "They're at the hunt camp," she said. "The forest Kira owns."

Aaron turned to me. "Where is it?"

I hesitated.

"*Where is it?*" he roared.

"Not far," I said. "A short drive."

"*Where?*"

I cringed as he took a step to hover menacingly over me. "Close," I said. "There's a sign, like those deer warning signs, the jumping deer, only homemade."

He turned on his heel to the door. "Let's go. Kira, grab Evie's diaper bag. We can get her dressed on the road." He pushed through the old screen door, carrying Evie. Olive followed.

I hesitated, looking down at Nathan. Thank god, he was still breathing, but he was out cold. He needed medical attention, now.

"We need to phone for an ambulance," I said.

"Get in the Jeep!" Aaron yelled.

"We can't leave him here like this."

"Move!"

I grabbed my purse and Evie's diaper bag, and took one last look at Nathan before stepping outside, leaving the door open behind me. Hopefully Teresa or another neighbor would see that the door was open and find Nathan.

"Aaron, what are you going to do?" I asked as I joined them outside.

"Get in my rental."

"We need the car seat for Evie," I said, going around to the driver's side of my truck, forgetting for a moment that the car seat was still inside, where Teresa had left it. From there, over Aaron's shoulder, I could see into Teresa's living room window. She was watching us, as I'd known she would be. She knew me well enough to know when I was lying. She held up her landline phone and pointed to it, asking, *Should I phone the police?* I nodded slightly, looking pointedly back at my summer house, hoping she would find Nathan and help him. Seeming to understand, she stood back a little, just out of Aaron's view should he turn to look, the morning light reflecting off the glass. *Please let her phone the cops*, I thought. But would she know where to send them?

"Leave the car seat," Aaron said. "I'm going to hold Evie. In case you get any ideas." He tossed me the keys as I reached his Jeep. "You're driving."

I opened the back door and threw my purse and diaper bag on the back seat beside Aaron's travel case. "You're going to hold her? That's not safe!"

He waved a hand by his ear as if that was too much to deal with. "I don't care! Just get in the fucking Jeep!" He got in the passenger side himself.

I slid into the driver's side as Olive sat in the back, in tears, clicking her seatbelt into place. Aaron held Evie, still naked and wrapped in a towel, on his lap. She whined and fussed, holding her hands out for me.

"It's dangerous to drive with her like that," I said again, knowing he was beyond caring. He had just threatened to drown Evie, several times.

"Drive," he said. "Straight to the hunt camp."

"Sarah and Madison may not even be there," I said. "As I said, they have likely left already."

"That neighbor of yours seemed to think otherwise. Drive."

I backed onto the street and drove up the laneway, turning off onto the main road. "Why do you need to see Sarah so badly?" I asked. "What do you want from her?"

Aaron kept his eyes on the road. "Shut up and drive."

"She's a threat to you in some way, isn't she?"

But what kind of threat? He'd managed to evade charges of abuse. Surely he couldn't be afraid of that now, after all this time.

His jaw tensed as he spoke quietly, to himself more than me. "I should have finished the job I started years ago," he said.

"You're not going to hurt Sarah and Maddy, are you?" Olive asked from the back.

I studied the side of his face a moment, the sharp angle of his nose. "Aaron, please, no."

Aaron flicked a glance at me but didn't answer. I put a hand to my throat, picturing the ring of finger-sized bruises that were blooming there. Aaron had dragged Olive by her hair and thrown her into a cellar. He had threatened to kill Evie. He had put his hand around my neck, just as he had with Sarah and Madison in the past. Whatever threat Sarah posed to him, he seemed bent on silencing her, and likely Madison as well. And—my god—the girls and I could well be next.

228   GAIL ANDERSON-DARGATZ

34

I drove slowly as we left the village, trying to stall to allow more time for the police to reach us in this rural area, but Aaron slapped the dash twice. "Get a move on," he said. "Faster."

"I told you, it's not safe to drive with you holding Evie like that. If we need to stop suddenly—"

Aaron held a hand at Evie's neck. "I said, faster!"

I pressed my foot to the gas, speeding over the rolling hills on this part of the road, my stomach lifting and then sinking in the dips. As we passed the dump, we met a Ministry of Natural Resources pickup towing a large rectangular box—a live bear trap—on a trailer. A yellow warning sign with a bear on it was fixed to the side. If I could signal the conservation officer in that truck, get him to notice me . . .

I glanced at Aaron, who stared back at me, his teeth clenched. "Don't even think about it," he said. He hovered a hand over Evie's mouth and nose, a threat, a warning to behave myself. Olive, seeing this from the back, took in a sharp, panicked breath.

"Please, no," I whispered, shaking my head.

The worker in the municipal truck lifted a hand and waved as we passed, and I nodded at him, giving nothing away, then watched the bear trap slide by. Aaron settled back in his seat, removing his hand from Evie's face, and I turned my focus to the road ahead. It was enclosed on either side by a wall of trees, creating the impression that the way ahead was getting narrower, collapsing in on us.

As we approached the hunt camp, I slowed to look at the section of road where I'd hit the deer the night before. As I had predicted, someone had hauled away the carcass in the night, and thanks to the heavy rainstorm, no trace of the accident remained.

"Is that the place?" Aaron asked, pointing ahead at the weathered sign my father had made, the leaping deer.

"Yes," I said.

"And that's the minivan you were talking about? Vicki's van." The gray minivan was parked where she'd left it the night before, near the entrance to the hunt camp road.

"Yes, that's Sarah's van."

"Good. Then they're here." They were probably asleep in the cabin, as it was still early. "Let's get this over with."

I started to park just beyond Sarah's van, but Aaron waved me down the overgrown camp road. "Keep going."

If we drove to the cabin, the cops wouldn't be able to see the Jeep from the road. Assuming they even thought to look here. If Teresa believed we were headed off the island, the police would undoubtedly focus their attention on the main road to Little Current and the bridge, or perhaps on the ferry, as those were the only two ways off the island. Even so, I had to make sure the Jeep remained visible. It was our best chance of being found.

"There's too much bush," I said.

"It's a Jeep," Aaron said. "It will get through this. Keep going."

Shit. I'd have to find a way to stop before we rounded the corner. I turned onto the camp road, mowing down the tall grass, still wet from the storm. The vehicle jostled as I navigated around young trees, flattening some. "It's too thick," I said. "We'll never make it."

"Just drive."

Up ahead, the girl, my young self, appeared in the middle of the road, nodding sideways at the old gray barn where my father had once hung deer carcasses. All at once, I knew what I had to do. I drove slowly ahead and then, just before the barn, swerved into the field, where I knew a large stump was hidden in the long grass. Aaron and Evie lurched forward as the vehicle got hung up on the stump and stalled, and I instinctively held an arm out so my baby wouldn't hit the dash. She looked stunned and then burst into tears. I smoothed a hand over her forehead to soothe her.

"You did that on purpose," Aaron said, pulling Evie away from me.

"No, I didn't—I told you, the road is too overgrown. I had to go around that young maple."

"Fuck." He pressed his lips together as he stared at the grass and bush growing on the road ahead. "How much farther is it?"

"Not far," I said.

"I guess we'll have to walk in." He lifted his chin to peer into the rearview mirror. "Olive, get out." He reached over and grabbed the key from the ignition, then stepped out of the Jeep himself. "And take Evie." He handed my baby to Olive, took off his suit jacket and threw it on the seat before slamming his door shut. Then he rolled up his sleeves as if getting down to work.

"I'll just get my purse," I said, reaching into the back seat. "And Evie's diaper bag."

"Leave it."

"I may need the keys to the cabin. And Evie needs some clothes."

"Fine. Just—let's *go*."

I leaned into the Jeep for my purse, slung it and the diaper bag over my shoulder, then grabbed Aaron's hardside travel case.

"What are you doing?" he asked. "Leave my luggage in the Jeep."

"I think you might need it," I said, and I lifted the case to swing it at him, hard. He looked briefly surprised, and then the case slammed into his skull. *Payback, for Nathan*, I thought. Aaron fell to the ground, grunting in pain and holding his head, then looked up at me from the grass, blinking, disoriented, as he leaned on one elbow.

I took Evie from Olive and held her tightly to my chest. "*Run!*" I told Olive. "To the barn. Quickly!"

As we sprinted to the barn, I glanced back to see Aaron still on the ground near the Jeep. But I knew that blow to his head wouldn't stop him for long.

"Hurry!" I said to Olive as we reached the old barn. "Inside!"

Once we were inside, I handed Evie and the diaper bag to Olive. "Go out the back. I'll close the barn door after you, but you'll have to slide the outside board down, to lock it from the outside." My father had put those boards in place on both doors to keep bears and other scavengers away from the deer he hung here.

"You'll be trapped inside," Olive said.

"I know what I'm doing." Sort of. I started to close the back door. "There's a deer path that runs from this barn through the trees and ends in the field behind the cabin. Take that. Stay off the hunt camp road. Be as quiet as you can. Let Madison and Sarah know what's going on. But stay in the cabin until I can get to you."

"What are you going to do?"

"Set a live bear trap," I said.

She looked at me quizzically.

"No time to explain," I said. "*Go.*"

I closed the barn door. Through the slats, I saw her swing the board down into place, barring the exit. She was right. If this went south, I was trapped.

Outside I heard Aaron yelling, "You *bitch!*"

GAIL ANDERSON-DARGATZ

He had never called me that before, reserving the title for Madison. For weeks, I had worried he would someday see me the way he saw her. Now here we were. And I didn't give a fuck.

I slid behind a stack of graying, water-damaged lumber next to the front door and crouched down, hiding myself there.

"You fucking bitch!" Aaron cried.

Through the slats of the wall, I saw him stagger toward the barn, holding his head. As he reached the barn door, he let his hand fall, revealing the huge red goose egg on his forehead.

"I saw you go in there!" he said, pushing the door open. He squinted, either from the pain of the blow or as his eyes adjusted to the dim light inside. Probably both. "What are you trying to pull?" He scanned the barn: the upper level that had once held straw, the tools my father had hung on the walls, the stacks of crates, the stalls that had once housed horses, the metal bar that stretched from wall to wall above our heads and, hanging off it, the hook on which my father had hung deer carcasses during the November hunt week, to age the meat before butchering it. "Come out!" he cried. "There's no use hiding. There's no way out." He picked up a short board, crusted with rusty nails, and wielded it like a club as he strode into the barn.

I waited until he was standing in the center, under the meat hook, before I slipped out from behind the stack of lumber. Hearing me, he swung around, raising the board and launching himself toward me. I quickly ducked outside and slammed the door shut behind me, swinging the board down into place just as he reached the door. He pounded on it hard, sending up clouds of dust. As if taking up the challenge, a pileated woodpecker began its *rat-a-tat-tat* drum on a snag somewhere in the forest.

"Kira, let me out of here." Aaron hammered on the door. "Let me out!"

I backed up and took a last look at the barn. The structure was weathered and water-damaged, the boards rotted along the base. A swift kick would likely dislodge any one of them. But trapping him here, even for a few minutes, might buy us enough time to make our escape.

I turned and sprinted down the hunt camp road. Just as I reached the corner before the final stretch of road to the cabin, I saw the hazy figure of my ghost, my young self, once again standing on the road ahead of me. I slowed to a stop as we stared at each other. After a moment, I glanced back over my shoulder for any sign of Aaron. When I turned back, the ghost was gone.

I ran the rest of the way, leapt up the porch stairs and pushed into the cabin. I locked the door behind me, even though Aaron could simply reach in and turn the knob.

"Kira!" Olive cried, wrapping an arm around me. Evie, in her arms and finally clothed, patted me, overjoyed to see me.

"Oh, thank god," Madison said. "From what Olive said, we weren't sure you were going to make it."

I took Evie from Olive and pulled back the faded curtain to look outside. "I locked Aaron in the barn," I said. "But it won't hold him for long."

Madison put a hand on my arm. "Olive said Aaron locked her in the cellar and threatened to drown Evie."

"He submerged Evie in the sink. Her face was underwater." I put a hand over my mouth as the emotion of the morning started bubbling up.

Sarah wrapped an arm around me. She smelled of perfumed deodorant and woodsmoke, from the fire the night before. "Oh, Kira, I'm so sorry."

I touched my neck. My throat was still tender from Aaron's grip. "He's coming for you, Sarah. I think he wants to kill you. We need to get the hell out of here."

"Why would he want to kill me?" Sarah asked. She looked at Madison. "I mean, why now?"

"I have no idea," I said.

"You were hard to find," Madison said to Sarah. "It was a matter of luck that I found you at all."

"Maybe that's it," Sarah said. "Now that I'm back in the picture, in Olive's life, I'm a threat to him again."

Madison nodded. "He must know you'd help me wrangle custody away from him."

"Yes, but why wouldn't he simply work through the courts?" I asked. "Why is it so important to him to track you down here?"

Sarah held up both hands, perplexed.

"We don't have time to talk about this right now," I said. "He could be here any moment. I think Teresa phoned the police, but who knows how long it will take them to find us. We need to get out of here. This is the first place Aaron will come looking. We can follow one of the deer trails to the road and try to catch a ride. It's not safe to head to your van because we'd have to go right past the barn."

"I'm sorry I got mad at Dad," Olive said.

"What are you talking about?" Madison asked her. "You *should* be mad."

"I shouldn't have told him I was going to live with you," she said. "If I hadn't done that, he wouldn't have got so mad and locked me in the cellar or tried to drown Evie or hurt Nathan. Then that lady, Teresa, wouldn't have heard me or come over—she wouldn't have said you were here."

"None of this is your fault," I said.

Maddy's face brightened. "You told him you're going to live with me?"

"It's nobody's fault," I continued. "Your father is . . ." I had no words to explain him. "He's dangerous," I said. "But I'm not going to let him hurt you or Evie or any of us."

"Me neither." Madison squeezed my hand and let go.

Olive didn't respond. She looked out the window as if resigned to the fact that there was little we could do to protect her. I felt the real weight of my failure then. I had spent more time resenting Olive's presence than getting to know her, and had completely misread what was going on between her and her parents. Worse, I had supported Aaron's agenda, standing between Olive and her stepmother and the help Olive needed. I had foolishly projected my ugly experience with my mother onto her. It had been my job to protect her, and I had failed. I wouldn't fail her again.

"We need to go," I said. But as I reached for the doorknob, we heard the distant rumble of a vehicle's motor turning over, sputtering to a stop, then starting up again. This time, it kept running.

"Shit," I said. "Aaron got out of the barn."

35

As we heard Aaron's Jeep heading down the hunt camp road toward the cabin, I clung to Evie and turned to Madison and Sarah. I saw my own panic mirrored in their faces.

"What are we going to do?" Olive asked.

"There's three of us against him," Madison said.

"But we've got the girls to protect," I said. "He knows he can use them to get us to do whatever he wants. He made me drive and threatened Evie all the way here so I would cooperate."

"Asshole."

"In any case, how are we going to stop him?" Sarah held up both hands. "Hurl rocks at him?"

No, not rocks, I thought. I opened the cabinet and took down hunting knives, handing one to each of the women and to Olive. Of course, knives were only useful at close quarters. I would have to be almost in Aaron's embrace to use one, and he was stronger than I was.

"Hold Evie for me, will you?" I asked Olive. She pocketed the knife and took my baby from me.

I fumbled in my purse for my keys. My hands shook as I unlocked the gun cabinet and took out my father's rifle and a box of cartridges. I opened the bolt and started loading the gun, pressing the rounds into the magazine.

"You're going to shoot Dad?" Olive asked, her voice rising in alarm.

"I'll only use the rifle to defend us," I said as I loaded the final cartridge into the chamber. I glanced at Sarah. "But he did say he was coming here to finish the job he started years ago."

Sarah touched a hand to her throat. "He said that?"

I gripped the rifle, aiming it upward as I pulled back the curtain on the window to see Aaron's Jeep roar around the corner, plowing down small trees, bouncing over rocks and leaving a flattened swath of grass and bush behind it. "You've got to get out of here," I said to the women, stepping back. I pulled a soother from my bag. "Here," I said to Olive. "Keep that sucker in Evie's mouth. It will keep her quiet. Hold her close. She knows you. She'll feel safe with you." I lifted my chin toward the back door. "Get out of here," I whispered to them all.

"You're not coming with us?" Olive asked, hugging Evie.

"I'm going to buy you some time."

"Then I'm staying with you," Madison said.

"No. I need you to take care of the girls."

Madison nodded, a pact, mother to mother. "We've come a long way in twenty-four hours, haven't we?" She grinned, and for a moment I almost liked her.

"Follow the path that leads to the outhouse," I said. "Keep going. You'll see a clearing. At the far edge, you'll find a tree stand, like a tree fort, but hidden. You won't see it at first, as it's camouflaged. Hopefully, Aaron won't see it either, should he come looking. Don't come down, out of hiding, no matter what. I'll call when it's safe." When the police arrived, I hoped.

GAIL ANDERSON-DARGATZ

"What are you going to do?" Madison asked.

I lifted a shoulder. "I'll stall," I said. "Try to keep him talking until the cops get here."

"That shouldn't be hard," Madison said. "But you said it yourself. He's dangerous, Kira."

I held up the gun. "I've got this if I need it." Though I couldn't imagine using it on him.

Madison put a hand on my arm. "You don't have to do this."

I kissed Evie's forehead as Olive held her. "Yes, I do," I said. My actions had led us to this. I needed to make it right.

I peered out the window again as the Jeep reached the clearing in front of the cabin. Aaron got out of the vehicle and banged the door shut. "Kira?" he called out. "I know you're in there. I saw you at the window." He stepped around to the front of the Jeep. "So this is your father's cabin? Not much to look at, is it?"

I gave Olive a quick hug and kissed Evie one last time. "Now *go*," I said.

Madison put a hand on Olive's shoulder as they followed Sarah out the door. When Evie started to fuss, holding her arms out for me, Olive plugged the soother into her mouth, then hurried down the trail to the outhouse behind the cabin, ushered by the two women.

"Kira? Vicki? Maddy?" Aaron called again, his voice closer now. "Come out and talk. All I want to do is talk."

I closed the back door quietly, then crossed the cabin and stepped out onto the front porch. "That's far enough," I said, holding the rifle upright with both hands.

He strolled toward me. "You know it isn't really over between us. I'm the best thing that ever happened to you. Look at what you came from." He glanced at the ramshackle cabin, with its broken windows. "And think of where you live now. Where *we* live."

Asshole, I thought. Did he really think I would stay with him for his money? "Stop right there," I said.

He laughed. "You don't even have the guts to point that rifle at me."

I cocked the gun, and he jumped a little. "Don't come any closer," I said.

But instead of frightening him, I had only managed to piss him off. He clenched and unclenched his fists as he slowly climbed the stairs. "How dare you," he said. "How dare you presume to threaten me? Or think you're better than me. You're nothing. You were lucky I took any interest in you at all."

"Stay back," I said, stepping back myself. "I will fire if I have to."

"Put that thing down," he said, as if chiding Olive or Evie. "You're not going to use it on me. I know how you feel about guns." He backed me into the cabin wall and pressed the muzzle down before tucking a finger under my chin. "I thought we had come to an understanding back at the summer house. I guess I was wrong." He softened his voice and put a hand on the back of my neck to bring me close enough that our foreheads touched, the gun at an angle between us. I struggled in an attempt to get out of his grip, but he held firm. "I loved you," he whispered. "I gave you everything—a child, a home, a life, everything you could want—and you threw it all away."

I finally broke loose and slammed the butt of the gun into his stomach. He grunted and bent over. Then, regaining his footing, he backhanded me to the porch deck, sending the rifle flying from my hands. I shook off the shock and the sting, then searched the floor for the gun, but he'd already grabbed it and was aiming it at me.

Shit.

I stood, pressing myself against the wood of the door. Glass, shaken loose from the window, tinkled to the deck at my feet.

"Vicki?" Aaron called past me. "Vicki, I know you're in there. I know you're all in there. I heard Evie crying. Come out. We need to talk." He weighed the gun in both hands. "All I want to do is talk. You hear me?"

"Sarah doesn't want to speak to you," I said.

"Well, that's a shame. We have so much catching up to do."

"What are you really after?" I said, to keep him talking. "Why drag Olive and Evie and me out here? What does Sarah have over you?" I squinted at him. "What are you afraid of?"

"Are you *trying* to piss me off?" he said. He looked behind me, through the gaping hole in the window to the dark cabin beyond. "Vicki, come out here *now*."

I tried to block him from looking through the window, but he took my arm, wrenched me away from the door and threw it open. "Vicki? Madison? Olive?" When he saw that the cabin was empty, he turned back to me. "Where are they?" He lifted the muzzle of the rifle to my chin. "I said, where *are* they?"

I wouldn't help him find them. I wouldn't. Desperate, I tried to grab the rifle from his hands. When I couldn't jar it loose, I put a foot behind his and, tripping him, shoved Aaron backward off the deck to the ground below. But he didn't drop the rifle, as I had hoped, instead clinging to it with one hand even as, winded, he struggled to right himself. Beyond him, I saw the ghost of my young self standing at the forest edge. She nodded to the side, then turned abruptly and disappeared into the bush. Before Aaron had a chance to recover, I jumped off the porch and raced across the clearing, following my fetch into the woods, hoping I could lure him away from Olive, Evie and the two women.

"Stop!" Aaron cried out, but I was already hidden from his view in the dense cedar bush.

There was a rifle blast, and I instinctively ducked, but I didn't stop running. I sprinted down the worn deer path that my father and I had taken that last day, bullying my way through brush at the corners, taking branches to the face and pushing on, leading Aaron away from Evie, away from Olive. I heard him crashing into the bush behind me, like a bear charging after prey.

"You can't run forever!" he shouted. He should have known better. I *could* run forever, pretty much. I was an endurance runner, a marathon runner. But then, so was he.

I sped up, and the girl, my young self, was there again, running down the path ahead of me as I had that day after hearing the shot in the forest. The girl looked behind her, through me, then continued on her way, around a corner, bounding ahead just like a deer on a hunt.

But this time, I was the hunted.

36

My fetch led me down the snaking path through the forest, leaping over windfall, pushing through low branches. I raced now, running harder, faster than I ever did in long-distance races, spurred on by the sound of Aaron trampling through the bush behind me, his feet cracking twigs. I scrambled over roots that cluttered the dark forest floor, instinctively heading toward the light of a clearing up ahead. On reaching it, I circled around it, keeping to the bush so Aaron wouldn't catch me exposed.

When I reached the far edge of the clearing, I heard the crack of the rifle and time seemed to slow. A flock of cedar waxwings lifted too leisurely from the trees into the sky, and I felt the spray of dirt as the bullet plowed into the ground near my feet.

"Stop or I'll fire again!" Aaron cried.

I was sure his aim on that shot was a fluke. I doubted Aaron had ever fired a gun before, other than in the video games he played. But he was close enough now that he didn't need to be a marksman to hit me. I stopped and held up both hands.

"Come out of the bush."

I turned to face Aaron, peering at him through low hanging branches, and in that instant, I realized where I was, where my child self had led me: to the clearing where I had found my father's body. This was the spot, right here, where I had started running all those years ago, and I had never stopped.

It had changed. The surrounding maples and cedar were taller and, of course, the circular clearing was thick with grass, fireweed and milkweed, and was not covered in snow as it had been on that November day, but this was the place.

"I said, come out!"

I stepped forward over windfall into the clearing, and as I did so, past and present merged. I was that kid dressed in camouflage, jittery and nauseous, my chest tight, looking down at my father's body. The pool of blood that oozed from behind his head onto the fresh snow. I braced my hands against my thighs to throw up, tasting the bitter coffee I'd had at lunch that day. I spit. Spit again. Then I looked up, blinking as I tried to get my bearings. I didn't feel right, like I wasn't myself, like I was rising above everything and watching a video of myself.

Aaron said something, but his voice seemed so far away, *he* seemed so far away, as if I were viewing him through a pinhole camera. In that instant, I was unsure who I was: was I that scared girl in the past or this terrified woman in the present? My sense of self expanded, diffused to encompass everything around me, as it so often did when I ran. As if looking down from above, I saw a woman—myself—and a man—Aaron—standing on either side of the clearing in the July sunshine, and between us was the girl I had once been, standing over my father's body sprawled in a circle of snow, a halo of blood around his head.

"I said, what the fuck do you think you're doing?"

I snapped back inside my own skin and found myself back in the present. Aaron was facing me across the clearing, gun in hand,

and my father's body was gone. Staring at the empty spot where he'd died, I experienced one of those rare, exquisite moments of clarity, and I finally understood why the ghost of my young self had brought me here. I had been so careful to hide this part of myself in the forest. I hadn't had the maturity to face my past. But now there was no outrunning it.

"I asked you a question!" Aaron roared. "What the fuck were you thinking, taking off on me like that? Do you *want* to die?"

"When I told you I was pregnant, you said you knew me," I said, my eyes still on the spot where I'd found my father's body. Then I looked up. "Do you remember that?"

Aaron seemed confused. "What?"

"You said you knew me. And I felt like I knew you too, because I did. You were so familiar. I thought, at the time, we were soulmates."

Aaron lowered the rifle and I dropped my hands as an expression of relief crossed his face. For a moment he almost looked like my old Aaron again. "We *are* soulmates," he said, and his voice took on that silky quality of reassurance that I had always loved. It hadn't occurred to me until now that it was his salesman's voice, that he used it on his clients as well. "We belong together," he said.

I shook my head at his audacity, that he could still believe that. I crossed my arms. "You know, you always order my meals at restaurants," I said.

He laughed a little at the subject change. "What?"

"You never let me order for myself. Why is that?"

"I don't know. It seems like the gentlemanly thing to do. And you often don't know what half the items on the menu are."

"And you pay all my bills, my credit card, give me an allowance."

"Are you complaining?"

"Why didn't you leave some of that to me? At very least, I could have taken care of the household bills."

He shrugged. "You weren't used to handling finances. You had never lived on your own before we met."

"Yes, exactly. You kept me dependent on you, just like my mother did. And I let you. I even thought I wanted that. Because it was all I'd ever known. I didn't think I was capable of taking care of myself, or Evie. I didn't think I was capable of making it on my own."

He laughed, as if we were just reminiscing about old times. "You weren't. And you had no idea how to be a parent. I had to teach you how to diaper your own baby, for Chrissakes."

"I honestly believed the only thing I was any good at was running."

"And you are." He took a step forward, carrying the rifle in one hand. "Babe, you could go back into competition right now and I would support you. I would take care of everything. I've always said you could be a contender."

Just like my mother had wanted. "And you would take care of me and Evie, keep us safe, as long as I am *obedient* to you. As long as you are in control."

"As long as you don't leave me."

"That was what my mother was afraid of," I said, more to myself than to him. "That I would leave her. She was so afraid of it that she lied to me about my father, just like you lied to Olive, to me, about Madison and Sarah. My mother was so afraid of losing me that she couldn't bear the thought that I could love anyone else— my father, or even myself. And my father died because of it. Right here, in this clearing." I tilted my head at Aaron. "The thing is, by hanging on so tight, my mother lost me. I couldn't really love her in the end. And now you've lost me too, Aaron. You've lost all of us. Evie, Olive, and me."

"No!" Aaron's anguished cry rang out across the forest and he swung the gun up to aim at me again.

"That's really what all this is about, isn't it?" I asked him. "The violence, the control. You're *afraid*. You're so afraid of being left alone that you threatened to kill us to make us stay. My god, Aaron, you're a *child*. A frightened, tantrumming child." He turned his head away and, emboldened, I took a step forward. "What the hell happened to you, Aaron? How did you get like this? It's because your mother left you, isn't it? She left you alone with a father who beat you. You must know that your father's abuse drove her off. But you're still so angry at her that you took it out on—"

"Shut up!" Aaron roared. "Just shut the fuck up." He fired the rifle at the ground to one side of me, and I startled, took a step back. "Don't think you know me," he said. "You don't know anything about me. My mother was weak, unfaithful, a *slut*. She deserved everything she got."

"What do you mean?" I asked. "She deserved what? What did your father do to her?" But even as I asked, I already knew. Aaron had replayed it with me and Evie that day. "Your mother *didn't* abandon you, did she? You told me she left you, just left one day and never came back. But that's not what happened, is it?"

Aaron's eyes traveled wildly over the dense bush around us, and I realized some part of him was lost in a forest of his own. "She *was* leaving," he said. "She packed our bags."

"But she was going to take you with her, and your father stopped her."

Aaron began rocking a little from side to side, as Olive so often did when anxious or afraid. He shook his head slowly. "The police didn't find her body in the lake until years later. When they did, Dad went to jail. He went to jail even though it was her fault. If she hadn't tried to leave—" He looked me full in the eye. "We would still be a family."

"And you lived with your father all that time, until he was imprisoned?" I asked. "You said he beat you. Did you know he murdered your mother?" Aaron let the muzzle of the gun drop as he rocked back and forth harder, shifting his weight from foot to foot. Then it hit me. "You were there when it happened," I said. "You saw your father kill your mother. He drowned her, didn't he? You *witnessed* him drowning her. That's why you threatened to drown Evie, isn't it? You were *reliving* it." Just like I had subconsciously arranged circumstances to relive my own childhood trauma.

"Shut up!" he said, aiming the rifle back at me. "Shut the fuck up!" Then he launched forward and gripped my upper arm hard, hauling me forward. "No more talk. Let's go. Back to the cabin."

I stumbled ahead of him as he poked me now and again with the muzzle of the rifle.

"Faster," he said. "Run."

I ran ahead and he kept pace, carrying the rifle in both hands.

"What are you planning?" I asked him as we reached the edge of the forest by the cabin. "You're not going to kill me."

He didn't answer.

"The police are on their way."

"Bullshit," he said.

"Teresa phoned them." Though I wasn't sure they would find us here. "And Madison, Sarah and the girls are already gone."

But almost as soon as I said it, I heard a girl's voice, Olive's voice, calling from beyond the cabin. "Kira? Kira, are you all right?"

Aaron stepped past me to scan the field and forest beyond, in the direction of Olive's voice, then tilted his head back at me, his eyes glistening intelligently, menacingly, like a crow as it tried to figure out how to get a worm out of a Coke bottle to eat it.

37

Aaron grabbed my arm again, dragged me to the cabin steps and pushed me to the ground in front of them. I scuttled backward, my eyes on the gun.

"Come out," he called over the roof of the cabin. "Olive, come out or I'll shoot Kira." When that didn't get an immediate response, he cocked the gun and fired it into the air. I heard Evie cry out.

"I'm coming!" Olive called. "Don't hurt her!" She stepped out from behind the cabin, carrying a sobbing Evie. The look on Olive's face was beyond terrified. Numb. Madison followed as Sarah lagged behind, hugging herself.

I saw the flash of the hunting knives in the women's hands. Aaron saw them too. He laughed. "Put those things down," he said, then, louder, aiming the rifle at them, "Drop them!" First Madison and then Sarah tossed the knives to the ground. With his eyes still on the women, Aaron scooped up the two knives and threw them into the bush.

"All of you, stand over there with Kira," Aaron said, gesturing with the rifle toward me.

As I stood and brushed myself off, Madison, Sarah and Olive joined me in front of the porch steps.

"I'm sorry," Madison said to me. "We saw Aaron chase you into the woods, then heard the gunshots. I told Olive to stay put, but she was so worried . . ."

"It's okay," I said. But of course, nothing about this situation was okay.

Evie, still crying, reached for me, but when Olive handed her over, Aaron intervened, taking my baby from me.

"No," I said, clutching at Evie. "Aaron, *please*. Don't."

But he wrenched her away. When Evie's cries grew louder, he shushed her and kissed the top of her head until she settled, then handed her back to Olive. He motioned with the gun for her to carry Evie over to the Jeep. "Wait in the car," he said.

"Daddy, I—"

"I said, wait in the car!" he yelled. Olive started and carried my baby over to the Jeep, but she didn't get in. She leaned against the vehicle, hugging Evie, her head down, but watching, as a frightened cat does from beneath the bed. I thought of her collection of stuffies then, all lined up against the wall, hidden beneath her mattress. It occurred to me that she had likely witnessed more of Aaron's violence against Sarah and Madison than any of her parents imagined.

Aaron held the gun with both hands as he looked us over. "Well, well," he said. "All my girls, together at last."

All my girls. Madison and I exchanged a glance. Aaron's girls. That was exactly it. He thought we were his property, to do with as he pleased.

He nodded at Sarah. "Good to see you again, Vicki."

"I wish I could say the same," she said. "I understand you wanted to talk to me?"

"No more talk," he said. "It's clear to me now that you've done far too much of that already." Aaron bounced a little on each step he took toward us, rage rippling through his body, the rifle gripped firmly in his hands. "I'm putting an end to all this shit once and for all. Not one of you three witches is going to take my girls from me ever again. You won't take my *family* from me."

Did he plan to shoot all three of us? He didn't have enough rounds left. But, my god, which of us would he take out? I had to buy us more time, distract him until, hopefully, the police arrived.

"How can you blame any of us for leaving you?" I asked. "After what you've done."

"What *I've* done?" Aaron said. He waved the rifle at Madison. "You tried to take my daughter away from me." He aimed the rifle at me. "And why is it you come up here any chance you get, huh? It's not for the beach, is it? It's Nathan."

"No, Aaron—" But I choked up at the mention of Nathan's name, picturing my old love unconscious on the floor. I hoped to god Teresa had found him, got him help.

"And you," he said, pointing the muzzle at Sarah. "You screwed around on me too."

"What are you talking about?" Sarah asked. "I never cheated on you."

"Don't give me that. You were with some asshole the day your kid nearly drowned."

"I was not."

"I *saw* you."

Sarah tilted her head as she scrutinized Aaron. "You *saw* me? What did you see exactly?"

"You were sharing a toke with some guy. Laughing and getting stoned while your daughter almost died."

"You're talking about Russell? He was there to help me pack up, to protect me if you returned early, because I was planning to leave you that day. He saw that I was stressed and afraid, and offered me a toke and told me a few stupid jokes to make me laugh. That's all. We weren't seeing each other." Sarah shook her head as she worked things out. "How could you possibly have seen me and Russell smoking that joint? That day—that shitty day—you didn't get home until after we'd come back from having Olive checked out at the hospital, after I revived her."

"You *revived* me?" Olive asked.

Aaron shifted his weight from foot to foot as he looked away from his daughter.

"Or did you?" Sarah asked. "You *did* come home earlier, didn't you?" Sarah squinted at him, scanning his face. "But we only smoked for a minute or two before I went to answer the door and found Olive outside, floating in the pool. So if you saw us smoking, you must have seen—"

Olive stepped forward, carrying Evie. "You mean, I actually *drowned*?"

Aaron shook his head slightly, like a doddering old man. But he wouldn't look at Sarah. He blinked rapidly as he stared at the forest that surrounded us.

I pictured Aaron arriving home to find a stranger's truck in his yard, knowing Sarah was leaving him and taking Olive with her. He would have reacted as he had earlier that morning when I said *I* was leaving him and he submerged Evie in the kitchen sink.

"It was *you* who almost drowned Olive, wasn't it?" I asked him. "Just like you threatened to drown Evie, just like your father drowned your mother—"

I shared a look with Sarah and saw grief consume her face as she understood. She launched forward to grip Aaron's wrinkled violet shirt in her fist, and her voice became shrill. "You tried to drown Olive? You *threw our baby* into the pool?"

Aaron's face darkened as he pushed Sarah away with the gun, gripping it with both hands. "I should have killed you instead," he said. "It would have saved me all this grief."

"What about me?" Olive cried. "You were trying to *kill* me?"

Aaron, caught, blinked. "No, but your mother needed to learn—"

"You were, weren't you?" Sarah asked. "You would have killed us both. What stopped you?" She paused a moment, remembering. "Russell's buddy turned up to help just before I discovered Olive in the pool. We heard the knock at the door, and as I went to let him in, I saw my baby—" Her voice cracked. "You knew you couldn't fight off both men, so you ran." She grabbed Aaron's arm, turning him so he'd look her in the eye. "You fucking coward, you ran and put the blame on me!" Sarah slapped him hard.

In return, Aaron backhanded her to the ground.

"Jesus, Aaron," Madison said, rushing to help Sarah up.

Olive pushed Evie into my arms and faced her father. "How could you do that!" she cried. A look of confusion passed over her face, and I knew the inner turmoil she felt in that moment. "It's not true, is it? You didn't really try to drown me. You wouldn't do that, would you, Daddy? Not to me. Don't you love me?" Her face was streaked with tears. She had witnessed this horror, all this evil, and yet she was still a little girl, just wanting her father's love.

Aaron saw it too in that moment, and his face changed into that of the loving dad I was used to seeing, wanting his daughter to keep gazing at him with those adoring eyes, thinking maybe he could still win her over and forget all this.

He reached out his hand to her. "Oh, Olive Oyl, of course I love you," he said. Keeping one hand on the rifle, he wrapped an arm around his daughter and kissed her head.

But then Olive pulled the knife from her pocket and stabbed him in the right hand.

"Christ!" Aaron dropped the rifle to grab his hand, blood oozing through his fingers.

Olive threw the knife to the ground and picked up the rifle. She weighed it in both hands for a moment, cocked it as the characters did in the games she played, and aimed the loaded gun at her father's head.

38

Still holding his bleeding hand, Aaron took a step toward Olive. "Are you really going to shoot me?" he asked. But he quickly jumped back when Olive put her finger on the trigger.

"Olive," Madison said. "What are you *doing*?"

"He wants to kill Evie, and you, and Kira and Sarah." She glanced at her birth mother as Sarah held a hand to her bruised face. "I won't let him."

"Baby," Aaron said, his face flushed. "Come on, baby, you don't want to hurt me."

"For god's sake, Aaron, sit down and shut up." I nodded sideways at the stairs. "Before you get yourself killed!"

Aaron hesitated and then slumped down onto the cabin stairs like a moody teen who'd been caught using his mother's credit card online. For porn.

I turned back to Olive. "Put the gun down, Olive," I said. "This isn't the way."

Madison reached out to her. "Please, sweetheart."

Sarah waggled her head as she stepped, distraught and panicked, toward her daughter. "Please, no," she said.

"I'm tired of all the fighting," Olive said, her voice rising in anguish. "I'm tired of you guys yanking me around, telling me I've got to live here or there. I'm sick of feeling scared all the time. I just want it to *end*."

"Not like this," I said. I handed Evie to Madison and stood in front of Aaron, shielding him with my hands out. "Olive, give me the gun."

"Get out of the way," Olive cried.

"No."

She lowered the muzzle. "You're protecting *him*?"

"I'm protecting you. Olive, you would never forgive yourself if you hurt him."

"But you killed your father!" Olive burst out.

I froze. Was that what she thought?

"I heard you talking to Nathan. You told me it was an accident, but you told him you meant to do it."

I took a deep breath and stepped toward her, slowly, as if I was approaching a skittish fawn. "I did mean to, for a moment. But that's not what happened."

I remembered that moment as if it were only yesterday, hearing the shot echoing through the trees.

"Jesus!" My father's voice rang out from the bush. "You nearly hit me!"

I dropped the gun to the ground and stepped back, terrified now, as my father stepped over a log and into the clearing, his brown camouflage almost indistinguishable against the foliage of the dormant November forest. But he was wearing his hunter-orange vest and cap. I had seen them glowing brightly in the bush before I pulled the trigger. Oh god, what had I done?

"What have I told you?" my father demanded.

What you see in the bush is rarely what's really there.

"You could have killed me."

"I'm sorry," I whispered, barely able to breathe. "I'm so sorry."

My father searched my face and all the air seemed to go out of him.

"You hungry?" he asked dully. He sat on a log and pulled out a paper bag, lightly stained with oil, filled with Finnish pastries. He held it out to me.

I took one out but then only held it, my mind clouded. I was shaking.

"It won't bite back," he told me, trying, without energy, to resurrect an old joke. "It's just a pig." A pastry loosely shaped, like my father's pancakes, to resemble a pig.

I took a tentative bite and put the remainder back in the brown bag.

"You don't like it?" my father asked.

"I'm not hungry."

He bit into his. "More for me, then," he said.

He poured coffee into the thermos cup and handed it to me, then reached for his travel mug and topped up his own. I sniffed the cup and sipped, making a face at the acrid taste.

"Here," he said, offering me a bag of sugar cubes. Then he took two for himself, setting them between his teeth and sipping his coffee through them.

I did the same, drawing the bitter in through the sweet. My father grinned at me, showing what was left of the sugar cubes, like two goofy teeth. An old game that was funny once. I didn't smile back.

"You're not enjoying yourself?" he asked. "You used to love our hunting trips."

When you're older, you won't have to go, my mother had told me. *You can decide for yourself not to visit him. But for now, he's used the courts to force you to take these trips with him. There's nothing I can do. Just be prepared to defend yourself when you need to.*

Not *if*, but when. I slept with a hunting knife in my hand beneath my pillow. My sleep came in fits, and I woke exhausted. The sound of my father chopping wood outside for a morning fire made me flinch.

Now, sitting on a log opposite my father, drinking strong coffee, my knee wouldn't stay still. It bounced of its own accord. My cup sloshed as my hand shook. "I'm just tired," I said.

He held my gaze for a long moment. "I heard the bullet whiz past my ear," he said quietly. "It was that close." He tossed the remains of his coffee to the ground and put the travel mug back in his bag. "But you know that," he said. "You saw my vest and cap. You looked me right in the eye." He knew what I had done—what I had almost done. He knew it wasn't an accident. Grief puckered his brow. "Do you really hate me so much?"

There were so many things I could have said, things that would have saved my father's life, and my own. But I didn't say any of them. I sat upright, both hands on my bouncing knees, and fought back my own tears as he sank his head into his hands and sobbed so hard his shoulders shook.

Finally, my father stood, wiped his face, his snot, with the sleeve of his jacket. I felt a rush of adrenaline as he picked up his rifle. Pure, raw fear. But then he said, "It's clear you don't want to be here. Go back to the cabin and phone Teresa, ask her to pick you up on the road. You can stay with her and Nathan for the night."

"Why can't you drive me?"

He hesitated, looking not at me but at something beyond me. "There aren't many hours of light left. I'm going to see if I can bag that deer." He focused his gaze on me and added, "I do love you, Kira. I'll always love you."

Then he turned his back on me and walked slowly away,

expecting me to do as he asked, to phone Teresa and catch a ride to her place, knowing I would be excited to see Nathan. But I was still stunned, terrified by what I had just done. I couldn't face Teresa or Nathan. I remained where I was, knees vibrating, watching as he climbed over the log at the edge of the bush and headed back into the woods the way he had come. He had walked away from my mother like that time and time again when they argued, as, frustrated or defeated, he reached his limit. In return, my mother had pointed a finger at the back of his head, thumb up, a pretend gun, and "fired." *Bang. Bang. Bang.*

An hour or so later, I heard the rifle shot ring out in the forest. When evening fell and I still saw no sign of my father dragging a deer back to the cabin, I followed his path into the woods and found him dead.

Now, fifteen years later, I shook the image from my mind. It was time for everyone to know the truth. My biggest secret.

"I shot at him," I told Olive. "But I missed. He knew I meant to hurt him, and it broke him. He killed himself. He killed himself because of me. That's what I have to live with, Olive. Believe me, you don't want to carry that sort of guilt with you forever."

Aaron, rising from the cabin steps, did a slow clap. "How touching," he said. "You don't want Olive to kill dear old daddy like you did. And here I thought you didn't care."

"Shut up," Madison said.

Despite her father's crude interjection, Olive slowly dropped the muzzle of the gun, and I thought for a moment that she was about to hand it to me. But then she tipped the rifle and pressed the muzzle awkwardly under her chin—something she must have seen in a movie, like she was acting. But I didn't doubt for an instant that she would pull the trigger. I understood. I had thought of taking my life many times, even before my father's death.

Madison, clutching my baby to her chest, uttered a desperate "*No*."

I couldn't let this happen again. I held out both hands as I faced Olive, trying to keep my voice level. "You say you don't want to feel scared anymore. You want it to end. Olive, all this, your father's abuse, it's over now. He made a big mistake firing that rifle at me, threatening to kill us, hurting Nathan. He's going to jail for a very long time."

"You'll live with me now," Madison said.

"Bullshit," Aaron said, taking a step forward.

"He'll just talk his way out of it," Olive said, but she lowered the gun a little.

"No, he won't," I said. "Not this time. Not with all three of us working together to stop him."

Madison nodded. "That's right, honey. He kept us isolated from one another. He told me your mother was dead—"

"And he kept me away from Maddy," I said.

"So we wouldn't talk to each other," Maddy added.

I held out one hand for the gun. "Because he knew that if we did, we'd end up working together, and we could bring him down. And we *will*."

Aaron scoffed and moved quickly toward us. I thought, at first, he was trying to grab the gun from Olive, but he went for Evie instead and easily pulled her from Madison's grip. Blood from the knife wound on his hand streaked down Evie's arm.

"Who cares?" he said, gazing at Evie as though he was a loving parent, not the monster who had tried to drown her. "Go and live with your junkie mother if you like. You're all welcome to each other. I have Evie, and she'll live with me. Then the rest of you can do what you like. But my girl stays with me."

Everyone looked at me. My heart was hammering. I knew there was only one thing I could do, one thing I could tell him that would make him give her back, something I had learned just that morning at the house, when I checked the mail. It might also make him hurt her, but it was the only thing I could think of.

"Aaron, Evie isn't yours."

"*What?*"

The stunned look on Aaron's face was so satisfying that I rubbed salt into the wound. "She's Nathan's. I wasn't sure, so I ordered a DNA test. And now I know. We can walk away from you, and she'll never even have to hear your name again."

"Evie's not my sister?" Olive asked, and the gun dropped in her hands. She looked, bereft, at Evie in her father's arms.

"She *is* your sister," I said, getting closer to her. "Even if she's not related by blood. You love Evie, and she loves you. That makes you family. Olive, I promise, you're not going to lose her. I'll make sure of it."

"You fucking bitch," Aaron snorted. "So you were just after my money. I should've known."

I kept my eyes on Evie in his arms, his hand near her throat. "No, it wasn't like that," I said. "Aaron, until today, I had hoped she was yours."

"I should have drowned her this morning."

"Jesus, Aaron."

Olive aimed the gun unsteadily at her father. "Dad," she said, her voice trembling. "Give Evie back to Kira."

Oh god. She had the gun pointed at him, and he was still holding Evie. "Olive, no!"

Aaron looked for a moment like he might challenge her, but then he turned to the road as we all heard the sound of approaching sirens. "Shit," he said. "Here, take your kid, then." He shoved Evie roughly into my arms, then yanked the rifle from Olive's hand and pointed it at me. "Take her with you to hell." He aimed the gun at the other women, first Sarah, then Madison. "You can all go to hell."

"Do you really intend to shoot us all before the cops get here?" Madison asked. "Are there even enough bullets left?"

Aaron's eyes shifted back and forth as he considered that. Did he know how many cartridges the magazine held? Likely not, though, of course, I did.

"If the gun is in your hands when the cops arrive . . ." I left the rest unsaid. The police cars had already stopped at the head of the hunt camp road. I could hear the officers talking as they made their way down the overgrown road.

Aaron looked briefly back at the forest, as if he was thinking of fleeing, then at the gun in his hands. He nodded as if he'd made a decision. "Who is it going to be, then?" he asked, pointing the gun at each of us in turn. "Huh? How many of you can I take with me? Should we find out?" He trained the rifle on Madison's head.

"Daddy, no!" Olive ran up, butting him from the side. Surprised, he swung away as he fired, and the bullet skimmed Sarah's arm. She fell to her knees, holding the wound, wincing in pain.

As Madison ran to Sarah, Evie, scared by the noise of the blast, started crying again. I bounced her, in tears myself, holding her close as I pressed kisses to her head. Up the road, I could hear the cops shouting in response to the shot as they ran our way.

"I'm all right," Sarah said, inspecting her wound. A rivulet of blood trickled down her arm. "It's only a graze." She looked up at Olive. "I'm okay," she assured her, though her face was ashen with shock.

I faced Aaron. "Why do you have to keep hurting everyone?" I demanded. "Does it really make you feel better?"

He slid the muzzle back to Evie and me, and I took a step back, pressing my baby to my chest, instinctively turning to protect her body with my own.

"This is all your fault," he said. "You shouldn't have said you were going to leave me. You ruined everything." His brows furrowed and his eyes watered as if he were fighting tears. I once again felt I was seeing the boy inside him, this dangerous child. He was hurt, I realized, and scared—terrified. Fear had driven his rage. "You ruined everything," he said again, and his finger pressed into the trigger.

I closed my eyes a moment and listened to my heart thunder in my chest as if I was nearing the end of a marathon. But hearing the shouts of the police, now only yards away, I looked him right in the eye. "You're out of time," I said. And cartridges. He pulled the trigger, but there was only a click. "It's over," I said.

One of the officers shouted, demanding that Aaron drop the rifle as he drew his own firearm. Aaron hesitated an instant longer, the muzzle of the gun hovering in front of my face, then finally dropped the rifle to the ground.

39

I sat on the concrete steps outside my summer house with Evie suckling at my breast. The oxytocin had kicked in and, especially after the turmoil of the day before, I felt exhausted but also blissfully at peace, like a cow lazily chewing her cud as her calf yanked a teat.

Teresa, seeing me through her living room window, opened the screen door of her house and joined me on the steps. "You used to sit out here when your parents argued," she said as she sat beside me.

I glanced back at the house, hearing my mother's and father's angry voices ringing across the years, but that seemed so long ago now, and the echoes faded away.

"Madison and Sarah are talking to the social worker," I explained, "hashing out what happens next with Olive. I'm just giving them some space."

"Sarah's all right?"

"She only needed a few stitches." I hesitated. "And Nathan?"

"They kept him in the hospital in Sudbury overnight for observation. His doctor wants to run a scan, so I'll pick him up this afternoon. We should be home around suppertime."

"So soon?" I had planned to visit Nathan in the hospital later in the day. "I guess that's a good sign."

Teresa nodded. "He won't be back to work for a few weeks, though. It was a pretty serious concussion."

Oh god. "I'm so sorry I got him into this, Teresa."

Evie unplugged and reached out for Teresa, and she hoisted my daughter into the air as I rearranged my clothing.

"There's my Evie!" Teresa rubbed noses with her. *My Evie*, she said, just like she was family. She *was* family. Evie was Teresa's granddaughter, though Teresa didn't know that yet. I would tell Nathan first, something I'd wanted to do as soon as I read the results the morning before. But I wasn't exactly looking forward to it. I had no idea how he would react to the news.

My kitchen door opened, and Madison made her way over to us barefoot, wearing a clean T-shirt and yoga pants she'd borrowed from me, and took a seat on the steps. Teresa lifted her eyebrows in a knowing look and carried Evie a little distance away, cooing to her, to give Madison and I privacy—while still listening in, of course.

"What's the word?" I asked Madison.

"As we expected, Olive will be back living with me. But I've invited Sarah to stay with us in the basement while she heals."

I raised my eyebrows. "Really? Is that a good idea?"

Madison shrugged. "She's committed to staying clean, and she knows she'll have to take things slow with Olive."

"You're not . . ." I paused, thinking of how to say it.

"Jealous of Sarah? Worried that I'll lose Olive?" She shook her head. "It comes down to what's best for my daughter. Olive needs to know her mother. I'd be lying if I said I wasn't uneasy about the idea of sharing her with another woman. I wasn't exactly thrilled with you coming into her life at first."

"Oh?"

She offered me a tired smile. "But if Olive wants to spend weekends with her mom once Sarah has a place of her own, I'm good with that."

Olive would never live with me again, of course. I had no rights to her. For months I had resented her irritable presence in my home. She could be mouthy, arrogant, a real pain in the ass, but now that I considered a life without her, I felt sick with loss.

I leaned over my knees, clasping my hands together like Madison did. "Listen, I meant what I said earlier. I really do want to stay in Olive's life." I glanced at Evie in Teresa's arms. "Olive *loves* Evie, Madison."

"I know. I have no intention of wrenching Olive away from you and Evie. Olive is going to need support from all of us if she's going to recover from this."

"She'll be seeing a therapist, I imagine."

"Yes, of course."

"Exercise will help," I said. "Let's get Olive off that phone and outside much more. I'm not sure she'll want to go running with me, but maybe I can take her swimming or biking or kayaking. Maybe you and Sarah can bring her up here to the island after things have settled."

"I think she'd like that." Madison bumped shoulders with me. "But let's keep her away from the rifles, okay?"

"Ah, yes." *And the knives and scissors*, I thought.

She took my hand. "Listen, you said something back at the cabin that's been haunting me: that you were responsible for your father's suicide. You weren't, you know. No child could ever be. For him to take his own life like that, he must have been fighting some pretty serious demons."

"Thanks for saying that."

"No, really, Kira, you can't keep blaming yourself for his death. Maybe it's time to let go of that?"

"Maybe."

Madison squeezed my hand, then smiled a little wickedly. "In other circumstances I would have liked you, I think," she said.

"Gee, thanks."

She let go of my hand. "I guess we don't have to like each other to do what's best for our girls, do we?"

"No." I grinned.

"But who knows? Maybe we can be friends, for Olive."

"Maybe."

Madison nodded, as if that was settled. "So, what about you?" she asked. "What happens now?"

I glanced at Teresa. "I'll have to talk to Nathan," I said quietly, a task I would take care of as soon as he returned from the hospital. "And then—we'll see."

At least I knew I wouldn't have to deal with Aaron any time soon, hopefully never. He had been caught holding a rifle on us, arrested and hauled away in a police cruiser. We had been told he would face many criminal charges. Once sentenced, he would be in jail for a long time.

Sarah opened the kitchen door, and Olive and the social worker followed her out. The Children's Aid worker was pretty in a wholesome, slightly overfed farmer's daughter sort of way. She must have seen domestic dramas play out countless times. And she had been kind. Still, it was all so very embarrassing, to have our private lives cranked open to scrutiny in this way.

I stood, noting that Olive was carrying her bag. "Time to go?" I asked.

Madison pushed up from the steps. "I guess it is."

I stood awkwardly for a moment as the other two women

chatted and said goodbye to the social worker and waved as she drove off.

"Well," Madison said, turning to me.

"Yes, well."

Sarah held my hand in both of hers. "It was good to meet you," she said.

And then we all laughed nervously. The circumstances of our meeting were so very odd.

"We'll see much more of each other, I'm sure," I said.

Olive threw herself into my arms, and I held her tight, tears stinging my eyes. Then she stepped back and took Evie from Teresa.

"You'll visit, won't you?" she asked me as she hugged Evie. "I'll see you and Evie?"

"Of course she will," Madison said.

"We were talking about getting you back up here this summer," I said. "And spending some time on the beach."

"Yeah," she said. "That would be cool." Olive rocked Evie back and forth. "She *is* my sister, right?" she said.

I glanced at Teresa, hoping Olive wouldn't say anything more on the subject.

"Yes, she is," I said.

Olive held on to Evie a long time, until Madison said, "I'm sorry, sweetheart, but we've got to go."

I took Evie from Olive, and she hugged us both again. "I love you," she said, whether to me or Evie, I wasn't sure. But it made me weep anyway.

"I love you too," I said. I pushed the hair out of Olive's eyes. "We'll see you soon, okay? Very soon."

She nodded and I wiped my eyes and snuffled. "Shit," I said. Teresa handed me a tissue.

"Okay," Madison said brightly, "I guess we're off." Then she surprised me with a brief hug. "Stay in touch," she said into my ear.

We both stepped back awkwardly. "You have my number," she continued. "Text any time. Let me know where you land so we can get the girls together."

"I will," I said.

Sarah squeezed my arm. "I look forward to getting to know you, Kira," she said, holding my gaze, and I knew she meant it.

"You too," I said.

"We should go," Madison said.

There was a commotion down at the river and we turned to watch as a small flock of Canada geese—parents and juveniles—first ran and then flew up the road as if it were a runway. Evie pointed at them as, one after the other, the heavy birds lifted into the air, flying so low as they passed that I could not only hear the whistling of their wings, but feel the rush of air dislocated by their labored flight.

40

I left the summer house carrying Evie, feeling nauseous with anxiety. After all the revelations of the day before, I had one more to deal with. I hadn't phoned Nathan, but I knew where he'd be now. Like other locals, he made a ritual of walking down to the beach in the evening to take in the sunset from the pedestrian bridge, a span connecting the boardwalk over the river.

I carried Evie there now, holding her hand in mine. Her tiny fingers were so warm, so small, so fragile that it made me ache. I had spent the nearly eight months since her birth wishing for sleep, for a warm supper, for a day without the countless interruptions a baby brings. Wishing for my simpler life before motherhood. Now I greedily stored up the moments with her as if they might never come again.

Nathan leaned over the railing of the pedestrian bridge, looking down into the water, his hair glowing ginger in the gilded light. His skin had the golden hue of summer. He often worked at his construction sites without a shirt and, on days off, sprawled on the beach without even a beach blanket, his hair full of sand. Teresa had always called him a beach bum.

"Hey," I said.

"Hey."

Evie held out her arms to him, and he took her from me. "Look," he said, pointing to the water below, and she pointed with him. A common merganser, a diving duck, swam underwater through the weeds beneath the bridge, hunting a school of small, silvery fry. The creature looked more like an otter than a bird as it zipped, slippery, through the water, snatching up fish after fish.

"How are you feeling?" I asked.

"Groggy. I've got a hell of a headache."

"Nathan, I'm so sorry."

"I'm the one who should be sorry." He touched the tender goose egg at the back of his head. "This wasn't your fault. I insisted on staying, protecting you from that asshole." He laughed a little and then winced. "Obviously, I didn't do a very good job. Oh god, Kira. If he had killed you or Evie—"

"None of this is on you. I'm just relieved you're all right. I felt horrible leaving you there on the kitchen floor."

"You didn't have a choice. And you gave Mom enough clues that she figured things out and found me right away. I'm just relieved for you that it's all over."

I nodded slowly, looking out over the water. *Mostly over*, I thought.

The town was quiet at this time of day. I only heard crickets and the low groan of bullfrogs below us, hidden in the grasses along the river. Fishermen were out in their boats in the bay. An elderly woman in a kayak bobbed on the shallow waters near shore.

Far up the beach, a slim young woman about my age ran toward us along the shore. It took me a moment to register that she was naked. One side of her head was shaved and her hair on the other side was long and dyed green. Even from this distance I could see that she had tattoos all over her body.

Nathan's eyes followed her as she headed our way, but he made no comment. Neither did I. Was this the nature of our relationship now, not speaking of the elephant in the room? In this case, the naked woman running toward us. Or maybe it had always been this way. Nathan and I had each lived two lives, one together, one apart.

Okay, out with it.

"Listen, Nathan, you once said you loved Evie as if she was your own. What if she *was* your own?"

"I don't know what you're asking."

I took a deep breath and exhaled. "Evie is yours, Nathan. She's your daughter."

He turned to face me, with Evie on his hip. "You're shitting me."

"I had a DNA test done. I just got the letter from the lab yesterday morning. She's not Aaron's. I can show you. But all you have to do is look at her."

He grinned at me, joy lifting his face. "*Really?*" He looked down at Evie in his arms. She was fair-haired, like me, but with a robust build like Nathan's. She had nothing of Aaron's, neither his dark hair nor his slender, patrician features. Evie reached out for Nathan's nose and he gave hers a gentle squeeze, then held his thumb between his index and middle fingers. "Got your nose!" An old game, one my father had played with me, one all fathers play. Evie squeezed his thumb, not really understanding.

"She *is* your daughter."

I felt relief start to settle in. He was taking the news better than I had imagined. But then his expression slowly fell as he worked things through. "But you knew, didn't you? You knew there was a chance she was mine or you wouldn't have gotten that paternity test."

"No, Nathan, really. I didn't know. You and I had only been

together once around that time, when I came up for a visit. But then you asked, remember? You wondered if she could be yours."

"You said no."

"I said no, but your question got me thinking about it." Worrying, actually, though I put off finding out. "So I sent Aaron's and Evie's samples into the lab."

Nathan stared out over the bay for a moment before turning back. "If all that shit didn't come down yesterday, if Aaron hadn't got himself arrested, would you have married him and never told me about Evie? Would you have kept my daughter away from me?"

"No, I . . ." I stopped there. The truth was, I didn't know what I would have done. Shit. Would I have kept Evie from her father, as my mother had tried to do?

"I'm so sorry," I whispered, barely able to breathe. "But I'm going to do my best to make it up to you and Evie. I'm moving up here so you can see Evie any time you want." It would be much cheaper to live on Manitoulin Island in any case, at least until I figured out how I was going to make a living. And I finally felt ready to make a commitment to the place, to build a community here, to get to know the locals, who already seemed to know so much about me.

Nathan ran a hand through his hair. "If you're thinking we'll get back together—"

"I know," I said. "There's no going back after this."

A look of hurt creased his brow, and I realized that was exactly what he was hoping for, to get back together, to build a family with me. But what did I want? Even though I still loved Nathan, I wasn't sure. I needed time to recover, to figure out who I was now.

"Then what exactly do you want from me?" he asked.

"Evie needs her father," I said. Just like I had needed mine. I lifted one shoulder. "And you need your daughter's love." Just as my father had needed mine.

Nathan nodded slowly. "I want to be in Evie's life," he said. "I'll support her, of course."

I felt my gut contract at the disappointment on his face. He wanted more from me.

"Maybe down the road you and I . . ." I paused. "We'll see." I smiled, holding his gaze, and his lovely sideways grin slid up his face.

Evie giggled at the merganser as it popped up to the surface again, a tiny fish in its mouth. It gulped it down and ducked under for another. Evie, enchanted, clapped her hands.

"You haven't told Mom about this yet, have you?" Nathan asked. "No."

"She'll be thrilled," he said. "Are you okay with me telling her about Evie? Or do you want to do it yourself?"

"I think maybe it's better if you do it," I said.

He looked up the road. "I'll go tell her now, then. Can I take Evie with me?"

"Of course. She's your daughter."

I kissed Evie on the cheek, and he carried her down the pedestrian bridge, turning once as he reached the steps. "My *daughter*," he said, a look of wonder on his face.

I waved and, in return, Evie open and closed her hand.

I watched them start down the road, then I turned back to the lake, taking in the view of the bay. Now that the naked jogger was nearly at the pedestrian bridge, I could see her tattoos clearly: a flock of tiny birds flew across one shoulder; an infinity sign spread over one breast. The word *vegan* was written in cursive along her arm. Her fingers were covered in tiny tattoos: roses, butterflies, a quarter moon. Her eyes locked with mine and she winked as she ran past at a leisurely pace, completely at ease with her nakedness, as if she was just any jogger out for an evening run. She splashed through the shallows where the river met the lake, laughing at the cold water. I wanted to be that bold, that *free*, to run for the pure pleasure of it, to celebrate the strength and power in my body, to feel the breeze on my skin. *I can*, I thought, feeling an excitement I hadn't felt in years. I could run for no reason other than this.

I tossed my hoodie over the railing of the bridge and, wearing yoga shorts and a halter top, jumped down into the sand of the dune. Then, racing along the shore, my bare feet slipping a little in the wet sand with each step, I ran as fast and as freely as I had ever run before.

GAIL ANDERSON-DARGATZ

41

I parked the rental beside my father's sign, the plywood cutout of a leaping deer that marked the road to his hunt camp, leaving the emergency lights flashing as I took Evie out of her car seat. Carrying her, I stepped onto my father's property, following the trail that Aaron and I had plowed down with the Jeep. The field around us was dotted with milkweed and alive with dancing monarch butterflies. Evie leaned away from me, trying to catch them as they fluttered up and out of our way, and then, as we entered the bush that surrounded the overgrown road, she held out a hand to the feathery tamarack branches. We passed the barn and rounded the corner, and there it was, the cedar-shingled cabin. My father's hunt camp didn't seem nearly so frightening now. The graying building was just an elderly gentleman left all alone for too many years.

I carried Evie past the cabin to the trail that led deep into the bush, into my father's old hunting grounds, and, as I had when Aaron was hunting me down, I began to retrace my father's last steps.

There was the seating area, just logs, where I had waited on him while he flushed out the deer. It was here that I had fired the shot that had nearly killed him, where we had sipped our last coffee together, through sugar cubes.

She sat there now, on a log, the girl I had been. She watched me and Evie as we passed and then jumped up to follow.

And there was the windfall my father had stepped over, the last time I saw him alive before he disappeared into the bush that dusky afternoon. I stepped over it now, pushing a tree branch out of the way so it wouldn't hit Evie.

I tromped on, carrying Evie, with my fetch following us through cedar, sugar maple and beech trees, deeper into the dim forest, until, finally, I saw a brightness ahead, the clearing. When I reached the threshold between bush and light, I put Evie on the ground, and she crawled ahead into the field to chase the butterflies that fluttered around the milkweed.

I looked over my shoulder and saw my young self, that frightened twelve-year-old girl, follow the path her father had taken through the forest, stepping into his footprints in the snow. "Dad?" she called. Then again, "Dad?"

She reached me and together, as one, we stepped forward, into the clearing.

My father's body was splayed over a crust of snow. A pool of blood fanned out like a halo beneath his head. I squatted down, next to his body, and took his hand, so much larger than my own. When I had witnessed my first kill years before—a two-year-old whitetail buck that my father had shot—I was surprised by just how long it took for the body to grow cold, for the life to drain from it. Thinking of that, I wondered if my father was still there in part, but draining away, little by little, along with the heat of his body. I imagined his spirit slipping away like a thread of fog carried on the wind.

GAIL ANDERSON-DARGATZ

"I'm so sorry," I told him now, on this fine July morning. Then I faltered for words. What could I say? *I'm sorry I hated you, or pretended to hate you, that I made you feel so unloved that you took your own life.* "I'm so sorry," I said again.

As Madison had said, I didn't make him take his life. He could have stayed, fought for me. Something else took him. He was ravaged by a mental illness that I would never fully understand. A wash of relief coursed through me as I realized, finally, that I wasn't to blame for my father's death.

I pulled a photograph from my pocket, one I had found at the summer house, of my mother, father and me around the firepit, and showed it to Evie. "My daddy," I said, pointing to him, but her attention was on the butterflies. She crawled through the field on all fours, trying to grab them.

As Evie played in the grass, I stared down at the photograph for a long time. I could feel my father's presence so strongly here in these woods that I could almost believe he was still with me. But then he *was*, in a sense—in me, in Evie, who was the spitting image of him.

"I love you," I said to my father's photograph, and to the winter ghost lying on the ground. "Please forgive me."

I needed to forgive him, too, for leaving me in that terrible way.

I stood and pocketed the photo, and the image of my father's body melted away. I closed my eyes and breathed in the heady summer scent of cedar bark heated by sun, forcing myself to be here in the present, and not in the past.

I heard a rustle in the bush. Something big. The bear that had been rummaging through the campground's garbage? I picked up Evie and searched the shadows beneath the trees in the direction of the noise until I saw a patch of white moving toward me through the bush. The beast grunted, a familiar sound I'd heard many times before in these woods, and stepped forward into the threshold between forest and field. Evie pointed at it. The large stag had an impressive set of antlers and was white. Completely white. A ghost deer. Its presence seemed like an answer from my father to my plea for forgiveness, and an apology of his own. Was I really seeing this creature, I wondered, or did it leap from my imagination as the ghost of my young self had? The vision was so strange that I inhaled a quick, shocked breath.

At the noise, the white stag stared at me, its eyes glinting within the shadows beneath the trees. For a long moment, we locked gazes. And then it lifted its head, heavy with antlers, snorted at my smell and sprang away. I saw flashes of white between the trunks of maple and birch trees as the stag ran off, and then it was gone. I stared after it, hoping for its return.

When it was clear that it wasn't coming back, I adjusted Evie on my hip and finally, after all those years, carried my young self out of that forest.

Acknowledgments

I offer my thanks, first, to my editor Iris Tupholme and my agent, Jackie Kaiser, for handing me the initial seed for this novel and allowing me to plant and cultivate it. The book would not have been written without you. I also offer my gratitude to my editors Helen Reeves and Julia McDowell for helping me realize the story you see here.

I had a cottage on Manitoulin Island for many years and love the region with all my heart. Setting the story on the island was my way of saying thank you as my husband and I let go of our life there. I hope my former neighbors will forgive the many liberties I took with reality to create my fictional community and its characters. And no, none of the characters are based on you. You're all much better people.

To build the characters in this novel, I found the following books useful: *Divorce Poison: How to Protect Your Family from Badmouthing and Brainwashing* by Dr. Richard A. Warshak (HarperCollins, 2010); *Mothers on Trial: The Battle for Children and Custody* by Phyllis Chesler (Lawrence Hill Books, 2011); *Adult Children of*

Parental Alienation Syndrome: Breaking the Ties That Bind by Amy J.L. Baker (W.W. Norton and Company, 2007); and *Will I Ever Be Good Enough? Healing the Daughters of Narcissistic Mothers* by Karyl McBride (Atria Books, 2009). I'd also like to thank registered psychotherapist Karen Essex for her invaluable perspective on the children of narcissistic parents and the adults they become. Any errors in the novel on any topic are, of course, my own.